British Li

FOREST SILVER

E. M. Ward

First published in 1941

This edition published in 2024 by
The British Library
96 Euston Road
London NW1 2DB

Copyright © 2024 The Estate of E. M. Ward
Preface copyright © 2024 Alison Bailey
Afterword copyright © 2024 Simon Thomas

Cataloguing in Publication Data
A catalogue record for this publication is available from the British Library

ISBN 978 0 7123 5580 3
e-ISBN 978 0 7123 6812 4

Text design and typesetting by JCS Publishing Services Ltd
Printed and bound by CPI Group (UK), Croydon, CR0 4YY

CONTENTS

THE 1940S

- Blackout regulations are imposed across Britain on 1 September 1939, two days before the official declaration of war. They remain in place until the end of the war, though softened to 'dim-out' regulations in September 1944.

- 1940 (December): All the students at the Royal College of Art are evacuated to the Lake District town of Ambleside.

- 1941 (February): The number of official evacuees in the UK rises to a peak of 1.37 million.

- 1941: *Forest Silver* is published.

- 1941 (December): A plan is considered to melt down 64,000 Belisha beacons for munitions – the pedestrian crossing lamps named after Leslie Hore-Belisha, Minister of Transport, and considered an attraction of Carlisle in *Forest Silver*.

- The Victoria Cross is awarded to 181 recipients for action in the Second World War, including 85 posthumous awards.

- During the six years of the Second World War, Penguin Books printed approximately 600 titles – presumably including Richard Blunt's 'dozen Penguin books in orange, blue and cherry coloured covers'.

❧ ❧ ❧

❧ **1946 (March):** The billeting scheme for evacuees is officially ended, though 38,000 people still have no homes to go to.

❧ **1948 (June):** The National Health Service (NHS) is launched in the UK with three core principles: to meet the needs of everyone, to be free at the point of delivery and based on clinical need.

&❧ &❧ &❧

E. M. WARD (1886–1955)

❧

Edith Marjorie Ward was born on 26 November 1886 in Leigh, Kent, daughter of Henry Ward and Margaret Maitland. The family lived in the coastal town of Formby, Merseyside, and Edith studied for a BSc and an MA at the nearby University of Liverpool.

Ward lived much of her life in Grasmere and chose it as the setting of *Forest Silver*. Other novels are equally closely tied to their locations: *Appledore Bay* (1941) focuses on Romney Marsh, *Dancing Ghyll* (1937) is set around Skiddaw in the Lake District, while *Voices in the Wind* (1944) and *Isles of Saints* (1943) are based in North Wales and Cardiganshire, now Ceredigion, respectively. She did go further afield: two novels, *Alpine Rose* (1934) and *Mountain Waters* (1935) are set in Switzerland.

Alongside novels, Ward wrote works of geographic interest, including *English Coastal Evolution* (1922) and *Days in Lakeland Past and Present* (1930).

One reviewer, in the weekly newspaper *The Sphere*, commented on *Voices in the Wind*:

> Even when Miss E. M. Ward is writing, as in her new novel, about Christmas parties, mad Welsh tramps or rich Armenians, there is a soothing quality about her work that makes it very attractive to the reader who may have to contend with the printed word in a crowded railway train, after a day's exhausting queueing or in an all-too-domestic centre.

Ward died on 14 March 1955 in Grasmere. Like several of the rediscovered authors in the British Library Women Writers series, little is known about the details of her life, and it is hoped that this reprinting of *Forest Silver* will introduce her to a new generation of readers.

PREFACE

Having broken his engagement only days before the wedding, Richard Blunt arrives in Grasmere unsettled and ashamed. Over the next two years, as he recovers from his injuries in combat, he joins a cast of characters – both locals and those seeking refuge from bombing – most notably the intense and ambivalent central figure of Corys de Bainriggs.

The first years of the Second World War with their blackouts, food restrictions and other privations (but postal delivery on Christmas Day!) form the background of the novel and there are elements of the jaunty tone of humorous works from the period.

However, the novel also explores the complex transition from childhood to adulthood, questions of gender and identity, and the unpredictability of relationships. Love – whether recognised, returned or unrequited – is more acute in the heightened atmosphere of war when life is precarious and time may be short. For women without economic security, engagement and successful marriage promise stability.

All this is rooted firmly in the Lake District setting and Ward's evocative descriptions of the landscape, colours and climate – where the power of the elements plays a major part.

The title reflects both the effect of shimmering moonlight on the lakeside trees and an ancient tax which allowed grazing. It also has a more specific relevance in the novel – which considers the history of

❧ ❧ ❧

the land and issues relating to development and conservation – while reflecting an acceptance of the contemporary social status quo.

Alison Bailey
Lead Curator, Printed Heritage Collections 1901–2000

PUBLISHER'S NOTE

The original novels reprinted in the British Library Women Writers series were written and published in a period ranging, for the most part, from the 1910s to the 1950s. There are many elements of these stories which continue to entertain modern readers, however in some cases there are also uses of language, instances of stereotyping and some attitudes expressed by narrators or characters which may not be endorsed by the publishing standards of today. We acknowledge therefore that some elements in the stories selected for reprinting may continue to make uncomfortable reading for some of our audience. With this series, British Library Publishing aims to offer a new readership a chance to read some of the rare books of the British Library's collections in an affordable paperback format, to enjoy their merits and to look back into the world of the twentieth century as portrayed by their writers. It is not possible to separate these stories from the history of their writing and the following novel is presented as it was originally published with one small edit. We welcome feedback from our readers, which can be sent to the following address:

British Library Publishing
The British Library
96 Euston Road
London, NW1 2DB
United Kingdom

FOREST SILVER

CHAPTER 1

Scowling and walking fast Richard Blunt came along the wet road towards Rydal. His haste and his scowl were due to no immediate sense of urgency or discomfort but to his recollection of what had happened on the previous day. Then, on a Thursday morning, he had told his betrothed, who had arranged that he was to marry her on the following Saturday, that he would not marry her, neither on that day nor at any other time. He had told her this in London, where she lived with her impoverished parents in Chelsea, and directly after doing so he had set out for the north, partly because the north was a long way from London and partly because he had an inherited fondness for the Lake District. And now, on Friday afternoon, he had walked from Windermere railway station nearly as far as Rydal and still felt himself emotionally ill at ease.

It happened to be one of those days, rare at the Lakes, when the falling rain, the low and formless sky and the sodden country-side were all of the same colour. The valley pastures were grey-green, the sky of a greenish grey, and the rain that joined grass and cloud, being transparent, appeared of the same sallow hue. The road glimmered with a metallic brightness in the gloom, reflecting a light that was nowhere else perceptible, and the full river swept beside it with a heavy sound that drowned the watery patter of the rain. However, when Richard reached that part of the way where the Rydal beeches and the cottages opposite them make of the road a green tunnel, dark even on a fine day, he stood still, the better to consider his sensations. The beeches being thoroughly soaked, the rain fell on him as steadily as if he were on the open road, but he was not conscious of wetness as one of his sensations; indeed, like any native of the district, he had long ago learnt to ignore the Lake rain.

Standing, staring at the beech trunks that showed in the green dimness like the shapes of vertical, pale, prehistoric monsters, Mr. Blunt was as little conscious of any sense of sin as of his increasing dampness.

As some of us avoid the use of the verb to die, so he, for many years, had unconsciously evaded any direct reference to sin. Yet, he felt shame and it was in the hope of finding out why he did so that he stood still in Rydal.

'I have undoubtedly behaved clumsily and not, perhaps, in the best of taste,' thought Richard, still unconscious of sin, 'but the only thing for me to be really ashamed of is that I got myself engaged to her. That was inexcusable, and so silly.'

He walked slowly on. In August, even on a wet day and in war time, there is no room for a pedestrian in Rydal village, and by walking slowly and not thinking about the traffic he caused, in five minutes, seven complicated traffic situations that were only prevented from developing into accidents by the fortunate adroitness of the fourteen drivers involved. Strolling thus, with bent head, and without scraping himself against the walls as do all other pedestrians in Rydal, he began dimly to wonder whether or not any of his actions with regard to that Miss Ozzard who had so nearly become his could, conceivably, have been what is called wrong.

'Fatuous, weak, but most necessary,' thought Richard, brooding on his engagement and then on his escape from it. 'But wrong? I cannot conceive that any part of the whole idiotic and deplorable affair was what a parson could call wrong.'

Emerged, though without conscious effort on his part, to the safety of the footpath beyond Wordsworth's Rock, Richard felt himself to be virtuous because he had not done wrong, by which he meant that he had not broken, so far as he knew, any of the ten commandments that might be deemed of importance. Yet, he still felt excessively uneasy. Many people, perhaps most people, would think that he had behaved to Miss Ozzard in an ungentlemanly way; moreover, there had been a look in her light blue eyes when he told her that he did not want her which he remembered with some discomfort.

'Well, anyhow, it would have been worse for me, married to her, than it can possibly be for her not marrying me,' thought Richard, staring abstractedly at Rydal Water, to the dimly luminous wetness of which the rain was adding, it seemed unnecessarily. 'She'll soon find another fellow, and one who likes curls.'

At this moment a heron came out of Heron Island, flying like a large and dilapidated daddy-long-legs, and Richard began eagerly and thankfully to think about herons.

'Can they be trying to re-establish themselves on the Island?' wondered Richard, remembering that he had read of a heronry that had been there at one time.

Where the road runs through the gorge between Rydal and Grasmere lakes there came another scent in the air. To the wild, soft smells that rise in rain from grassland, fern, wet roads, and leafy trees was added that of wood smoke. Invisible at first the smoke yet smelt, sharp and wary, with warning and invitation in its scent, but so faintly it seemed a miracle its tenuous breath could be sustained in the weight of falling rain. Then the dim pallor of smoke began to show, vaporous, transparent, curiously astir with a formless movement of its own, and with the smoke came those cracklings and hissings of flame that, like the scent of fire, spread warning of it, urgent and unmistakable. Blunt was now walking fast again and he soon came to sight of the fire. An old man with a sack over his shoulders stood in the wood to the left of the road and so close beside a great pile of burning brushwood that the smoke, here, at its source, rolling up in rounded billowings, solid as cumulus cloud, continually hid and revealed him. Up into the streaming rain darted and flared flames, quick as a lizard's tongue, and dark within them, suspended from a branch as yet unburned, hung a can of tea so that its steam sent up a little pale cloud. The old man was cutting thick slices from a chunk of bread and eating, staring as he ate into the glowing heat that dried the windless deluge as it fell. Blunt stopped and watched him, fascinated by the glory of flame in the midst of the falling waters and by the tranquil homeliness of the old man, eating, and drinking his scalding tea as if his fire were that of a cottage hearth. Around him felled trunks, neatly stripped of branches, and piles of fire logs, yard wood and twigs were disposed in so orderly a manner as to add to the odd sense of domesticity, and when the old woodman turned his face toward Blunt, warned of his presence by some sense other than those of hearing and of sight, there was in it the unquestioning tranquillity that brightens the look of a well-cared-for dog or horse.

'You lovely old chap!' murmured Richard and raised his hand in a greeting of homage and admiration.

The old man saluted in reply and his unchanging look followed the stranger's head and shoulders above the wall as Blunt went on again through the ceaseless rain.

Grasmere, like Rydal lake, lay dead calm, the blackness of its still surface broken by the rain into countless and minute silvery splashings. The opposite shores were hidden by the deluge; the waters looked boundless and the Island, dimly visible within them, of so vague a darkness that all colour and solidity must, it seemed, have been washed out of it. Wet, almost cold, and tired more by his thoughts than by nine miles of walking in the rain, Blunt paused at the garden gate of the Prince of Wales Hotel. Should he go in for afternoon tea before seeking a more rural lodging? Lights shone from the lounge windows and were reflected from the puddles on the drive; through the steady roar of the rain he heard voices and the laughter of guests; beside him lay the lake among the boat-landings, silent and wan, and the thin twigs of a leafy birch above it perpetually bowed and rose again in the windless air as rain beat upon and then slid from them.

'I tire of winds and waters and pale lights!' quoted Blunt, to himself, and he went up the drive into the hotel.

Mr. Blunt had his reasons for ardently desiring privacy. He had served with distinction in the Royal Air Force from the day that war broke out until he had won the V.C. and been desperately wounded at the same time. His photo had been in the newspapers because his widowed mother had proudly distributed it to every one who had shown even the most obviously feigned sympathy with her maternal emotions about her only child; he had been unconscious in hospital at the time and so unable to restrain her. His recovery from what had been thought to be several mortal injuries had made him more interesting to the general public, always fascinated by surgical details, than had his V.C., and the same photos of Wing-Commander Blunt, V.C., now happily more or less recovered, appeared in the newspapers months after they had first done so. Then he had got engaged and the photo of him was reprinted, and now he had broken his engagement and he much feared they would do it again. Those months of desperate illness that had left him so changed that, at thirty-four, the R.A.F. had no more use for him, had scarcely affected the charming, ugly vigour of his face, and he knew himself to be too easily recognizable. Yet, he felt a great need of tea and so he walked into the Prince of Wales Hotel and stood, dripping, in the hall.

He had read that the Lake District was full of visitors from the less peaceful parts of England, yet he felt a vague surprise and resentment at the excessive fullness of the Prince. So far as he could see all the ground floor rooms were full of people, from upstairs came ceaseless sounds of voices and doors and running taps and laughter and nailed boots, being dropped outside rooms, and between downstairs and up passed yet more people, surging up and surging down again in polite and energetic waves. After more than a year of war his return to civilian life had given Richard a sense of unreality and bewilderment that still strongly affected him, and the cheerful clamour and brightness, sheltered from the lonely rain by the walls of the hotel, had, for him, something of the remote animation of scenes in a film. However, eventually he found a chair and a waitress brought him tea. She told him that not only the Prince but the whole of Grasmere was full to the last camp-bed.

'You won't find nothing, nowhere,' said the waitress, who had been bombed out of Birmingham. Thus, she felt friendly towards the homeless and there was, besides, something about Blunt that made most women feel motherly towards him. 'There's a gentleman leaving here to-day,' she said, hesitating, as well she might, at meddling with what was the business of the young ladies in the office. 'He comes from Liverpool and he says he can't stand another night of them owls. Says he'd rather have a blitz every time. It's a little bit of a room, but you might try for it?'

Blunt reflected. He felt miserably convinced that every one in the room recognized him and that to-morrow they would read that he had jilted

Miss Ozzard. Naturally, his conviction was wrong and, so far, only the middle one of the three Misses Sweeting had realized who he was, with that kind of thrill wisely and briefly described as indescribable.

'Heavens!' said the middle Miss Sweeting to herself and began to wind her way, elegant as a blue fish, among the little tables in search of her sisters.

These three ladies, aged respectively sixteen, seventeen and eighteen, were, nevertheless of the same height and resembled lit blue candles owing to their extreme slimness, and their clothes, and their hair, which was of so pale a yellow as to be whiter than flame. They had been bombed out of London and had lived with their parents at the Prince for the last nine months, so that Grasmere was by now well accustomed to seeing their pale heads moving, like will-o'-the-wisps, high over the bogs and bracken of the fell slopes. Mrs. Sweeting frequently read the poems of Dante Gabriel Rossetti and she had named her girls Cecily, Gertrude and Magdalen, in the hope, so far disappointed, that they might be followed by a Margaret and Rosalys, and it was Gertrude who had begun the habit of cutting from periodicals the portraits of men she liked the look of. Cecily and Magdalen had at once done the same, and it was a tribute to the charms of Blunt's face that his photo was in each of the three collections.

'Essie! Mag!' said Gertrude, who was always called Rudie, in an urgent whisper, as she beheld her sisters eating ice-cream cornets in the passage to the kitchen. 'Oh, you greedy beasts. You've been out, and never told me. Girls, listen, there is some one in the little lounge, some one perfectly great. Come and look, quick, because I think he is discontented and won't stay long.'

That evening after dinner a breeze from the north came down the valley, wandering as breezes do among the hills. It whispered in the spruces at Thorney How, drifted silently on, whispered again in the pine and the spruce opposite the book-shop and then, passing voiceless over the valley flats, stirred the wet woods of Bainriggs with the sound of lightly falling rain. Before it, the usual miracle happened. The rain, mist, cloud and darkness that had filled all the space between the earth and the higher heaven vanished, evaporated, or driven away to soak and overshadow some other place down wind. There was the brief glow of a clear, orange sunset behind Far Easedale and, before it was quite faded, the full moon rose above Rydal Fell.

'Please, Mr. Blunt, will you come up White Moss with us?' said the eldest Miss Sweeting. 'The moon is lovely.'

Though she alone spoke in words the looks of the other two spoke as urgently. 'Oh! do, *do*, DO come,' said the tremulous, flushed faces of Rudie and Mag.

Thus, while meteorological miracles (or what seemed so) had been efficiently and almost silently accomplished things, perhaps equally mysterious, had been influencing Richard Blunt and the Sweeting sisters. Richard Blunt, suddenly oppressed by an odd, primitive fear of being left homeless in the rain, had taken the small bedroom left empty by the Liverpool gentleman who found owls so lugubrious. And the Sweeting girls, urged by impulses as old as life upon the earth but which they accepted as casually as the breath which the sight of Richard had caused to quicken, assailed him with overtures so friendly, shy, diffident and yet childishly confiding, that by the time the moon was well up the wary Blunt began to feel, though with astonishment and some misgivings, as if he were their elder brother.

'These pleasant creatures, these sweet Sweetings, are not women, but delightful children,' thought Richard. 'And, anyhow, there are three of them, constantly and everywhere three of them together. One cow is usually reckoned as no cow,' reflected Richard, now accompanying the sisters down the front steps of the Prince, 'but one woman is all women whereas two, and still more three, young females are no woman at all.'

The little windows of Dove Cottage were in shadow, dark and blank as if the light had gone out behind them very long ago. The Sweeting sisters did not read Wordsworth. They asked Blunt why they should do so. He was grieved to feel that he had not yet regained enough vitality even to begin explaining to them why they should. After his long walk of the afternoon the hill road up White Moss made him too well aware that his heart had been damaged, irreparably so had said the doctors, with that wealth of picturesque, anatomical detail that doctors call being frank with their patients. He might live to a good, even to a great age, had said the doctors, but only if he never forgot that his this and his that were out of action and those other fitments damaged and the whole thing doing, with the grindings of effort, what should have been done with the effortless rhythm of health.

'You'll lose something if you don't read Wordsworth,' said Richard at last, and stood still, taking care of his heart.

'Plenty else to read,' said the Sweetings, and they all went on again.

From the narrow road they looked down through tree branches to the lake, that lay rippled and silver bright behind the dark trunks. Almost at the top of the hill they turned off by a little path that led to a gap in the roadside wall. Through the gap they could see into the solemn wood of Bainriggs, now colourless and vague but so sodden with the day's rain that, except in the black tree shadows, everything was changed to silver. The moonlit rocks, the wet sponge of moss upon the ground, leaves, lit spaces of the beech trunks and the stems of birches, always silver but now brighter than in any noontide, all these shone and glittered with a light so wan and yet so brilliant that it seemed like the phosphorescence of a world long dead.

'Forest Silver!' said Blunt, observing all this and thinking of the tax paid long ago by tenants for the right of pasturage in the lord of the manor's woodlands. 'What's that?'

The forest had been as still as it was silent; save for the almost imperceptible shifting of the shadows as the moon rose towards its low, summer zenith, nothing had been astir there. But now something moved in the mingling of tree shadows and glittering light; up the slope towards them came a figure, human no doubt, but one that came with such swiftness and silence that it seemed it must be as insubstantial as the fall of moonlight. It looked like a tall boy, for it was wearing shorts, and Blunt could see dark, short hair and an open-necked shirt. Then it must have seen them for, with a sudden swerve that made the first faint clatter of a disturbed stone underfoot, it sprang away from its unseen path and disappeared, silent again and hidden immediately by the hill slope.

'Who or what on earth was that?' said Blunt, but the three Sweetings, wrapped in glamour, had all been looking at him and had seen no one else.

As they strolled back down the hill they talked of the leaping apparition.

'Could it have been a hiker?' said they, and answered themselves, all together, as was, apparently, their cheerful custom. 'Oh, it couldn't have been. All the hikers have to be in the hostel by half-past ten. Oh! Do look! There is Jownie Wife at it again! How furious P.C. Smith will be!'

Far below, through the moonlit wood, the lake was visible again and the Island in it. Dim, like a phantom ship, it lay in the silver waters and from the nearer end of it shone a narrow rectangle of light, a tiny rectangle of dull light that was so dull and red and smoky looking that it seemed sinister in the bodiless and blanched moonshine. It looked like a bale fire, a beacon fire, a fire of warning that the red cock might soon crow again upon the roof-trees as it did when the Scots fired the Border long ago.

'Does anybody live on the Island then?' asked Richard, in surprise.

'Yes, in that old barn. She is called Jownie Wife. She's what they call a roadster here, or partly so. But she lives for weeks in that barn. Every one hates her in Grasmere and we do, too. She is like a weasel,' said Cecily and Rudie together. 'And she will show that light, not every night, but just now and then, and P.C. Smith goes quite mad and rows out to the Island and she locks him out and hides the light, but as he comes back she shows it again, as often as not,' said Mag. 'He is going to have her run in, some time.'

'She lives on the Island!' said Mr. Blunt, dreamily, and not thinking about Jownie Wife. How desirable a place to live must be the Island! How quiet! How surrounded by and lapped in the healing solitude of water! Surely on such an island, if anywhere, he could find time to adjust those spiritual wheels of his which, like the wheels of his heart, revolved only with dolorous grindings. Moreover, he had a small investment income and could afford a long holiday and his civilian work as an architect had come to an end when the war began.

'Who owns the Island?' said Richard, abruptly.

Shocked at such ignorance, even in so new a comer as Mr. Blunt, the pretty Sweetings spoke, solemnly, and with something of reproof. 'Why, Miss de Bainriggs, of Bonfire Hall, of course!' said the Sweetings, all looking at him, but with such moonlit faces that the weight of their gravity became bodiless as the night.

'Miss de Bainriggs!' said the Sweetings, hushing their earnestness because of the expectant hush of the moonlit world so that to Blunt it seemed that horns of elf-land dreamily sounded the name, this harsh name, that was new to him.

'De Bainriggs!' echoed Blunt, quietly too.

CHAPTER II

The next morning in Bonfire Hall across the lake Miss Corys de Bainriggs woke, as was her custom, at six. It was also her custom, immediately on waking, to scramble out of bed, swim out into the lake, there look round upon the enclosing fells and swim back again. This morning, however, she lay still, aware that, for the first time since she had had 'flu last spring, she did not want to get up.

'That wretched Jerry kept me awake at least an hour,' reflected Miss de Bainriggs, 'so I dare say I am tired.'

The German aeroplane had circled around Grasmere about two in the morning, grunting noisily, fading away above the fells and then coming back urr-ump, urr-ump. About two-thirty, the moon having clouded over, he had dropped a flare which, as Miss de Bainriggs had observed with rapture through her uncurtained window, fantastically lit the country-side. Then he had grunted himself finally out of earshot and had dropped twenty-three bombs in the sea and gone off home, as Miss de Bainriggs heard a week later from a farm-girl who had a boy-friend by the sea.

When she had thought about the Jerry Miss de Bainriggs suddenly remembered the water-supply. The Bonfire Hall taps had run dry last night. Before yesterday's rain there had been weeks of dry weather and some of the bracken on the fells was already changing colour; thus, bits of dry fern fronds blew about, and where the Hall water-pipe took off from a Loughrigg beck a grid, designed to keep out twigs, trout, and rolling stones rather than any less obvious impurities, was quickly closed by a mat of drifted fern. There were other problems that Miss de Bainriggs might profitably have considered, such as the ploughing of that part of the Bainriggs estate which had grown wheat in the eighteenth century, and the destruction of the bracken that was spreading its sterile wastes over the fell pastures. Instead, she got into her bathing-dress and an old overcoat and went off up the fell to clear the grid, a job almost as wetting as her usual swim in the lake.

In Bonfire Hall behind, and soon far below her, old Mrs. de Bainriggs, her grandmother, woke and began to wonder how she could get her own way about giving the Herdwicks' corn ration to the fowls while making it appear that it was Corys' way, and the other Mrs. de Bainriggs, mother of Corys, woke too, in her case from a haunted sleep in which she had dreamt of London and her husband in it. The Jerry in the night had made vivid once again her memory of those London nights, with Miles her husband, in the basement of the block of flats and, once again, she thought of them as happy compared to the endless hours spent in this safe solitude to which he had sent her.

'For solitude it is without Miles, Corys and Gran notwithstanding,' thought Blodwen.

Her name was Blodwen because she was Welsh. By birth she was an ap-Conan and her family was descended from Maelgwn, who had been king of Gwynedd in the sixth century and had died of seeing a yellow spectre in a marsh near Llandudno. Until she married she had lived in an ancient hall, at Corris, surrounded by dark, shiny mountains of slate waste. So she had called her baby Corys, for the Welsh name of her birth-place is Abercorys, and now that she had been sent away from London she sometimes longed to walk again by the waters of Tal-y-llyn, and shop in Machynlleth, and go behind the waterfall to the Chamber of Hwmffra Goch. Now that her naturally rosy face was blanched by years of town life, its pale oval emphasized the darkness of her eyes and her dark-brown, straight, soft hair, and gave her somewhat of an exotic look. And even her realistic acceptance of life could not quite dispel some faint air of tragedy that seemed associated with her unusual colouring and the persistent echo of what had once been a Welsh lilt in her speech.

'There goes Cory,' thought Blodwen, now observing her daughter climbing energetically up Loughrigg. 'How well she always seems. We were wise, I think, to let Bainriggs have her.' Then Blodwen, it seemed from her expression, fell into one of those Welsh meditations that, perhaps, helped to give her her air of remoteness and serenity. Yet, after a few moments, her look grew graver. 'I wonder, were we?' reflected Blodwen. 'And has Bainriggs got her, soul as well as body? I begin to think it has.'

Miles de Bainriggs was an official in the Ministry of Health, and life in a London flat had induced, apparently, in the infant Corys a state that was rather lack of health than any positive disorder. Anyhow, a long holiday at Bonfire Hall had given her something that had been withheld and her parents had decided that babies, like dogs, were undoubtedly at their best in the country. So Corys had been left behind when they returned to town. Bonfire Hall had become her home, and the little estate of Bainriggs, which a de Bainriggs of the fourteenth century held of the lord by fealty and a pound of cummin yearly, had become as much part of her as had the sound and shimmer of the lake, the singsong of her nurse talking the local dialect or the smooth feel of the polished oak partitioning at the Hall.

'There is Cory,' thought old Mrs. de Bainriggs, staring from the window of her room up at Loughrigg as she hooked about her opulent figure a strip of something in natural coloured wool, designed partially to restrain it. A spasm of discomfort altered her face: never could she forget or forgive that strange act of her late husband when, dying, he had made a will that left Bainriggs and the Hall to Corys, then thirteen years old. To his wife, nothing but the right to live at the Hall and an annual pittance. To his son, nothing at all.

'Well, anyhow, it is a mercy that foreign woman didn't get anything,' thought old Mrs. de Bainriggs, of that brown-and-white stranger from Wales who was her daughter-in-law.

Old Mrs. de Bainriggs, then a Miss Danger, had married the Miles de Bainriggs of her day when she was eighteen. She was the daughter of a scientist who had spent all but brief intervals of his adult life in the far north of Canada, studying meteorology and Eskimos and the response of the latter to the former. That she was also the daughter of a young woman of good English family who had played the piano admirably and died before she was thirty was very generally forgotten since her mother had, it seemed, been but the means of transmitting, unaltered, the characteristics of Mr. Danger. However, a few discerning people attributed the sensitive and yet casual attitude to life that distinguished the scientist's daughter, long before she became Mrs. de Bainriggs, to the piano playing of her mother. Her vagabond habits, her frequently uncontrollable temper, her love of good food and wines, her tolerance of sins of the body and intolerance for sins of mind and spirit, came to her, it was believed, entirely from her father.

At nineteen Ungava de Bainriggs (for her father had, unfortunately, insisted that she be called Ungava because in that rather forbidding land he had discovered something hitherto unknown about the marriage ceremonies of Eskimos) had given birth to her son Miles, now the father of Corys. After that, both with and without her husband, she had roamed about the world a great deal. She was not well able to pay for her roaming and when Miles her husband died she had been hard up in Tierra del Fuego and had had, as a result, a tiresome journey home. She was by this time sixty; her once magnificent health was somewhat damaged by fever and insect bites acquired in the Amazon jungles and by her habit of always eating as much as she wanted; with her usual courage she decided to give up travelling and become a Grasmere lady. Indeed, her husband's will being so odd, that was all she could afford to do.

'I hope she won't get any more bracken shoots,' thought old Mrs. de Bainriggs, on this August morning, still watching her granddaughter up on Loughrigg, and remembering the stresses and strains set up within her when Corys had insisted they should eat bracken shoots instead of asparagus.

That morning the old maid, Jane Peascod, woke later than any of them. She had acted as father and mother to the present Miles since his parents, when not in Bolivia or Korea, had felt ill at ease in his infantile, watchful, self-possessed presence. When Miles' child, Corys, had been left at Bonfire Hall it had been Miss Peascod who took entire charge of her with an expert ease that was in no way affected by the thirty years that had passed since the infant's father was a baby himself. However, though she had a way with babies, Jane was not of an affectionate disposition and this morning, as she lit the kitchen fire and then sat by it drinking tea, made from her little kettle she filled overnight, she thought not of any de Bainriggs but of two bad Herdwick sheep, more vagabond even than such sheep normally are. These rogues had been ravaging all the gardens Back o' Lake. Had they, in the dawn, eaten her favourite blackberry bushes at the edge of the wood? 'Miss Cory wouldn't drive them away,' thought Jane, bitterly, as that lady came in through the kitchen, dripping beck water on the clean slate flags, and marched in silence to the scullery tap. 'Miss Cory thinks it's patriotic for sheep to eat blackberry bushes,' mused Jane resentfully, and she made no reply when her former nursling said Ha! in her deep voice and triumphantly, as water gushed once more into the sink.

That morning Mr. Blunt had breakfasted early, too early for a holiday hotel, for he had demanded anything they could give him at eight o'clock and had then gone out, saying he would be out all day. Even so, he had not succeeded in dodging the pretty Sweetings, for all three of them, hearing him call for his boots while they still lay abed, had dressed in ten minutes and then met him, in the most casual manner, they hoped, on the front drive. However, he had shaken them off, by being vague about his plans and morose in his manner, and he had then walked to Pelter Bridge and strolled back along the Loughrigg Terrace Walk. By the time he reached the seat above the river between Rydal lake and Grasmere he knew that he was tired, too tired for the day of desultory rambling by which he had hoped to attain solitude. He sat down discouraged, and stared at Grasmere lake. Its still waters, under the clear summer sky, had a dark, purple-blue sheen like that of wild hyacinths. In the sunlit green of pastures and woodlands it lay, mysteriously coloured, hiding a world alien from the land and holding its Island, green as a frog, within its opaque and glossy surface.

'There,' thought Blunt, regarding the Island, 'I could be quiet. If any one landed I could shut myself in the barn and throw boiling water from the loop-lights.'

He strolled slowly on, aware that after yesterday's walk his heart must now be taken, gently, back to the hotel where his body must be suitably fed and then stretched prone—or is it supine? wondered Richard with vague memories of a First Aid course in his mind—upon a bed. However, after he had come out upon the road Back o' Lake, he was involved in a row. He began to hear shouting, faint and distant, but quickly getting louder and less distant. The shouting had an almost rhythmical quality that suggested some one emitting bellows timed by the panting breath of haste. Then a young person appeared some way ahead, hurrying towards Blunt down the green tunnel of the road. Leafy branches arched above, tall moss-grown walls on either side, the green fronds of bracken and polypody, and the wild scent of all of these gave to the air a green and scented dimness that made the young person appear rather spectral. In grey stockings, grey flannel shorts and a silver-grey, sleeveless pullover he (or she) looked remotely like a tall minnow, moving in an unusual posture under water. Not from this person came the shouting and, no doubt, this person sought escape from it and perhaps the black-and-white dog, held close against the grey pullover, was also a fugitive. In a few moments, so quickly did the young person walk, he (or she) had reached Richard, but only when she spoke did he feel certain that the dark-haired, thin creature in grey was a girl.

'The tall boy, girl I mean, in the wood last night!' thought Richard, suddenly convinced of the young person's identity.

'Hold her, please,' said the young person, now recognizable as female. As she spoke she pushed the dog against Richard's chest. 'She's terrified of him. Hold her and walk away a bit, if you don't mind. She shakes all over when she hears him. If I know she's safe with you I'll wait for him and send him off.'

'But—' said Blunt, awkwardly clutching the dog, which certainly was shaking as if its bony little body was too full of a terrified heart. 'But can't I deal with him, whoever he is? He sounds large and irritable—'

'No, no, go on! I know him, and he knows me,' said the girl, pushing back a spike of her straight, short hair as if she swept her face clear for battle. 'Do, please, take poor Jet farther away.'

Most unwillingly Richard retreated a few steps and then stood, clutching Jet and prepared, if it seemed necessary, to do what he could verbally, and perhaps by throwing the dog at him, to help quell the violence he expected from the shouting man. Fight him, he could not.

'How awful it is to know one is helpless,' thought Richard, bitterly conscious of his labouring heart. 'Ah! There comes the brute!' And in spite of those heavy, slow thumpings in his side he took a step forward, and lifted a stone off the wall beside him. It would be easier, kinder, and would not vex the girl so much if he threw a stone rather than the dog.

The approaching man looked immense and rather distraught, but the girl's voice, as she began to address him, reassured Blunt. She spoke with the crisp decision of authority; in the voice of one who had never had need to fear shouting men and proposed never to do so.

'Now, Jos Blaine, that's enough,' said the girl. 'Stop following me and stop shouting like that. I won't have it. Stop, I tell you. Don't you hear me?' Upon this, the slim creature stepped forward and she must have managed, somehow, to make the movement menacing, for the man stood still and his shouts, though still loud, became articulate.

'Gimme my dog,' said the man. 'What do'y mean by it? Taking my dog! What for do'y want to bodder a poor farmer, a young lady like you?'

'You know well enough what for,' said the lady. 'You're not fit to have charge of a dog. This time, I'm going to keep Jet. You shall never have her again.'

At this the man Blaine began to dance, though without any forward movement.

'I'll have the law on you,' said Mr. Blaine, dancing. 'You can't thieve a poor man's dog nowadays. I'll have the law on you and the gentleman who's got my dog. Here, gimme my dog, you!'

Shouting the last words at Blunt the immense Blaine began again to display hysterical symptoms. Obviously he was working himself up to commit violence and Blunt realized that his own presence was making things worse for the young person in shorts. Yet, how could he withdraw? Hesitating in great distress of mind Blunt heard, again with relief, the voice of the girl, still as calm and dictatorial as it had been. Evidently she felt capable of defending not only herself and Jet but also of counteracting the infuriating presence of a male stranger.

'Be quiet! Listen, Jos Blaine, once and for all, before it's too late,' said she. 'What about that ewe, left dying for a fortnight in your intack? What about your mare, beaten and starved till she dropped dead on the Raise? What about those fowls, shut in on a foot of muck and with no food or water? What about those calving heifers, crushed into a wagon so that two were dead? You kicked Jet, brutally, just now in Red Lion Square. Every one saw you. Every one heard what I said to you. Every one knows what you are to your unfortunate animals. I shall have plenty of witnesses. I took Jet from you and I'm going to keep her. If you make any more trouble about her, the least little bit more trouble, I'll get the Bench to make it illegal for you to keep any dogs at all.'

The last words were spoken slowly and with a hatred and contempt that made them sound like a series of blows, deliberate, deadly and meant to be so. Certainly Mr. Blaine seemed to find them shocking. He ceased to dance and for a moment he stood silent, staring at the young woman. In this pause Blunt observed that a weasel or stoat was as interested in the scene as was he himself. It was in the dry stone wall beside him, looking out from a cranny, disappearing, looking out from two rows higher up, disappearing again to poke its sharp nose from between two stones, down at ground level. It made Blunt think of some one inquisitive, careering about inside a tall house and peering out from one window after another.

'You never would!' said Mr. Blaine, at last, and in quite a gentle, argumentative voice. 'The real gentry'd never play such a trick on a poor man. Why, I couldn't get my living without my dogs.'

'And a good job it would be if you didn't get it,' said the girl. 'You'd do less harm if you were dead, unless, of course, there are animals in hell.'

The immense Mr. Blaine at this, threw up his huge, knobbly hands. 'What a way for a young lady to speak!' said he, and then, savagely again, 'A man'd think you were God A'mighty, but let me tell you—'

'You've got Him to deal with as well as me,' said the girl, briskly interrupting, 'And he'll never let go of you. Now, be off. Remember I shall do what I said if I have any more trouble with you, and more than I said, too.'

She looked for a moment at Mr. Blaine, in what seemed to Blunt a meaning silence and then turned her back on him and held out her hands to Richard for the dog.

'Give her to me, please,' said she, eyeing with disfavour the way in which Richard, his agitated feelings tightening his grip, held the shuddering Jet. 'And don't stand looking at that brute,' she added quickly. 'Ignore him. Turn your back on him.'

'I thought perhaps he was going to kick up some kind of shindy,' said Blunt, rather reluctantly doing as he was bid.

'Not if you ignore him. He's a Cumberland man, and nowt good comes ower t'Raise,' said the girl, cuddling Jet and beginning to walk forward again but now more leisurely.

'They say the same north of the Raise,' said Blunt, with a chuckle. 'Can you really get his dogs taken away from him?' he added, walking by her side and aware of a complete silence behind him.

'I dare say not, but he may believe I can. And, anyhow, I know quite a lot more about him, as he well knows. Moving stock when there was foot and mouth, not notifying sheep scab, selling lots more butter than he gets coupons for, and once—' here, the young lady paused, perhaps unwilling to recount to a stranger the further crimes even of a Cumberland man. 'I don't think he'll dare to make any more fuss,' added she. She was looking down at Jet as she spoke, into Jet's timid, misty, trustful eyes. And as she looked she began suddenly and silently to weep so that the dog's rough coat shone with her tears.

'What a fool I am!' said she, angrily, and rubbing her hand across her eyes. 'But it's the thought of all the others, everywhere, that I can't take care of—'

'And a bit of a reaction after the row,' reflected Blunt as he said, gently: 'I know, it's horrid. But perhaps they'll get a bit of their own back, one day. How do we know?'

'I turn off here,' said the girl, abruptly. 'Good-bye, and thank you very much for holding Jet.'

She went through a gate and began to walk along a track that led down towards the lake. In spite of her dress she did not walk like a boy. There was a precision and grace in her movements that had nothing of the clumsy, elastic uncertainty that gives a sense of power to a boy's stride.

As Blunt went thoughtfully back towards Grasmere he remembered a young robin he had held, one spring long ago, in his hand. In its first speckled brown feathers it was soft as a powder-puff and not much bigger than a walnut, so that his sense of touch was too coarse and blunted to respond to its minute pressure. He could not feel it, lying in his palm, till it kicked him, with undaunted tramplings that felt like a butterfly dancing. This child, in boy's clothes, reminded him of that robin; so young; so valorous; imbued, like the feathered atom, with that great mystery of a brave spirit, come from who knows where to animate the helpless flesh.

'Plucky kid,' thought Blunt, as he neared the village without overtaking Mr. Joshua Blaine and, also, neared the day's newspapers that must surely have arrived by now and would, perhaps, have his portrait in them. 'I wonder who she is.'

CHAPTER III

The day's newspapers had his portrait in them, though very small because of the paper shortage. Exasperation drove the thought of the girl who was like a boy out of Richard's mind and he was grateful that evening for the mild distraction of going with the Sweetings to the Island, and the more so since these three ladies apparently thought no worse of him for having jilted his betrothed. The late sunset of Summer Time still glowed, though dusk already climbed the fells from the shadowed valley. Behind the clear edges of the Easedale fells shone a cloudless glow from the hidden sun and on the eastern heights, on the tops of Seat Sandal and Fairfield, Stone Arthur and Rydal Fell lay a vivid red-gold light, clear and brilliant and still as if evening had crystallized fells and sky in a stainless and unchanging brilliance. The lake, shadowed, like the hollow in which it lay, by the western wall of fells yet reflected the bright sky from every faintest ripple and as they rowed to the Island upon the dark reflection of Silver How this was broken by their passage into a stir of sunset light.

On the Island there was a scent of dew on grassland and the flat scent of lake water; dead calm the water lay black about it, hiding all it held; from the road came the intermittent roar of passing cars and the church clock struck ten from the hazy shadows of the valley bottom. On the far shore, lower down, Bonfire Hall showed, shut in between the vague darkness of climbing woods and the clear, metallic blackness of the shadowed lake.

'There's Miss de Bainriggs, lighting up,' said the three Sweetings, all together, as a light, bright and pale as moonlight, shone from some window that had been hidden until now.

Blunt thought they were going to tell him what they knew of Miss de Bainriggs, but they were interrupted, to his annoyance.

'Oh! Look! There's Jownie Wife in her hogg'us! Isn't she an old scream!'

said Rudie and Mag, giving the local name to what off-comes call the barn upon the Island.

There indeed was Jownie Wife, in the hogg-house that had been built for the growing lambs that are known at the Lakes as hoggs. The door was shut; there was as yet no lamp lit in the little old building but first from one loop-light and then another looked the face of Jownie Wife, a narrow, withered, tight little face with black eyes, proportionately small and restless, that scanned suspiciously the four strangers who stood upon the rocky turf beside their boat.

'She's exactly like a stoat or weasel, running about in an old stone wall and looking out,' said Blunt, vividly reminded of the little beast that had watched the scene with Mr. Joshua Blaine that morning. 'Has she any right to live there?'

In bed, half an hour later, Blunt lay thinking of the Island. Before they left it the sunset light had lifted even from the fell tops and above the shadowed country-side the sky had glowed alone, immense, remote, darkening slowly as the shadow of the earth's rim climbed its vaporous heights. Jownie Wife had disappeared within her stone walls. No cars passed upon the road. The silence had seemed waiting for the moon, for as they rowed home it rose about Rydal Fell and filled the valley with its shifting network of light and thin shadows.

'I suppose crowds might land there by day, but if I could get rid of Jownie Wife I should, anyhow, be quite alone at night,' reflected Richard and kept himself awake with visions of a watery solitude.

Next morning, tired but determined at least to ask for what he wanted, he set out for Bonfire Hall.

'She, this Miss de Bainriggs person, might anyhow let me have a tent on it for a week or two,' thought Richard, staring down upon the Island from Back O' Lake.

From the road that went on over Red Bank Blunt took the turning that led, he had been told, to Bonfire Hall. It was that which the girl with the rescued sheep-dog had taken yesterday. A rough cart-track sloped down to the level of the lake and then followed the shore past an old white cottage and so, a few hundred yards farther on, to the Hall.

'Queer old place,' thought Richard, regarding it. 'And, surely, sunless all winter.'

Bonfire Hall was a small house but had been smaller, for irregularities in its ancient roof and straggling ground plan showed that additions had been made to it at one time and another. Most of it was white plastered. It was roofed with local green slates, rough and thick. From one of its round stone chimneys, grown here and there with moss and fern, rose a vaporous blue pencil of wood smoke. Small, stone mullioned windows, dark with tree shadows, showed no curtains and gave no sense of welcome as Blunt approached, rather hesitatingly, for he was beginning to realize how absurdly he would be disappointed if Miss de Bainriggs put an end to his dreams of an island life. Only a narrow strip of closely cut grass lay between the Hall and the lake and no wall or fence shut it off from the hill-side and the wood of oak, ash and birch that grew close up to its southern walls. In front of the nail-studded oak door that had been the front door since the Hall was built in 1601 Richard hesitated a moment more, his hand half lifted towards the knocker. Some fold in the fell sides cut off the sunshine so that the house was still in the cool morning shadow; there was a faint scent of mould and damp moss from the wooded slopes and their green darkness enclosed the back of the Hall in the silence and leafy mystery of wild, uncared-for woodland. Yet, to the left, the calm lake, in full sunshine, lay bright upon its grassy banks beside the Hall as if some invisible barrier in the air divided the land shadows from the lit and shining waters. Midway between the forest dimness and the bright lake stood Blunt and knocked, with a loud rap that was echoed back from the wall of trees.

Jane Peascod's face showed commonly no expression and it showed none now as she heard Mr. Blunt ask for Miss de Bainriggs and led him across the stone-flagged hall.

'A gentleman,' said Jane, opening a door and speaking to a person or persons within it, and so subdued did Blunt feel by now that he was sensibly gratified to hear this commendation.

The room was a long one. A window on the right of the door looked into the wood and this end of the room was dim with its green shadow; at the other end a window was open to the shining, blue, spacious brightness of the lake. In the middle, surrounded by immense round baskets, sat two solemn gentlewomen, facing the door so that the left sides of their faces were tinged with a faint, green shadow and the right oddly lit by the light reflected from the waters. Piled high in some of the baskets were heaps of grey-green, woolly-looking stuff and the hands of the gentlewomen were filled with the same fluffy substance. Perhaps, thought Richard, with an idiotic earnestness, they were solemn because of this fluffy stuff or because they were dark on one side and light on the other.

'Miss de Bainriggs?' said Richard, putting into his voice as much of its most persuasive music as he thought it would hold.

Grandmother de Bainriggs was no spinster; Blunt felt sure of this though he cautiously directed his voice between the two of them. Perhaps the thin, pale, inscrutable lady was a Miss; she was so tall he thought she might be, but did not ladies who married often become inscrutable?

The solemnity of the two Mrs. de Bainriggs had been real as well as apparent. They had both been feeling ill-tempered. Grandy, as Corys had always called her grandmother, had had one of her tiresome fits because she regretted not being in the Falkland Islands, as she had been in August thirty-five years ago. All the morning as they picked bits of rubbish from the grey-green sphagnum moss she had been comparing Grasmere very unfavourably with those wind-swept, sheep-ridden pasturelands so resoundingly beset by stormy seas.

'Here,' had said old Mrs. de Bainriggs, 'here, in this foul hollow of a valley, we are simply smothered in trees. There are no trees in the Falklands and there is some air there. If a decent breeze ever gets into this valley it can't get out again because of hills and trees. Dark, damp, diseased trees, smelling of rot and full of screeching jays, that's what we're shut in by. If your father-in-law hadn't gone mad or been got at while I was in Tierra del Fuego this place would have been mine, as it should have been, and I'd have had all the trees cut right up Red Bank. But Corys is as fantastic as you are about trees; what possessed my son to beget such a child I can't imagine.'

Picking over the masses of sphagnum moss that Corys had gathered in the last few sunny days Blodwen resorted to her usual habit when Grandy was in a tantrum and silently repeated to herself a Welsh englyn before making any reply to the older lady's abusive grumblings. She had had to repeat one at three different times before Richard Blunt's arrival and her curious serenity was being invaded by an intense irritation that might have relieved itself in an explosion of temper as quick and fiery as Grandy's own had he not come, looking so appealing and pleasant and asking for Corys, which seemed so odd. Strange men never came asking for Corys.

'Neither of us is a Miss, thank heaven,' said Grandy, replying, and with complete amiability, to Blunt's query. 'We've been spared that anyhow. Must you have a Miss de Bainriggs? Because she's either up Loughrigg or cleaning the duck-house.'

'I was told that it is a Miss de Bainriggs who owns the Island,' said Richard, 'and I wanted to ask her about the Island.'

'Do sit down,' said Blodwen, getting up, 'and I'll try and find my daughter—'

But Grandy had her own way of calling Corys.

'Cory!' said Grandy, leaning back and shouting in a great melodious bellow towards the open window. 'Cory! Cory!'

These two latter shouts were directed respectively to the ceiling and towards the polished oak panelling of the wall that faced the door.

'You can hear everything, everywhere, all over this old rattletrap of a house,' said old Mrs. de Bainriggs. 'Practically all the inside walls are wood partitioning.'

Richard sat down, reflecting that if this charming, foreign looking younger woman were the mother of Miss de Bainriggs the latter lady could not be the middle-aged countrywoman of his imagination. And as he sat, reflecting this, the door opened and a dirty, tall child, wearing boy's overalls, came in.

'What on earth are you roaring about now, Grandy? I was just cleaning—' began the child and fell abruptly silent, staring at Blunt with what seemed an alarmed defiance.

Mr. Blunt felt himself bewildered and wondered if he was bewitched.

This tall creature, in stained blue overalls, with a muddy smear across its right cheek and hands that looked as if they had just delved into those various mucks so delightfully eaten by ducks in the poem, had a strong resemblance to the clean girl in shorts who had dropped tears on Jet yesterday. Yet, surely, this was a child; even when washed it must remain a tall child, whereas the young person of yesterday had had a dignity and poise that were quite unchildlike.

'I thought you would be in the duck-house,' said Grandy, apparently gratified at her prescience. 'Here is a gentleman, come to see you. But if he dislikes the smell of ducks as much as I do you had better go and wash before he sees you much longer.'

'My daughter does a great deal of farm work about the Hall; it is difficult to get help in these war days,' said the younger woman as the dirty child left the room. She was faintly flushed and her manner a little apologetic so that grandmother, glancing askance at her, remarked loudly that dirty bodies did little harm in the world.

'Her daughter! Then, can that child be Miss de Bainriggs?' thought Blunt, incredulous but already feeling annoyed. It seemed that he was being purposely bewildered and baffled by these queer people. How could any man make a deal about an island with a child, even when it was clean?

'The de Bainriggs estate belongs to my daughter, Corys,' said the younger woman. 'She is older than she looks; she is almost seventeen.'

Mr. Blunt realized that the child's mother was aware of his feelings but the old lady spoke before he could reply.

'My husband went mad and then wrote a will,' said she, with a side glance at the visitor from her long, blue-green eyes. 'I was away at the time, in Tierra del Fuego,' said Grandy, 'and so he undoubtedly went mad. He always said I should unbalance his mind and I told him it would be better if I did, but, of course, I was not thinking of wills.'

Now, the child came back. Perhaps the smell or smears of ducks had penetrated the blue overalls, or perhaps it was shyness that had made her put on her school cloak. Corys had been to school at Rydal Hall until two months ago and she, like the other girls, had worn one of those long dark blue cloaks with a coloured lining to the hood that made them all look so delightful walking on the Rydal road. Her hood was lined with apple green silk, and as it lay softly upon her narrow shoulders she looked like a graduate, precociously about to receive a learned degree. Her face was now clean, though a little shiny because it was damp. Her eyes, long, but a deeper blue than her grandmother's, regarded Blunt with a remote and watchful gaze. He learnt, much later, that she feared he had come about her seizure of the dog Jet and, if he had, it could be only because he had silly scruples about its legality.

'I have been wondering whether you would let me rent the Island and live on it,' said Blunt, feeling that brevity and directness were required of him by the young Miss de Bainriggs' earnest look.

'Oh, no,' said Corys, her voice and bearing, the sudden clutch at her cloak and quick look at her mother, all showing an alarm that seemed unnatural. 'Oh, no! Of course not!'

'But why not?' said Richard, his kind look, so weary and tolerant, yet stiffened by the authority of his age and sex.

'Every reason not,' said the girl, looking away from him. 'I am sorry, but it is, of course, impossible.'

Later that day, reflecting on the argument that followed, Richard thought that he had felt as a dog must, chasing a small bird through undergrowth, for all the while he was conscious that the child might escape, mentally and perhaps even physically, at any moment into some airy distance that he could not reach. She had power; she had motives mysterious to him; he had nothing but persistency and patience. He won, or thought he did, but at the end, highly flushed, tired and so excited that her deep voice had grown small and husky, Corys said: 'It's time I got some of my own back from Jownie Wife,' thus leaving him uncertain whether his pleadings or his personality had had anything to do with his victory.

As to her intense reluctance at first even to consider his proposal he felt himself a little enlightened when, to save him a longer walk back to the Prince, she rowed him across the lake to the private boat-landing on the de Bainriggs' land near Penny Rock. Old Mrs. de Bainriggs had suggested that she should do so.

'You've been ill, and your heart is doing queer things at this moment,' had said Grandy, dispassionately regarding him. 'I've had a lot to do with hearts; in China especially; loving and diseased hearts, both of them, in plenty.'

On Penny Rock Corys looked automatically to the right to see if old John Benson the woodman had felled the sixty-year-old birch yet, and then up the wooded slope where friends of hers, a greater spotted woodpecker and a red squirrel, lived, not at all in harmony with each other.

'You see, we've had Bainriggs since nobody knows when,' said she, after this observant silence and with something of a childish pomposity. 'It, all of this, is part of us, somehow.'

'Don't people want to buy building sites with lake frontages?' asked Richard, aware that she had been trying to explain her reluctance to let him rent the Island.

'They have done, before the war,' said Corys, 'but people are queer, some people, aren't they?'

Across the sunlit lake Blodwen de Bainriggs looked at her mother-in-law.

'What can have made her consent?' said she. 'I was never so surprised in my life.'

'I think when he offered a pound a week she began to think about it,' said Grandy, reflectively. 'Fifty pounds a year didn't seem to interest her. And, of course, she has got her knife in Jownie Wife, well in. But when all's said and done, Blodwen, I believe it was because he is a man and Corys is female, whatever she may look like. She's not in the least conscious of being female and won't be, perhaps for years at the rate she is going, but she is and some day she'll know it.'

'But goodness me, Grandy, the man is old enough to be her father,' said Blodwen, amused and yet a little irritated.

'Perhaps, just about, and I don't mean that sort of feeling, exactly, Blodwen,' said Grandy. 'I mean that, even now, Corys responds to a man's influence differently from the way she would if a woman had wanted the Island. And she may have been sorry for him, too, because he looks ill but I doubt that.'

'She is saying good-bye to him now; they are shaking hands,' said Blodwen, who was long-sighted. 'A pound a week will be very useful, Grandy,' she added, sensitively trying to evade any further reference to her daughter's sex.

Beside the little old stone boat-landing at Penny Rock Corys shook hands, formally, and in what she hoped was the correct style between landlord and tenant. The rocky ground was dark in the shadow of the beech trees, and mottled by little circles of sunlight; the lake waters lay upon the rock and shingle, clear and brown; beyond the trees there was a sunny stillness that seemed held in the green hollow as the lake was held.

Mr. Blunt was almost uncomfortably conscious of this stillness and thought of the war that went on beyond it. Corys did not think directly of war, though her thin face was grave and thoughtful as she looked at the sunlit meadows across the water, and then at her tenant.

'I am thinking of having an acre of cascara sagrada bushes planted over there,' said Corys. '*The Times* says it might be worth while unless the war stops soon. Do you know where one can buy cascara, the bushes I mean?'

CHAPTER IV

Moonshine is at least as mysterious as it looks. At the full moon it does queer things to some people. At Bonfire Hall it gave Grandy palpitations of the heart; she would wake, in the silent, moonlit night and palpitate. She was not surprised at this since she knew of natives, in the West Indies she said, or it might have been the East Indies, whose insistence that some tropical plant must be harvested at the full of the moon was proved by scientists to be correct since the moon, when full, did something salutary to the sap or tissues of the tropical plant. If it could do this, what might it not do to human hearts or anything else that was alive?

On the Island Jownie Wife could not sleep. The moon looked through one of the loop-lights in the hogg-house and Jownie Wife wriggled about on her bed of dry bracken and felt the old, familiar call of the road.

In the Prince of Wales Hotel, across the lake, Mr. Ernest Lovely, known to his hundreds of acquaintances as Ern, also lay awake, wriggling, but in his case on a mattress delightfully full of springs.

'Can't you keep still, Ern?' said Mrs. Lovely, but Ern could not, because of the full moon that made him feel in his bones that the Prince would shortly be requisitioned and where would he and Mrs. Lovely and their admirable son and clever daughter go then? Being a townsman he did not know that his immediate troubles were due to the moon, so he replied to Mrs. Lovely that he could not keep still because of the rum butter he had eaten too much of at afternoon tea. He did not wish to worry Mrs. Lovely, who was not strong, and so he lied thus and went on, silently wriggling and thinking of the Prince. The Lake District was full already. Many people from bombed cities had come there. A bomb had bounced off the roof of Mr. Lovely's house in Lancashire. Mr. Lovely had spent the last war in the trenches of Flanders and so he disliked bombs even more than did his wife.

'Oh, dash this war!' said Mr. Lovely, silently, in his head, and said worse things too as, wriggling, he saw the full moon, a bomber's moon, shining at him through a narrow, illegal space between the black-out curtains.

On the Island Jownie Wife, less ignorant and more resolute than Mr. Lovely, yielded to the moon some time before dawn. Her father had been a charcoal burner in the woods of High Furness and her mother a gipsy, so she knew she would have to yield and did so early. She got up, kicked out her smouldering fire of stolen logs, wrapped in a bit of sacking the few things she would want on her wanderings, and rolled the remainder of her possessions in newspaper and poked the bundle a little way up the chimney. Then she locked the padlock on the hogg-house door, hid the key in a cranny in the stone wall and rowed herself across to Back o' Lake. There, in that uncanny time before moonset and sunrise when there are no shadows, she hid her boat in its usual place among reeds and alder bushes and set forth, climbing towards the pale western sky-line.

Old John Benson, the Bainriggs' woodman whom Richard Blunt had greeted beside his bonfire in the deluge of rain two days ago, spoke with Jownie Wife a few minutes later. Old John was fetching water for his breakfast from a spring in the wood and Jownie Wife passed him, climbing quickly by a path, overgrown, and forgotten by all save such as she.

'T'se gaan off,' said Jownie Wife and was hidden at once as the green hazel bushes closed in again behind her.

The deluge of the day of Blunt's arrival had done no perceptible good to the country-side. After weeks of drought, polypody and parsley ferns in the stone walls were still withered and brown; the waste grasses upon the fells were burnt to a scorched pallor that looked from some way off like sunshine, uncanny beneath a clouded sky; the valley meadows had lost their perennial greenness; grass on the wall tops stood blanched like the white hair of age and young silver birches, with their leaves dry and brown, gave an uneasy look to the green woods, as if disease or some strange disorder of the seasons had stricken the country-side. On the morning that Jownie Wife went away the water failed again in Bonfire Hall and, a second time, Corys had to clear dry bracken from the grid in the beck. Coming down Loughrigg she met Old John going to his work and he told her of Jownie Wife's departure.

'She's got watter and to spare round hogg'us,' said Old John, who had found his spring nearly dry that day. 'What does she want to go off for, like that?'

Thus it came about that Corys, still completely absorbed in thoughts of her tenant, rowed herself across to the boat-landings at the Prince of Wales Hotel and told the news to Richard Blunt.

'Jownie Wife has gone off, on one of her long tramps, no doubt. She may be away for weeks,' said Corys. 'So will you come now and have a look round the hogg-house?'

As she rowed inshore Corys had seen Richard, lounging in a hammock chair on the little green lawn by the lake, and surrounded by the pale heads of the Sweeting sisters. He had jumped up at her approach and come to meet her with the tall figures of Essie, Mag and Rudie forming an elegant screen behind him. For this was Miss de Bainriggs, they understood, and if so how odd she was, but how exciting it would be if they could get to know her. With not one of the natives of Grasmere had the Sweetings, as yet, become even acquainted.

'Of course I'll come. I longed to go yesterday but you rowed me the other way,' said Richard, smiling at the grave young landowner and wondering why she was dirty again.

Corys hesitated. She was unused to accounting for her actions or trying to explain what she felt. Moreover, though she did not know that her hair had bits of dusty bracken in it and that a slimy alder twig from the beck had smeared her left cheek, she felt vaguely uneasy in the presence of the Sweetings. Very trig, fashionable, worldly and sure of themselves, and overpoweringly feminine did the Sweeting sisters appear to Corys.

'Well, Jownie Wife is a pig and a wretch but I didn't exactly want to tell her she's got to go,' said Corys, at last, and mumbling rather. 'I hoped she'd go off soon, it's ages since she has, and now we can decide everything peacefully.'

Behind Blunt the Sweetings were hovering; behind them hovered Mr. Lovely. Mr. Lovely had an aptitude for finding out things. From across the lawn he had found out that Corys was Miss de Bainriggs, who owned land in Grasmere.

'Pardon,' said Mr. Lovely, his short, fat legs carrying him quickly past those Sweeting girls. 'Pardon,' said Mr. Lovely again, and this time to Corys and Mr. Blunt, 'but you're Miss de Bainriggs, I understand, and I've been wanting to ask you if you'd care to sell me a bit of land. A bit I could build a country cottage on, if you take me, and at a war price, of course. I don't mind what I pay if I want a thing, or if mother wants a thing either. You ask mother about those sables!' Here, Mr. Lovely jerked a stubby thumb towards his wife who sat, under a weeping tree, smoking, and screwing into her ear-lobes ear-rings of the same scarlet as her painted lips.

Corys looked at Mr. Lovely and then at Mrs. Lovely, vaguely expecting to see sables, hot though the day was. She had not met any one like Mr. Lovely before, for Bonfire Hall was secluded. Moreover, she still felt confused and baffled by the sight of the three Sweetings, yet she found time to wonder if ear-rings and scarlet paint were really so much more barbarous than other forms of adornment as they appeared to be. Before she could make any audible reply to Mr. Lovely there came a loud shriek from Mrs. Lovely, who had heard father talking of her sables.

'Always boasting, father!' said Mrs. Lovely, shrieking again but only because it was her custom to shriek, when greeting any one or responding to greeting. As she shrieked she rose and came and put her arm round Rudie Sweeting's waist.

'Where do you keep yourself, inside this?' said Mrs. Lovely, squeezing Rudie. 'Queer to think her, and father there, are both human, isn't it?' added Mrs. Lovely to Corys, as Rudie wriggled resentfully away from her.

'This is Miss de Bainriggs, mother,' said Mr. Lovely, but as if he did not believe it himself. 'I was just asking her about a bit of land for a summer cottage, as you might say.'

Mr. Lovely thus elusively referred to remote plans in his secret mind since he did not wish to alarm his wife about his full moon premonition that the Prince would be requisitioned.

Corys hesitated, uncertain to whom and to what she should reply. Her grave look returned to the Misses Sweeting before she gave her serious regard to Mr. Lovely, for it was they who seemed to demand her watchful attention.

'I am sorry, but no part of Bainriggs land is ever for sale,' said Corys at last, and she turned to Mr. Blunt.

'Haughty young miss, that, if she is a miss,' said Mr. Lovely, biting his finger-nails in turn and staring after Corys and Richard, now rowing away from him. 'And what is she taking him to the Island for?' Here, Mr. Lovely fell silent, suddenly wondering if the young miss had double-crossed him and was going to let that Blunt fellow buy the Island and build a bungalow on it. 'With electricity and telephone cables taken across on the bed of the lake it might do for us,' reflected Mr. Lovely, of the Island, and thought he would have a talk with Blunt later and buy him off, if it should seem advisable.

Asking permission and at the same moment taking it as granted the Sweeting sisters leapt, but lightly and with skill, into the blue boat their father had bought for them in Bowness and followed Miss de Bainriggs and Blunt across the lake. Once on the Island they were all observed, from the lawn at the Prince, to disappear within the hogg-house and stay there, while the Sweetings' Blue Bird silently slid its bow off the Island beach and drifted away, trailing oars that were fortunately pinned to the row-locks.

'Ah! Ha! That old barn on the Island!' said Mr. Lovely, to himself. 'A bit of roughcast, and one or two bow windows thrown out and a bathroom, perhaps built out on Gothic pillars, and it might do, for a bit anyhow.'

So pondered Mr. Lovely, who had never been on the Island, and then he began to think of Gerald and Myra, his elegant son and daughter, who studied, he in Cambridge and she at Liverpool University and thus grew, both of them, daily more elegant and learned, and he sighed.

'Don't bite your nails, father,' said Mrs. Lovely, with a disapproving shriek.

Out there in the hogg-house, Corys looked anxiously at her tenant, realizing that the thought of a pound a week had become most pleasant to her.

'If you don't like it, of course, the bargain is off,' said Corys, wishing those dressed-up girls would not chatter like starlings and stand, gaping, at the roof and the floor and Jownie's bed. 'It must be swarming with fleas in here,' added Corys, to the sisters but, having no doubt only a slight experience of fleas, the silly things did not run away.

'There are no proper windows, and the earth floor will be cold, and the floorboards of the loft are a bit rotten, and you'll have a job rowing fuel across,' said Corys, again to Mr. Blunt. 'And it will have to be fumigated, after Jownie Wife. She—she's not always quite clean, though her face is, and usually her apron,' added Corys, hastily, desperately anxious not to be too depressing.

Mr. Blunt had heard nothing that any of the girls had said but had observed his future home and made up his mind as he did so.

'It'll do for me all right,' he now said, aware that the child de Bainriggs seemed to expect him to speak. 'It'll be a bower of beauty by the time I've got it tidied up. But from outside you'll have no idea it isn't still full of fleas,' he added, hastily, seeing apprehension shadow the smeared face of his landlady. 'I'll not do a thing to it that'll make it look as if it weren't full of hoggs, as well as fleas, and I won't tread a path, or lop a tree or move one stone on the Island. It'll be just the same green, prehistoric hump covered with seventeenth-century hoggs with me on it as off it.'

By now the Sweeting ladies had become almost inarticulate with excitement and it was through their squeaks and exclamations that Corys said, in the deepest tones of her deep voice, 'I believe you,' and looked at Blunt as she spoke with trust and understanding.

Soon after, Corys rowed out to the Sweetings' boat, towed it to the Island with a bit of string, and they all returned to the Prince. That night Richard Blunt felt well content. He had spent many holidays, tramping and camping, before the war. He had no doubt he would make himself comfortable in the hogg-house. He had no doubt that, in a week or two, he would be alone on the Island, day and night, for when autumn came and the summer visitors left Grasmere, rowing on the lake would cease till next year. Surrounded by that great ring of pure and endless light that was the shining of the lake waters surely, Richard thought, he could the more profitably meditate on Eternity and, but this was quite a new idea, read up, and write a treatise on, the history of Bainriggs.

'There must be libraries,' reflected Richard, 'and old documents, perhaps in the church. It would be rather fun and please that odd, long, competent infant who is my landlord.'

Half smiling as he thought of Corys, Richard glanced at the letter board as he went by on his way to bed. There was a letter for him, put there only recently because the postman had dropped it in a bush, owing to a wasp. He had dropped all letters, for the Prince, but only Richard's had been left, deep in the bush, until a Miss Smith, who lived in the hotel and was mad, went looking for autumn birds' nests at dusk. Now, all sense of content left Richard. Miserably he opened and, yet more miserably, read the letter and all night the thought of it shadowed what had been that calm, bright eternal ring of waters that was to lie between his uneasy mind and the suffering world. For the worst had happened: the letter, sent on by his mother, was from Miss Ozzard in Chelsea and in it she forgave and blessed him.

'Curse her!' thought Richard, writhing in bed, but not because the moon was full. 'Blast the wretched girl! She couldn't have written anything more utterly exasperating.'

All through September Grasmere was quite full of visitors, dry, and very hot. Those were the wise houses that closed windows and drew dark curtains after the first coolness of morning was over. Bonfire Hall, thus shielded against the cloudless glare, kept the freshness of night all through the sunny day so that to go into it felt like the entering of some cave, dim and cool with the coolness of shaded stone. All over the vale of Grasmere sheep lay in the shade so that from the dark shadows of trees and walls, and the dry stream beds under bridges, their pale faces looked forth, stirred by the hurried breaths that shook their woolly bodies. There were grass fires on the fells and some said spies set them alight to guide German raiders. So windless was the weather that on the fell tops, even on the summit of Helvellyn, there was the same dim, hazy heat as in the valleys and it seemed that the sky must be absorbing sunshine all through its vaporous heights.

By the end of September the hogg-house on the Island had been cleansed and its chimney cleared of Jownie Wife's bundle. The Lakes Urban Council had given a grudging consent to its temporary occupation as a dwelling-house, and Blunt had bought a few necessaries in Ambleside. At last he moved into his new home, accompanied by several boat loads of odd bits of furniture, saucepans, bedding, two oil lamps, seven pounds of candles and a dozen Penguin books in orange, blue and cherry coloured covers. That night, as on every fine night, the flat smell of lake water and the wild scent of dew on grassland came, with the bodiless motion of scent, into the hogg-house at every loop-light and through the open door, and he saw the new moon over Silver How. Its thin brilliance shone on his bed through one of the higher loop-lights but only for a moment or two as it and the moving earth voyaged in space.

'Why do they move? What started them?' thought Blunt, half asleep, and something of the mystery of the universe seemed to move behind his dreams, as stars move behind the homely branches of apple trees.

Nearly a fortnight later the Hunter's Moon shone, immense and the colour of a tea rose, above the valley. It shone also above Jownie Wife, at that time half asleep in a barn on Torpenhow Common. It would be full in a day or two and she felt it stir familiar tides of unrest within her meagre bosom and, this moon, they set towards home.

'I'll get back to my hogg'us,' said Jownie Wife to herself and knew that, once there, she would settle for the winter. Her urge to wander was appeased. At dawn, this time while the moon shadows still lay long and dark from the west, she set forth towards Keswick with Skiddaw immense against the sunrise and grey lag geese, homing as she was, calling over her head.

CHAPTER V

In most particulars Mr. and Mrs. Sweeting were in no way remarkable save for their parenthood, for, indeed, few husbands and wives have three daughters so decorative as were the Misses Sweeting. However, Mr. Sweeting was different from most men in that he had made enough money to be rich and retire at the age of forty and Mrs. Sweeting looked much younger than her age even when overheated, as she frequently was in this extraordinary weather. Those capabilities that had made Mr. Sweeting rich had made him, also, alert, and he began to muse upon the possibility of the Prince being requisitioned soon after Mr. Lovely had been oppressed by the same idea. What was worse, he talked about his misgivings, greatly to the annoyance of Mr. Lovely who justly feared that the Prince's guests might, as a result, compete with each other all over Grasmere in bidding for houses, barns, sheds, disused stables, furnished apartments with attendance and even those without it. So Mr. Lovely, thinking that a messy, boyish young female like that Miss de Bainriggs would be more susceptible to persuasion than some impersonal land agent, prowled, trespassing as he did so, all about the Bainriggs estate and finally decided to make what he described as a firm offer for a nice, rocky bit of land with beeches on it and a lake frontage just where the road goes round a blind corner on the Rydal road.

'Between you and me, mother,' said Mr. Lovely, 'that's a valuable bit o' land and I'll give her a tidy price for it, but not what it'll be worth, say, ten years on. Trust me for that. And there'll be nobody else after it, for who wants building land in war time?'

'But the creature said she'd not sell, any bit of land, anywhere,' said Mrs. Lovely, closely regarding the miniature face that looked back at her from her hand-bag mirror. She gave a shriek, partly to end her sentence, partly because she looked, in the mirror, so old, frightful, and delightfully modish. 'Anyway, what you want land for is beyond me,' said Mrs. Lovely, with another outcry that expressed amusement and bewilderment and sounded like a jay's shriek where there were no jays, for the Lovelys sat on the top of White Moss Common.

By the time that Mr. Richard Blunt was ferrying things across to the Island where he had, with such disgusting secrecy and adroitness, found a harbourage, Mr. Sweeting, Mr. Lovely and seventeen other war-time residents of the Prince began, with the earnestness proper to efforts at self-preservation, to seek for other quarters in Grasmere.

Mr. Sweeting had found a cottage Back o' Lake that he liked the look of. It was excessively minute, ancient, shaded by trees and so set under the western fell that it probably got no sun in winter. Thus, his liking of the look of it must have been due to the fact that he had, so far, found no vacant house, rooms, or even hotel bedrooms in Grasmere, so that this cottage assumed to him the pleasant guise of a refuge. It was occupied. It had no board saying To Let or Apartments. But he felt in his bones that he could have it if he wanted it and so, one frosty day in October, he stood on a mat of wet leaves, with others falling noiseless and golden upon him, and knocked upon its green front door. It was green, partly because, until recently, Grasmere house painters could not, comfortably, use any other colour and partly because of a thin growth upon it of some minute kind of moss or lichen. When Miss Trusty opened the door he smiled at her with a confidence that was certainly not due to her looks, which were fierce, and asked if she would give him a cutting of her exceptionally fine forsythia.

'I have never seen a finer bush,' said Mr. Sweeting, looking at it and wondering whether it was a blackbird's or thrush's nest that he saw, long abandoned, within it.

Miss Trusty was eighty-four and lived alone in the cottage that had been occupied by the Trusty coachman when all the surrounding country-side had belonged to her father. Now, the Trusty money, land, coachman and family had vanished, been sold, died or emigrated and she and the cottage were left behind, waiting. She knew she was waiting. She knew it was absurd, and incredible that she should live like this, alone, poor, sometimes even hungry and cold. And, surely not so very long ago, there had been father, and mother, and seven brothers and sisters, playing and calling in the woods as she heard them sometimes now. And so she waited, for if they could not come back surely she must go forward and find them all again.

'Yes? What did you say?' said Miss Trusty, looking at Mr. Sweeting fiercely but vaguely too. 'He thinks me very old,' thought Miss Trusty and resented it, for she had been half asleep and back in the old nursery again, and how odd it was that little Felicia Trusty should be old!

However, Mr. Sweeting's bones had not misled him. He got his cutting, and did not throw it away till he was back in the village, and he got his cottage for he offered Miss Trusty five pounds a week for it. Her income was ninety pounds a year and she disliked her cottage as much as Mr. Sweeting, looking at it, had surmised she must. Thus, she said at once that she would clear out and live in a hut above Chapel Style where she went whenever she let the cottage in summer.

'It was built to be a hen-house,' said Miss Trusty, 'but it's all stone, walls and roof, and has a good door and window. Anyhow, I couldn't afford to go anywhere else on your five pounds a week.'

Mr. Sweeting knew he had got his cottage so he did not offer her any more, and he did not trouble to feign interest in any stone hut or other receptacle in which she might house herself. Instead, he gave her five pounds, as a deposit, he said, and promised to send her an agreement to sign next day. Then he went back to the Prince, well satisfied, and told everybody he had got an antique furnished cottage, where it would be amusing for his daughters to live a simple, hard-working life, taking care of their parents, if and when the Prince were requisitioned.

All this infuriated Mr. Lovely; indeed, he suffered greatly, and was so convinced that his blood pressure was rising daily that he feared something horrid would happen to him unless he could outdo that foppish young sprig, Sweeting, and find for his own females a retreat superior to that now provided for the Sweeting females. Thus he determined again to ask that girl, if she were a girl for he thought of her as something neuter, like a mule, if she would sell him land, much or little land. How much or little mattered nothing to Mr. Lovely as long as the little would have room to support a house. If it were very little the house would have to be taller.

After all this it was unfortunate for Mr. Lovely that he knew himself to be not on the top of his form when, for the second time, he asked Miss de Bainriggs to sell him a building site. He got himself rowed across to Bonfire Hall and had there been told that she was out, in the Bainriggs wood across the end of the lake. So he had been rowed back to the Prince and had then hurried along the road and gone wandering, heated and stumbling, up over the rocky ridges and down the marshy valleys that were so bafflingly overgrown with Bainriggs trees until he had seen the lady he sought far beneath him, with that fellow Blunt who had got the Island. The two stood on the bank of the river, a few hundred yards below its outlet from the lake, and Mr. Lovely, from his tree-grown ridge, went straight down to them. It was the brambles that made Mr. Lovely feel even worse than he had done on the top of the ridge. They grew out of the ground, formed a wiry, prickly loop and then grew in again so that his short, woolly legs were continually trapped while taller trails, climbing about on their own bushes, clutched at his woolly body and held him, like the sheep from which his Harris tweeds had, no doubt, been derived. Like the sheep he struggled and pulled and, unlike a sheep, got himself free, but just before he reached the foot of the slope his feet were caught in another loop and he fell, downhill, and shook himself quite dreadfully.

'I am so sorry,' said Corys, admirably grave. 'Those brambles are frightfully dangerous. Are you hurt?'

'Yes, I am hurt,' said Mr. Lovely, 'badly hurt, but not injured. I fall light because I am fat. I weigh more but I fall lighter since I got fat, which is interesting, I think. Now, Miss, I want to ask you again, and very earnestly for you won't get a better offer with no building being done and the income-tax what it is and going to be worse, for a bit, just a bit, or a square mile if you like, of land. Listen, now. I'll give you three hundred, and you can make it guineas if you like, for a plot no bigger than a sizable little house down by the lake, back there, where there's an old boat-landing.'

'Oh, no,' said Corys. 'Thank you very much, but I won't sell any land.'

And then she began to try and get him to join her and that Blunt fellow in searching for signs of the mill that she said had once stood here.

'It was first mentioned in 1493,' said she, looking at Mr. Lovely as earnestly as if anybody cared two pins about her old mill. 'It was a fulling mill, for the local cloth, and you can see a bit of the mill-race and I think part of the weir in the river, but I wish I could trace the outlines of the building. Every last stone of it must have been carried away.'

'Very interesting,' said Mr. Lovely, for he lied easily when he thought it politic to lie. He stared vacantly at the ditch she called a mill-race and began again: 'About that land, Miss de B. I am sure your friend here will tell you to close with a good and a firm offer before I go elsewhere for what I want.'

It seemed to Mr. Lovely that Blunt had become her friend. 'What's he going to get out of it, beyond what he's got with his Island?' marvelled Mr. Lovely, reflecting that the two seemed as silly as children about the old mill and the pack-horse track from it up into the wood. They showed him the latter and he followed it when he left them and thus easily regained the main road.

'You'll be sorry about this when you want a tidy bit of the ready, as we all shall, very soon,' said Mr. Lovely, sternly, in farewell.

'He couldn't build, even if he got land,' said Corys, as she and Richard stood a moment, watching the grey-green, pin-cushiony appearance of Mr. Lovely as he climbed the ridge. 'He is awfully like a sheep, isn't he?'

'I don't think he could, but money can do a lot, even in war time,' said Richard doubtfully. 'Yes, he looks round and woolly but his brain isn't. Corys, the water-wheel must have been an undershot one.'

'Yes, I know,' said Corys. 'And Old John says there are the foundations of a biggin, he means a building, just above there, where the track winds round. It may have been a house. Lots of houses have disappeared about here; there were once two tenements and a capital messuage on the Bainriggs estate and there was a house across the river in Benson's Coppice. I love looking for them, for their sites, I mean.'

Meanwhile, the Hunter's Moon was growing nightly rounder and shining brighter through the faint October haze that smelt of burning leaves. The old roadmen of Grasmere swept, every day, the red and golden and brown leaves against the wall bottoms and then set them alight, so that the pale smoke hung in the valley like a fog long after the flames were out. On the evening before the full moon Jownie Wife smelt dew and frost and bonfire smoke high on the Raise as she came with her long, flat strides over the pass and down to Grasmere. The scent made her walk quicker for it told her that winter was near. Tomorrow the valley would be white with hoar frost and at any time now the first snow would show on the fell tops, dim as pale cloud in the moonlit sky. Jownie Wife thought of her snug home in the hogg-house; of its solid, slate roof; the fire in it, with her enamel teapot in the hot ashes; her bed of dry bracken; her bundle that she would find in the chimney, full of treasures that she had half forgotten. She was well content as she strode through Grasmere village, hungry too, but supper could wait. She would have a late meal by firelight and moonlight, and then curl up for a long sleep, like a hedgehog or squirrel, in her winter home. She found her boat, hidden where she had left it. It leaked, for it was derelict when she took it from the boat-landings at the Prince, as were most of the things she stole. She baled some of the water out of it, took the oars, which were derelict too, from the reeds and rowed herself across the moonlit lake to the Island. It was by now nearly midnight and the hollow of Grasmere hushed in that white silence which makes the glare and bustle of day seem something for ever done with. Jownie Wife broke the stillness without a tremor. Her key was gone from the cranny in the wall: the hogg-house door was fastened on the inside; the scent of smouldering wood ash, sinking in the cold air as it drifted from the chimney-top, told her some one was within. With her right foot in its heavy, man's boot, she kicked the door. With her bony fists she hammered on it. She kicked again, and swore aloud.

Inside the hogg-house Richard Blunt, waked from sleep, swore too. Corys had warned him that so would Jownie Wife come home, some time. She had been apologetic about Jownie Wife and about her weakness in having allowed the little weasel of a woman to occupy the hogg-house. 'She's got to come back and realize it's all up and then perhaps she will clear out for good,' had said Corys, hopefully, but she had given him no hints on how to deal with the wanderer when she did appear.

On this night Richard had a cold in his head. He lay warm, listening to Jownie Wife. If he opened the door she would be a nuisance and probably scratch him. He lay still and, after a while, her noises ceased. He heard a gentle gurgling, as if some one drank from a bottle, gruntings, rustlings of paper and then stillness came again as if the windless silence of space had closed in upon Jownie Wife as a lake surface closes over the splash of a stone.

When the sun rose and a frosty steam began to move, like breath, about the hogg-house roof and the sunlit rocks beside the lake, Mr. Blunt opened his door, cautiously. Even so he did not prevent Jownie Wife from falling in across the lintel. Her gin bottle was empty; her bit of dirty newspaper still half-filled with the crusts, cold potatoes, carrots, and sticky lump of porridge that she had got, begging from house to house, on her way from Keswick. She was incapably drunk. Richard, sneezing because of his cold, and shuddering because of his disgust at her, put her in her boat and rowed her to Back o' Lake and cast her out among the hazels, where it seemed tolerably dry. Then he walked round to the Prince and had himself taken across to the Island in time for breakfast.

'It's a problem,' said Corys, that evening, 'and I was weak and wicked not to face it sooner. But I did so want that pound a week.'

'And you were sorry for me, wanting the Island so badly?' said Blunt, watching her face.

'Was I? I don't think I was,' said Corys.

They all sat in the long parlour at Bonfire Hall. It was not yet time to draw the dark curtains against the raiders that might come, in these days, through the skies as raiders as savage came long ago over the Raise. In at the north window came a dim, tawny glow from the lake, shining with the frosty sunset in slopes already dark. Through the south window came no light but the deep shadow of the russet, autumn woods. In the midst of the room shone the wood fire, red and quiet, and in its glow sat Corys, with her long arms round her knees and her long back bent, and Grandy and Blodwen and Blunt and Jet, the drover's dog, with her nose against Corys' arm.

'At seventeen, as Cory will be to-morrow,' said Grandy, 'no one is sorry for any one. At seventeen other people's troubles are vague and very foolish. Such troubles can never come to oneself, thinks sweet seventeen, which Cory will never be, however long she may be seventeen. No one could be sweet and look like Cory.'

'I wonder,' said Blodwen, unexpectedly.

Richard wondered, too. Corys was all hunched in her chair so that it seemed no part of her young body but was bent except her thin shin bones. Her hair, so dark, so straight and so untidy, somehow seemed the right hair for that look on her sunburnt face, a look stern and watchful and, perhaps, impatient as if Corys felt life a wary business, lacking something that seemed a long time in coming.

'I think, if I were miserable now and wanted something, Cory would be sorry and help me, even if it didn't mean a pound a week,' said Richard, reaching out to let his hand rest on Jet's head.

'I would,' said Corys, and smiled at him.

Tall and lanky, unkempt, too thin, without a boy's charm and yet with not a single girlish one, there was yet in Corys' smile something that spoke of quite a different Corys.

'Good child!' said Richard, and smiled back at her.

That evening they came to no conclusion on the problem of Jownie Wife but the friendship between Corys and Mr. Blunt grew a little stronger, as it did every time they met. Old John was consulted next day and after reflection he said he thought he could stop Jownie Wife going over to the Island. Choosing that time in the evening when the lady usually went into the village for a drink he went to her boat. Beside it, he looked carefully round amongst the hazel bushes, for he had no wish for even an off-come to see him. He then sank it by putting large stones on its floorboards.

After her evening drink Jownie Wife had intended to go across and make another row at the hogg-house. If she went on making rows she thought, from what she knew of gentlemen, that Blunt would tire of them, get disgusted and go away. She found that her boat was sunk. She saw it clearly through the still, inshore water and the great stones inside it. She realized, as clearly, that she could not get it up again. Old John, being very good, was also, as are some good people, unfortunately guileless. He had left the imprints of his boots in the soft ground about the boat and so Jownie Wife knew at once who had sunk it, for Old John was the only man in the neighbourhood who wore clogs.

'Curse you, and you, and you,' said Jownie Wife, shaking her fist at Old John's cottage, then at Bonfire Hall and then at the hogg-house. 'May your sins be a black rope round your neck and a burning fire in your inwards.'

This incantation suggested to Jownie Wife an appropriate activity so she went and set alight a mound of dead leaves in the road-side beside the gate into Old John's bit of meadow. She did this after every one but herself was in bed and during the night the flames destroyed the gate as well as the leaves. After watching to make sure the leaves would burn up wind, as she wished, Jownie Wife went off to bed herself, in a shack, of corrugated iron and old wooden boxes, up on White Moss that had formed a temporary home for such as she since its owner had walked over the edge of a quarry one dark night.

CHAPTER VI

Though by now the summer visitors had gone away, like the wheatears from the Raise, the vale of Grasmere was still full and every bed not occupied by a native was thankfully slept upon by an off-come. Many of these had had no earlier holiday and there were no sirens at Grasmere, except an inaudible thing like a motor-horn. Certainly the policeman went about blowing a whistle on some nights, but only those living in the village itself heard these dolorous sounds, and apart from the occasional resounding passage of aeroplanes over the dark valley most households slept undisturbed. Thus was Grasmere become a quiet haven and its residents cooked, washed and cleaned for their guests, drove them in the taxi, sold them in the shops all that the natives did not want, delivered their endless letters, regarded them with a tolerant kind of pity and curiosity and, though increasingly exhausted as time went on, made a lot of money out of them. The Gift Shop and the Little Café, normally closed in winter, added to the somewhat austere gaieties of the village by remaining open; the famous gingerbread could be bought three times a week, and distinguished war guests from London gave concerts and recitations and, when hard up, taught the natives and each other whatever seemed suitable to the parties concerned.

Naturally, the war-time visitors had not very much to do. They roamed the valley in little groups, looking at woods and streams and old farms, delighted to talk to any one, but especially to the roadmen and farmers and, when it was wet, they made things in assemblies of each other that were called work parties and were usually presided over by a native. Old John Benson's cottage was a popular goal for afternoon walks. Many of the off-comes, oppressed by homesickness, burdened by war anxieties, weary with enforced idleness, looked at Old John's cottage and felt an easing of their burden. Its white plastered walls, little windows and moss-grown roof enchanted them. From its round chimney-stack drifted up wood smoke, smelling as delicately as its thread of vapour was outlined against the autumnal trees. Under the wide eaves on the side that faced the road was an outside gallery, the only one in Grasmere. Up to its white walls grew turf, always green, always close-cropped by wandering sheep, and on the far side of it lay the lake, dark, or blue, or shining as the wind and weather changed.

A John Benson had bought a tenement in Grasmere in 1480, but Old John's cottage, Oak How, had not been built till 1621, at which date one Robert Benson, having become rich by means of the local cloth trade, acquired the little customary holding of Oak How and built a stone house on the site of the previous one of wood and thatch. Since then there had always been a Benson at Oak How, and though its woods and pastures had now passed into the hands of rich strangers who came and settled Back o' Lake Old John, a bachelor, and the last of his family, had as passionate a devotion for his little house and the patch of grassland about it as had any of his more prosperous ancestors. He lived alone, cooked, washed and mended for himself, kept Oak How spotless, and earned enough as woodman on the de Bainriggs estate to satisfy himself.

Mr. Sweeting took Mr. Lovely to see Fold-in-the-Wood, which was the name of the grey, damp cottage with walls of water-worn stones from the river Rothay, which he had rented from Miss Trusty.

'They tell me it may fall down at any time, owing to the rounded stones in its walls, but Miss Trusty says it is a hundred and fifty years old so I dare say it will stand for as long as the war lasts,' said Mr. Sweeting, depreciating his prize in the aggravating way of those who know they have secured one. 'And if the Prince is taken over by some Governmental person or persons I think we shall be thankful to have somewhere to go.'

Mr. Lovely thought so too.

'Dashed, smug, conceited Daffy-down-Dilly,' said Mr. Lovely to himself, for Mr. Sweeting, being tall and very fair and apparently languid, was known by this pretty nickname at the Prince.

'Of course I wish I could have got Oak How,' said Mr. Sweeting, strolling on again as if it were nothing to him to gaze upon his precious refuge. 'You know Oak How? A real old statesman's home, more or less prehistoric but sound as a bell. However, Old John wouldn't stir out of it if you offered him a thousand. I know that, because I did.'

Then they both looked at Oak How and, contrary to other off-comes, felt depressed, Mr. Sweeting because he could not get it for money and knew of no other way to do so, and Mr. Lovely because he was hating Mr. Sweeting quite distressingly, as it is common to hate people whom we envy.

And that night, after depressing off-comes for the first time, Oak How was burnt down.

Jownie Wife had now been ousted from her island hogg-house for three weeks. She had suffered little physical inconvenience since she drank herself into her nightly stupor as comfortably in the shack on White Moss as she had done in the hogg-house. But emotionally she suffered acutely, and to relieve her rage and sense of injury she did various frightful things as the Hunter's Moon waned, and grew less and rose later, until the nights were dark. Meeting the three pretty Sweetings, strolling in the dusk to see Blunt's light shine out from the hogg-house, in those few minutes before the black-out when lights might shine, she cursed them.

'Daft watties. Jammy lang necks,' said Jownie Wife, scowling at them. There was a right of way behind Bonfire Hall and Jownie Wife would walk upon it, at midnight, and shout and scream and curse so that she woke every one but Corys.

'Bring her to me and I'll soon stop that behaviour,' said Grandy, grimly. 'I know more about Jownie Wife than she thinks on.'

But no one could bring Jownie Wife because she was so difficult to catch, and it might not really be legal to do so, though this did not trouble Grandy.

Then, Corys found a jagged hole in her boat and, the morning after that, a horrible emptiness in the duck-house. Somebody had opened the little door of the duck-house during the night and a fox had gone in and killed the seven tall white ducks and carried away all but one head and two yellow legs. The ducks had been pure-bred Indian Runners and they had spent every day in running, in a tight little white clump, about the lake-side meadows, and Corys had loved them deeply. The one whose head was left had been broody in the summer. She had built herself a high nest of straw and feathers and sat in the top of it, on three of her own white eggs. It had been a hopeless business since all the ducks were ducks, but Lilywhite had not known this and she had been very happy and had ruffled her feathers and gone limp and changed her voice to a loving whisper, just like a hen in like circumstances. Corys had found her irresistible and now she was dead.

That morning Richard found Corys savagely cleaning the empty duck-house, with her white face all smeared with tears and mud and the head of Lilywhite and the two legs in a cardboard box, awaiting burial.

'That is, I mean that head was, Lilywhite,' said Corys, with another sob. 'She had quite a different expression from the others.' She paused and rubbed her wet cheeks with her hand. 'It was Jownie Wife, of course,' added she, in a less muffled voice. 'But how can I prove it?'

With a sympathy that was genuine, for he had kept ducks himself, Richard helped with the funeral rites.

'You are a comfort to me!' said Corys and, hearing this, he suddenly realized what a comfort this child was to him and how, in a world that held such young creatures, fundamental things must be sounder than he had thought.

After this Jownie Wife was not seen for some days and no more mischief was done. When she appeared again it was, once more, on the right of way behind Bonfire Hall, where she diligently swept up dead leaves into little mounds all one afternoon. Grandy, greatly incensed by this behaviour, went out in her rough, hodden grey overcoat, with her white hair blowing in the damp wind.

'Come here! You, Jownie Wife! Come here, woman!' called Grandy, but Jownie Wife nipped into the woods and, directly Grandy had gone, came back to her job.

That evening Jownie Wife set fire to her mounds of leaves, one after the other, and they flared into the moonless sky long after black-out and brought P.C. Smith on his bicycle from the village to scold Miss de Bainriggs for showing a light. Nobody had seen Jownie Wife set them afire. No one could prove that she had done it. Corys and P.C. Smith put out the fires, and when they had disappeared Jownie Wife came secretly out from the woods and lit them again. Next day P.C. Smith said Miss de Bainriggs would be summoned for a breach of the Defence of the Realm Regulations because part of one of the burning mounds had been off the right of way and on her land.

Two or three nights later Richard Blunt meditated upon the top of the Island. The crescent moon had set behind Yew Crag but the sky was full of stars. There was a light breeze. He heard the sound of little waves, breaking upon the Island, and the breeze whispered in the Scots pines beside him. Perhaps few sounds seem more like the remote echoes of some eternal harmony than do those of waves and pines and, hearing them, Richard thought of life and death, of pain and the starry heavens and felt comforted by his ignorance of these immensities. From what bright, ultimate solution of his problems might not the ignorance of man shield eyes as yet too dim and ears too dull to perceive mysteries?

'Who knows? Anyhow, who knows anything about anything?' pondered Blunt and had his wandering thoughts suddenly and sharply focused by the sight of Oak How in flames.

Reflected in a broadening path across the rippled lake the flames seemed already to involve the little old house as if they had burnt unhindered within. The roar of them came with the breeze and muffled the sound of waves and wind. From an upper window they suddenly burst forth, streaming like a golden banner, and the pale smoke of their burning rose in a dense cloud above the dark roof. Richard ran to his boat and rowed frantically over the fire-lit water. By now the trees across the road from the cottage were alight and through the closed door that faced the lake came the steady, rushing sound of fire and the glow of it showed round the edges of the door.

'Try a window, you'll never burst that door,' said a voice in his ear, and there was Corys in a dressing-gown, bare-footed, and with Jane Peascod's little chopping axe in her hand. She had seen the flames as she was beginning to get into bed and had seized the axe and rushed off, over the dewy meadows by the lake, to Oak How.

Richard broke the kitchen window, climbed in, and found Old John insensible on the passage floor. He had evidently been trying to escape and the smoke that had made him collapse hung over him, sinister and motionless. There was Corys again, now beside Richard, helping to drag Old John out from beneath the burning oak beams. As they laid him beside Richard's boat part of the roof fell in through the burnt rafters and the flames escaped, roaring, into the night air. By now the Grasmere fire brigade had arrived, and A.R.P. wardens, more worried about the light than the flames since an enemy plane was known to be prowling near. But no one could save Oak How or more than partly dim its burning brilliance. Some of the men helped to put Old John in the boat and extinguished the burning branches in the edge of the wood. They left a guard to deal with the danger of burning fragments, that were sucked high in the air by the draught of the fire, and the others tramped back again, while Blunt rowed Corys and the old man to Bonfire Hall.

By now Grandy and the younger Mrs. de Bainriggs were hurrying along the lake-side towards the fire, but they turned back on seeing the boat and were at the landing to meet it.

'Put on your shoes,' said Blodwen, giving the blue slippers she was carrying to Corys. 'Is he badly burnt? I've got a hot bottle and blankets on the parlour sofa.'

Grandy was very strong. She took half of Old John's weight and Blunt took the other half while Corys carried one of his limp and heavy arms. They laid him on the sofa. He had no burns, so Blodwen read aloud what should be done to people who have been gassed, an instructive leaflet about this having come on the previous day.

'Stuff and nonsense. He's just had too much smoke. He'll be all right when he's been sick,' said Grandy, watching Old John. 'Unfortunately. Perhaps if we let him alone he may die. It would be kinder to let him. The loss of his cottage will kill him, more painfully, if this doesn't.'

As the days went by it began to seem as if what Grandy had said was true. Old John recovered from the smoke and shock. The doctor said he had perfectly recovered. His colour came back and his appetite: he slept well in the attic at Bonfire Hall and cut down trees all day just as he had always done. He was rather more silent than usual and he never went near the ruins of Oak How, not even to see if there were any bits of furniture worth recovering, but otherwise he seemed normal enough. Then, one wild evening in November, he did not return after his day's work.

'Where is Old John?' asked Corys, going into the kitchen to make sure that Miss Peascod gave him cheese with his tea.

'Eh, I don't kna where's he at,' said Jane. 'Miss Corys, will you have a few podish to-night? There's nowt else.'

Blodwen had a bad cold. Grandy had sciatica.

'You must not go alone,' said Blodwen to Corys, anxiously. 'And, besides, where would you look? You've no idea where the old man may have got to.'

So, in the clouded moonlight, Corys rowed to the Island, the rough lake slapping against her bows and the stir of wind and water filling the night. There, with a painful sinking of her heart, she found that her friend Richard was giving a supper-party in the hogg-house. In the bright, soft light of two oil lamps and the flaming log fire sat he and the three Sweetings and a young man and a young woman, whom Corys had not seen before. Richard had shouted 'Come in!' when she knocked and now she stood with darkness behind her and the wind and its clamour hurrying past her into the warm room.

'Oh! Richard! I'm so sorry, but Old John is lost,' said Corys, looking at him and forgetting that any one else was there.

'Lost! What do you want me to do?' said Richard.

He and Essie Sweeting had been frying sausages over the wood fire, sausages that stuck to the pan because, it being war time, they were dry and full of breadcrumbs.

'We must all go and look for him at once,' cried Essie. 'At once!' echoed Rudie and Mag, seizing the frying-pan and dumping it on the earth floor.

'I thought he was working up for something,' said Richard. 'Will you all think me very rude if I go with Corys? Miss Lovely, you must be hostess and the Sweetings troupe will cook and Mr. Lovely will eat and then perhaps I shall be back again.'

But the Sweeting sisters made a great outcry at this so that Mr. Lovely's son and daughter, who were tall, dark, handsome, inscrutable, and completely unlike both their parents, had to decide between eating sausages by themselves or ranging the dark country-side with these local lunatics in search of somebody or other who would not be worth finding. However, anything was better than being left alone with each other, so they got into the large boat that the Sweetings had hired and every one rowed to the Bainriggs landing at Penny Rock.

It was two hours before they found the old man. Gerald and Myra Lovely had come to the Lakes for a week or two because of bombs on their colleges. They soon got disgusted with scrambling about in what they called the dark. Corys could see perfectly, and Blunt, as much as enabled him to get about safely, while the Sweetings did not mind whether they saw or not as long as they were with Richard and Miss de Bainriggs. Gerald and Myra eventually made their difficult way over the ridges and through the hollows of Bainriggs wood on to the main road and then walked back to the Prince, silently reflecting upon the remarkable enterprise upon which they had been engaged.

'Quite mad, all of them,' said Gerald, screwing up his eyes so as not to walk into the wall. 'What does an old man or two matter anyway? And what was that long creature who came for Blunt? It was local apparently, but was it really female?'

'What they want is halibut liver oil for night blindness,' Corys had said, standing on a miniature crag and watching the Lovelys go away. 'They'll fall if they go down just there. Oh, they have. Are you hurt?' Corys ended with a shout but Gerald and Myra, vaguely hearing it, had been too irritated to reply.

Old John was nowhere in the Bainriggs estate. That, they had established before midnight. If Corys had not suddenly remembered a mysterious hovel, somewhere over the top of White Moss, they would not have found him.

'It's a queer, flat, stone place and they think White Moss quarrymen made it to save coming every day from Langdale,' said Corys, as they climbed the slope with the Sweetings following, largely on their hands and knees. 'You could sleep in it, if you weren't fat. Old John told me about it himself; the ford over the Rothay bothered the Langdale men in wet weather, he said, before the footbridge was built.'

'But why should he suddenly go off and sleep in a flat hovel?' asked Richard.

'I don't know, but they do, Grasmere men I mean, when they get turned out from their homes. They just go up the fells and sleep anywhere. They won't be beholden to anybody,' said Corys. 'And perhaps when you are heartbroken you do queer things. Old John is heartbroken. It would cost £500 to repair Oak How. I asked the local builder for an estimate. I haven't got it, or of course it would be all right.'

'You'd spend five hundred on the old fellow?' asked Blunt, and could not keep incredulity from his voice.

'Spend it? Twice over, if I had it and he wanted it. Oh, Richard, he's here!' said Corys, her voice going husky with relief.

When Essie and Rudie and Mag reached the quarrymen's flat hut they were breathless, bleeding from various cuts, scratches and abrasions and had lost some of their hair which they left, caught in brambles, like Herdwick wool but a good deal cleaner. They were not dismayed by their sufferings and found themselves able, by now, to see almost as well as their adored Richard Blunt. Old John had been sound asleep and he was still in his shelter and refusing to come out. His feet were visible near the front, which was open to the air, and the rest of him hidden within for the quarrymen, to save labour, had made the little place just high enough for a man to crawl into and lie down.

'T'se a' reet. Let me lig,' said Old John, drowsily.

'Shall I pull him out?' asked Richard.

Corys hesitated.

'John, are you warm and dry, and will you come to the Hall for breakfast?' said she, stooping low to the entrance.

'T'se a' reet, Miss Cory. Let me be,' said Old John.

So they all turned and began to come down over White Moss.

'It's no good. We'd better leave him,' said Corys. 'He'll go all wild now. He'll do his work, probably, but he'll live anywhere and anyhow. He's not done it before and it'll kill him, but I know what he feels. He won't be under anybody's roof but his own.'

Greatly depressed and aware now of a fatigue that made even the bemused Sweetings more conscious of their injuries, they went home. The Sweetings had a friend in the night-porter at the Prince and they got in without waking their parents, who thought them still with Blunt and the young Lovelys upon the Island. Blunt rowed Corys home and then repaired to his hogg-house. The moon had set. The night was overcast and dark and it had fallen calm so that there were no voices, of eternity or anything else, about the Island. Yet Richard felt restless and uneasy. He thought of Old John and wondered what instinct drove him away from his room and friends at Bonfire Hall. What wild, imperious compulsion, as little understood, no doubt, by him as by his friends, made him behave so? Blunt listened to the silent night and thought we move in it no more blindly than we do among the impulses that sway us, this way and that. Then, suddenly, he remembered how Corys in her trouble before they found Old John had slid her hand, as a child might, into his and had walked so till they had to scramble again, up a ridge.

'It seems odd that her father should be content so long away from her,' mused Blunt, and took his left hand in his right to see if he could remember just how Corys' hand had felt in his.

And on the next day others suffered something of the same bewildered shock that had overcome Old John Benson at the loss of his home for, on the next day, the Prince was requisitioned.

CHAPTER VII

'Have you always dressed like a boy?' asked Rudie Sweeting, blushing as she did so because she thought she was being rude, but felt she could not stop herself from asking.

On the evening of the day after Old John had been found in the quarrymen's shelter she and her sisters had gone across to the Island to see how Richard was feeling after his exertions.

'You're *sure* it's no worse?' had cried Essie and Rudie and Mag, when he said that his heart seemed much as usual, and then Corys de Bainriggs had come ashore from her old boat and interrupted them. And perhaps a feeling of vexation at this had made Rudie so ill-mannered and inquisitive about Corys in boys' clothes.

'Always, except when I was at school,' answered Corys. Last night, in the dark woods, she felt herself the superior of the Misses Sweeting, but now her old feeling of being on the defensive before the charming sisters had come back. Now, as usual, she felt abashed by them and ashamed, though of what she did not know. They were such girlish girls and Corys, who had always felt herself more boy than girl, wished to despise them for this but could not. Instead, she felt herself to be somehow in the wrong and Richard, amusedly watching her downcast look, wondered if nature was suggesting things to Corys. Nature was single minded and direct; was she asking Corys what would happen if all the girls turned boy? Was she whispering, somewhere behind Corys' defiant eyes, that Corys was a traitor and a coward and turning her back on life?

'Oh, well, but she's only a kid,' thought Richard. 'There's time enough.' And he felt he liked Corys just as she was, whatever nature might think about it.

'We're being frightfully rude but we should *so* love to know why you pretend to be a boy,' said Essie and Mag, 'but don't say if you think we are, are rude I mean. It's only because we're so interested.'

'I don't pretend to be a boy,' said Corys, coldly, and she turned to Richard. 'Old John has worked as usual all day but he won't sleep at the Hall any more. He won't say where he is going to live, only that he'll be all right if we let him alone,' said Corys, to Richard, with her back to the sisters. 'But he won't; he'll die. I can see death in his face now.'

'Anyway, no girl looks like a boy from behind,' said Rudie, meditatively surveying Corys and now wishing to be rude.

To Richard's relief the war interrupted any further conversation at this point. Some body, or bodies, both human and official, in London had decided a week ago to take over the Prince of Wales Hotel, thinking that it would help them to win the war. Word of this decision had reached the Prince by that day's post and late in the afternoon the guests were notified that they must leave in a fortnight. So Mr. Sweeting, irritated, but also much pleased because he had rented Fold-in-the-Wood and was now proved to have been wise and far-seeing, rowed across to the Island to fetch his daughters.

'Hi! Kids! Come home. We've got to pack up and begin to lead the simple life,' called Mr. Sweeting, looking more like Daffy-down-Dilly than ever as he came over the green grass towards his primrose-headed offspring.

That night in bed, Corys felt as if the Misses Sweeting were in bed with her, sharp and painful as dry biscuit crumbs. They had wondered why she dressed and behaved like a boy and now, when she had time to think, Corys wondered, too. She had always read boys' books. She had hated sewing. The young governess who had taught her before she went to school had painted her face, and gone all queer when there was a young man anywhere near, and used scent. This behaviour had been disgusting to Corys. If such behaviour were common to females Corys would not behave like one. With her mother in London and Grandy either in Timbuktu or Manaos there had been no sensible, sober-minded gentlewoman to counteract the shocking behaviour of the young governess. Moreover, boys' pursuits fascinated Corys and to follow them she must dress as a boy for who, in girls' clothes, could saw tree trunks, drive the dung-cart, or help Old John with dry-walling? Her two years at school had come too late, for none are so obstinate as are the young. Dressed as a girl, behaving as a girl, all the time Corys clung to her conviction that girlish things were tripe and sawdust and clung the tighter because she was at bottom as little sure of herself as were her more feminine schoolmates.

'What it all comes to is this,' reflected Corys, much annoyed at being still awake at eleven o'clock. 'Those tow-headed, dressed-up dolls with idiotic names like being girls and have gone all frightfully girlish. I hate being a girl. I will not go girlish and make eyes at the Prince's chauffeur. I am a landowner and shall behave like one. Oh, dash, there's another Hun plane, and can I have got a flea from that wretched shack of Old John's?'

In the morning began that great agitation among the Prince's guests which drove them about the vale of Grasmere like dead leaves in the autumn gales. Those with cars drove in them, but the motive power was the same. Panic had seized upon the Prince's guests. Besides Mr. Lovely and Daffy-down-Dilly one or two of the more anxious-minded among them had already begun to make tentative inquiries about accommodation elsewhere, but most of them had drifted along, trying not to worry and remarking that the war would be over some day, or so it might be supposed.

In the quiet of Grasmere it had seemed, fantastically, to the Prince's guests that all the rest of England was constantly being bombed and set on fire, and when any of the more level-headed guests dared to go a journey their reports that everything seemed more or less normal, except the meals in trains, were listened to with open unbelief. Thus, to most of those at the Prince, it seemed desirable and even urgently so, that they should not be cast forth from the Lake District and, as Mr. Lovely had foreseen, they went about calling at the same lodging-houses, consulting the same house agents, advertising, and answering the same advertisements, trying to persuade residents to take them as paying guests, telephoning to hotels at Keswick and Cockermouth and Grange-over-Sands and, all the time, suffering torments and receiving not much sympathy from anybody.

The sight of Daffy-down-Dilly, with rather more than his usual air of a dandified insouciance, ferrying his family and luggage over the lake to that dark spot among trees that was the roof of Fold-in-the-Wood, filled poor Mr. Lovely with a ghastly sense of failure. For him and mother there was no roof, however moss-grown. For his Gerald and Myra, so clever and modern and utterly superior to those pale-headed slips of girls that Sweeting had got, was there no safe refuge from the academic and other trials of Cambridge and Liverpool in war time. He, father, had failed them. He, clever old fox that he might be, had yet provided no burrow for his family and, using this metaphor, Mr. Lovely was not too distraught to wonder if the dog fox really did this or did he pinch one from rabbits?

Mr. Lovely was no hand with an oar, having been born and brought up in a Lancashire town called St. Helens. Thus, early one morning, he had himself taken out to the Island and there put ashore, with some difficulty as the bow wobbled so when he tried to step out. There, he found Mr. Blunt, apparently in a kind of stupor under a Scots pine and with a sheet of newspaper and various scribbled bits of notepaper scattered about him.

There was no wind and the sun shone but it was not warm, and Mr. Lovely wondered why Blunt chose to write out of doors and then sit, staring at the bright lake, as still as an image.

'The Financial column of *The Times*! Ha!' said Mr. Lovely, observing the sheet of newspaper. 'Trying to make out how to get an income in spite of income-tax by bettering your rate of interest? It can't be done, my boy. I know, for I've tried.'

'I'm not going to try,' said Richard, wishing he had not let his financial calculations be so strewn about. These words, in his big, untidy handwriting, were too visible on a piece of paper by Mr. Lovely's right foot: 'If I sell out £500 stock 3½ per cent Conversion Loan I lose—' With no one to talk to Richard had written thus conversationally to clarify his ideas. Of course Mr. Lovely read the words though he could not see the maze of figures that followed them.

'Certainly don't sell out that,' said Mr. Lovely, serious at once. 'But that's odd, my boy. If you want a bit of ready cash perhaps what I have to say may help you, as well as me and mother, out of a difficulty.'

It appeared that Mr. Lovely wanted the hogg-house. He was prepared to pay Mr. Blunt any sum, in reason he added hastily, if he could have the tenancy of the hogg-house transferred to him. 'It wouldn't make any difference to that Miss across the way,' said Mr. Lovely, jerking his head towards Bonfire Hall. 'In fact, I'd offer her a bit more rent, just to make things friendly like. And you're a single man and single men can always find a shake-down somewhere. People are glad to get 'em, women I mean, landladies I mean, though so are other women. Ha! Ha! Now, my dear old man, what do you say, and what'll you take, though that sounds like the drink I'll stand you at the Prince when it's all settled.'

When Mr. Lovely had left him, which was not till half an hour later, for father was as persistent about the hogg-house as mother had apparently been about the sables, Richard sat on under his pine, meditating, and contracting meanwhile a chill that gave him a horrid pain inside that night. Why had he felt it quite impossible to let Mr. Lovely or any one else have the Island? He thought that if he had urged Corys to accept a new tenant she would have taken his advice, for Mr. Lovely had vowed he would alter nothing in the hogg-house except for putting bits of glass on the inside of the loop-lights where they wouldn't show at all. And, nowadays, Corys often did what he suggested to her, and she would probably offer to take him in at Bonfire Hall. Certainly he, Blunt, could more easily find accommodation than could four Lovelys, even if Corys did not ask him to occupy one of those two empty rooms at the Hall that weighed upon the conscience of her imaginative mother. So remote from the centre of Grasmere was Bonfire Hall that no one called there, begging for a bed, but Blodwen felt the homeless like a cloud between her and the sun. Not so Corys, who cared nothing about them.

'I certainly think I am a hog about my hogg-house,' thought Richard, at last getting stiffly to his feet from the fallen tree trunk where he had sat too long. 'But the long and the short of it is I won't give up my Island. I believe I ought to, but I won't. Some things one ought to do one can't do, and then perhaps one oughtn't. Perhaps instinct may be more right than conscience sometimes. And I'm afraid I can't afford to give Corys that £500 either. What a curmudgeon I am!'

Mr. Lovely went back to the Prince, had his lunch and was then rowed to Bonfire Hall.

'Quite like Venice!' said Mr. Lovely, in the drawing-room and with a superficial gaiety. 'Being rowed about everywhere to-day, though I must say that Wilson chap who rows me isn't my idea of a gondolier. How are you, Mrs. de Bainriggs, and you, Mrs. de Bainriggs—I believe I am right in thinking there are two? And is Miss de Bainriggs about? I would very much like to see her.'

Another strange man to see Corys, thought Blodwen, going to look for her daughter. Grandy, silently regarding Mr. Lovely under her bushy grey eyebrows, did not on this occasion shout for Corys.

'Is it the war that's bothering you?' said Grandy, after her inspection. 'It does bother some, though not me.'

'Well, it's this way,' said Mr. Lovely. 'Mother and me are at the Prince and we've got to go, do you see, and that bothers me. Not that the war doesn't bother me, for it does, and mother too, but the war's a good way off, you know, to any one here, I mean, and so I feel more badly, like, about the Prince. Do you think now you could persuade Miss de Bainriggs— young folk are difficult sometimes—to let me have a bit of land, anywhere about?'

'No,' said Grandy and looked at Mr. Lovely as if she expected him to go on talking.

'Well, you see, as things are—' began Mr. Lovely, desperately trying to do what she wanted.

He was thankful when Miss de Bainriggs came in with the pale, nice lady who appeared to be her mother. Miss de Bainriggs looked more female than he had yet seen her. She wore a green velveteen jacket and trousers and had a velvet ribbon of the same green tied round her head. Of course Mr. Lovely did not consciously see any of this but only that she seemed more female, like.

'I'm a desperate man, Miss de Bainriggs,' said Mr. Lovely, shaking hands.

Indeed, he appeared so when he left the Hall only ten minutes later. Corys had said No again and with a vehemence that surprised her relatives.

Corys was not usually vehement. Her mother had noticed that she was pale this afternoon, and cross. Corys was seldom cross. She seemed in a dream and yet she got quite wrought up over silly trifles. When Grandy told her, at lunch, that she looked like an Eskimo because her hair had gone flat and yet droopy Corys had left the room and banged the door. Certainly, the green ribbon was a kind of apology for this conduct, but it was not like Corys to apologize, either.

'Got a temper, that young jack-a-napes,' murmured Mr. Lovely so that the boatman heard him and grinned.

'I should say!' said the boatman, who was a Grasmere man but had spent twenty years in Canada.

However, at ten o'clock next morning Miss de Bainriggs called at the Prince and asked for Mr. Lovely. He was out. The hall porter said he was out house-hunting. The lady in the bureau knew more: she said he had gone up the Raise to look at that old cottage which was the Isolation Hospital not long ago.

'Is it for sale?' said Corys, horrified, as are all Grasmere people when any old house is for sale, because who knows what an off-come may do to it?

'Yes, and twenty acres with it,' said the lady in the bureau. 'But it's sold by now, I should say. Some one was after it yesterday.'

Corys went out of the Prince and hesitated. She was feeling odd. She had lain awake through much of the wild, wet night and had suffered in those lonely hours what seemed to her the utmost extremity of anguish, indecision and conflict. She had not known that it was possible for one part of her to fight another part as had happened that night. Even now, she did not know which part of her had won; she had decided nothing. The thought of right and wrong in her conflict had not occurred to her and would have seemed unimportant if it had. All that mattered were Bainriggs and Old John. Now, as she stood outside the Prince, Bainriggs and Old John still filled her mind, and still she did not know what she was going to do. After a few moments when she had, apparently, been looking intently at the wind in the pale gold rushes that stood at the head of the lake, she set off, tramping up the valley towards the Raise road. It showed like a dim thread climbing that dark cup in the hills which holds the northern sky in it, an invitation and a menace.

It took Corys, walking fast, nearly half an hour to get to the top of the Raise. Mr. Lovely had just been over the cottage, slowly, with long pauses for thought in every room. Was it too isolated for mother? What about a water-supply? Could electricity be brought up the Raise—he feared not. Would there be tramps, begging day and night? Had not some one said they might be buried in snow and that for three weeks last winter the Raise had been blocked? Meanwhile, mother sat in the warm car, reading *Home Notes* and talking to the elderly Lovely chauffeur who did not hear anything she said because he was deciding to volunteer for a war job next week, before he was fetched.

Mr. Lovely, coming despondently out of the cottage, was indeed enraptured to see the Bainriggs Miss.

'Ah! Ha! my young lady! You've thought better of it,' said Mr. Lovely, most genially. 'You've come all this way up here to see me? Ah! that means only one thing.'

'Does it?' said Corys, not at all sure, even now, that it did. And yet, though she was not sure, she began to speak as if she were. 'Mr. Lovely, do you still want to buy some of the Bainriggs land because, if you do, I might let you have some,' said Corys, finding it difficult to make herself clearly audible because something queer seemed to be inside her throat.

Mr. Lovely looked at her, sharply, and knew that he was not sure of his lake frontage yet.

'Well, of course, I should have to build some kind of a house, and that's a hard job these days,' said Mr. Lovely, 'and there's this place here, not what I'd choose for mother but already built and fairly habitable as you might say. What piece of land had you in your mind, Miss de B.?'

'I had been thinking of a nice bit up on the Wishing Gate road,' said Corys. 'A good big bit, with marvellous views, because I must have £500 for a building plot if I decide to sell one. You can't have this cottage anyway; Will Dixon has just told me it's sold.'

'Is that so? Dear, dear, what things people will buy in war time,' said Mr. Lovely. 'But £500, Miss de B., is a tidy sum and I couldn't give it for anything but a good plot, on the main road and with a lake frontage. I couldn't indeed. Now, for that bit of land I asked you for before, what they call Penny Rock about here, I'd give a good price, but not £500 unless you threw in a bit more so that I could have a river frontage too, for a hundred yards or so. I could fancy a bit of river frontage along there very well; I'm fond of running water. Shall we say an acre or thereabouts, till we can get it properly measured up? £500 for an acre of rubbishy, waste land all rock and bog and half dead trees, and when nobody but me could build a house on it, isn't too bad at all, my dear, with things as they are and the income-tax what it will be. Now, what do you say, Miss de B.?'

Behind Mr. Lovely was the northern sky beyond the Raise and in it, showing above the near grass slopes, the top of Skiddaw. There was snow on Skiddaw and light from the partly clouded sun rested on it so that it looked to Corys like a far, gold torch, bright with some heavenly message above the shadowed valley of Thirlmere. She wondered if Skiddaw were speaking to her but Mr. Lovely put his head on one side, the more ingratiatingly to regard her, and his head hid Skiddaw.

'You can have it, what you say, for five hundred … guineas,' said Corys still husky until she threw the last word at him like a blow.

'Bless the girl! She drives a hard bargain!' said Mr. Lovely, much elated, and he put his arm about Corys' shoulders and drew her towards mother in the car.

'Ouch!' said Corys, and, wriggling herself free, shook her shoulders as if she still felt Mr. Lovely's hand, heavy as a heavy burden.

CHAPTER VIII

Half an hour later Corys appeared on the Island. Mr. Lovely had whirled her down the valley in his big Bentley; even down the Raise they had whirled, owing to Jones, the chauffeur, having his mind still set on next week when he would volunteer for a fitter's war-time job. Corys had then, at once, rowed as fast as she could to the Island which she reached a little after eleven. Richard was at this time beginning to consider how best to deal with kippers. He had bought six in Ambleside the previous day and the fishmonger had told him they were the last of the kippers, owing to there being a war on. So Richard felt he must do the best he could for them, and himself, and he proposed to put them in a saucepan by half-past eleven and then let them simmer in a good lot of water till lunch-time. Things so mahogany-coloured and feeling so cool and leathery to the touch must, he thought, want a lot of simmering.

'I don't know anything about kippers,' said Corys, glancing at them, in their darkly glimmering row. 'But, Richard, please, will you come with me to speak to Old John? I must get him while he has his dinner, because when he is working he won't stop, and I have something I must tell him at once. Somehow, I feel I can't do it by myself.'

So Mr. Blunt put his six kippers on the smouldering fire to simmer and went out with Corys. Loose, dull coloured clouds flew from the east above the fells and between them gleams of pale yellow sunshine wandered over the slopes, bright and yet wan almost as moonlight. Now and then the wind that drove them came out of the sky and roved, roaring, in gusts about the valley, gusts that were followed by long periods of calm that seemed threatening and unnatural beneath that tumultuous passage of cloud.

'Old John has moved,' said Corys as she directed her boat towards

Back o' Lake. 'There is an old hovel up over the top of Red Bank, going on down towards The Oaks. There was a coppice wood there once and some woodman lived in the hovel while he cut it down, cut the coppice down I mean. Old John has gone there. He said the quarrymen's shack smelt of fox. Oh, gosh! Hold on!'

A squall swept down on the lake, on the middle of the lake as if it fell straight out of the sky, and at once waves rose about the boat and the air was full of rushing sounds and the flappings of water. Dead leaves from the Island flew out like a cloud banner, red and gold, and from the pine trees came that steady sound which is harsh and yet has that in it which calls to the listener as if from some place he knew once and would know again.

The Island pines called to Corys as she rowed and the strained look on her face softened a little.

'It'll take us about a quarter of an hour,' said Corys, tying her boat to a hazel bough and then looking up to where the hill sky-line stood, dark with trees, against the flying cloud.

Over the top of Red Bank they found Old John, in that upland country of Loughrigg where the great fells, Wetherlam and Bowfell and the Pikes, overlook every rock and cottage, little field and patch of coppice as if the dark austerity of their silhouettes were due to anything but height and distance. He sat outside the old hut and, beside a fire, ate and drank as Blunt had seen him do in Bainriggs wood three months ago.

'Hallo, John! I've come to tell you something,' said Corys, bending to speak because the old man sat still, looking at her, and the wind made mad, whirling sounds over the crags. 'Oh, bother your smoke!' said Corys, as it blew straight in her face. She stood up and looked rather piteously at Richard. 'Richard, please, will you tell him I've sold an acre of Bainriggs for five hundred guineas and I'm going to rebuild his cottage at once. I can't shout; my voice is gone queer somehow.'

Indeed, her voice sounded uncertain and had those abrupt changes of tone which meant that childish tears would drown it if Corys did not somehow hold back her grief.

'Sold an acre? Which part?' said Old John, still sitting but now staring up intently with his can of boiling tea gradually tipping in his hand so that it began to splash, in scalding but unnoticed drops, on his other hand.

'Which part?' said Richard to Corys.

'Penny Rock, and down along the river for a bit,' said Corys, almost inaudibly.

'Ah, no good standers there, only the sixty-year-old birch and some beech, not good for mich,' said Old John, who apparently had heard Corys well enough when his attention was really caught. 'And so Miss Cory is going to build up my cottage. Well, that's good hearing to be sure and I'll be glad to be back there, there's nea doubt.'

Looking down at Old John in the light of the flames and the strange, stormy light that brightened and faded too, Richard saw how he had altered since the burning of Oak How. There were hollows below his cheek-bones, his eyes seemed to have sunk and there were dark shadows under them, he who had always been shaved as clean as a young chap had chin and jaw covered with a stubble of white hair, and his old hands shook as he sat. When he looked up at Richard and Corys and said, so quietly, that he would be glad to be back in his cottage there was not gladness but only a pitiful questioning in his eyes as if they had looked so closely on ruin that not yet could they focus on anything else. Corys was right, thought Richard. Soon, Old John would have died, like a plant with its roots pulled up.

'Anyway, Miss Cory'll have Oak How when I'm gone,' said Old John, 'if so be she's really going to mend it up.'

The little silence had frightened Old John, but two griefs had been overwhelming Corys, her own, for that precious acre of her most precious Bainriggs, and her pity for Old John who had drawn so near to death. His alarm helped her to control her voice.

'In a few weeks Oak How'll be itself again,' said Corys, 'and so will you, John dear.'

'That's as may be,' said Old John, but placidly now. 'There's nea doot but I've been feeling a bit woffy. Miss Cory, timber'll be bad to get. What abut that oak I felled in thirty-nine, by t'owd mill? It's been ligging safe and it'll be grand stuff for beams.'

When Richard and Corys walked down the hill towards home they did so in silence. Corys stared straight ahead of her, so straight ahead that she nearly stumbled on the woodland footpath down Red Bank. By looking so she did not see the lake, a silver pond far below, or the dark Island in it, or the rocky, blunt headland of Penny Rock, dark with trees, across it. Instead, she looked steadfastly at Rydal Fell and thought of herself as walking, henceforth, on heights heroic and austere.

'I lay in dust life's glory, dead,' quoted Corys to herself, from some hymn she had half-forgotten, and felt a solemn joy in being so sad and so magnificent.

Glancing cautiously and sideways at her Richard recognized the look on her face. Just so had he felt, once or twice in youth. 'No fear of tears now,' thought Richard, 'but later there'll be all the more.'

Once again, thinking of Corys, Richard was reminded of the baby robin that had kicked him. He marvelled that somewhere in Corys' long, immature body should be hidden a spirit so powerful. Because of this immaturity she would suffer all the more. Not yet, for Corys, were those comforts of the body, everyday, commonplace comforts like hot tea, a fire, a good bed at night, of any avail. Not yet could Corys set a joy against a sorrow and think herself lucky that the sky was not all black. To Corys, too near childhood for the act of heroism that her youth had eagerly embraced, the sky would be all black. He was aware by now that Corys had still for Bainriggs that enchanted intimacy of a child with the surface details of its playground: up that grey, broken crag, at least six feet high, she had gone rock climbing; in the fork of that oak branch she had set her doll, Queenie; that minute track among mosses and dead leaves that a hedgehog had made she had followed with her painted horse and cart, small as he. Where the rock sloped, smooth as grey silk, she had sat and slid down it, rushing beneath green branches to land in clumps of parsley fern. In the lake edge, along the low rocks and shingle beeches of Penny Rock she had built little harbours and floated boats of twigs and dead leaves. And now so many ridges and hollows, tree grown, so many grey rocks, so much lake shore and reedy river bank she had sold. She would not be able to walk there any more. Into the slow rhythm of forest life, unchanged for generations, would break Mr. Lovely; building himself a house; making himself, no doubt, a garden; planting trees from Africa and the Rockies; felling trees, not because they should be felled but because he wanted a view, or a summer-house or, even, poles for a pergola. And from Bonfire Hall, across the untroubled lake would stand Mr. Lovely's house, right on that beech-grown hump of Penny Rock where the red-gold leaves and the rain had fallen, and the lake waves lapped ashore, without any works of man to break the gentle sound of their falling.

Thinking of all this Richard began to doubt if Corys, being the kind of child she was, would be able to bear her affliction. If not, what would become of her and what would he, Richard Blunt, do? What did one do with an unbearable affliction?

'The first time I saw you there was moonlight in Bainriggs wood,' said Richard. 'Everything was wet and glittering. It made me think of Forest Silver, the tax that was paid for letting beasts run in the forest. Now, you are going to save Old John with Forest Silver, from Bainriggs forest.'

'I always think what a pretty name it is, for a tax,' said Corys.

Corys rowed Richard to the Island and there they found that the six kippers, simmering, had amalgamated themselves and become a bony paste, firmly stuck to the pan. So she took him on to the mainland, where he could get lunch at the Prince, and there, by the boat-landings, stood Gerald Lovely. He and his sister Myra had been blown off Helvellyn, he said. Actually, it appeared they had been blown on to it, or rather on to those slopes approaching it which lie on the way to Grisedale Tarn. Twice had Myra been blown off her feet, and on to the hard ground, and once Gerald had been blown off his. So they had turned back and come down again, bruised and tired, and here was Gerald, idling about by the lake, wanting his lunch and wondering where those Sweeting girls were. He watched Corys neatly bring her boat alongside a landing in spite of a squall that lifted columns of spray from the inshore waters and sent them flying across the lake.

'They tell me it is what they call a Helm Wind,' said Gerald, sauntering out on the boat-landing and holding the bow for them as if he were the boatman.

Gerald Lovely was twenty-one and not in the army because he was an engineering student. He was tall and slim. His hair was dark and, owing to hair cream, seemed all in one piece, like felt. The skin of his lean, good-looking face was as brown as if he led the life of a gipsy, and he had excellent teeth and lively, light grey eyes that showed he knew himself to be a charmer. He wore, at this moment, grey flannel trousers and a sage green pullover and he bent over the bow of the boat as if his body were all muscle, elastic as his youth.

Mr. Blunt was tired, because of having climbed Red Bank. He was empty, for there had been lumps in his breakfast porridge and he had thrown it into the lake. As he got out of the boat it jerked, in spite of Gerald, and the gust of wind that had jerked it seemed to hit him in the face. He blinked, stumbled on the edge of the boat-landing and might have slipped had Gerald not caught hold of him. Looking past his back Gerald, thinking Richard an old crock and how amusing it was that he had nearly fallen down, made a comic grimace at Corys, who might be an almighty freak but was, anyhow, young.

'Thanks,' said Richard, to Gerald, but with animosity rather than gratitude and he freed himself from the young man's insufferable care and stood up straight.

It was then that he observed Corys, who was looking at Gerald. She sat, holding her oars, ready to back herself out when Gerald should push, but she was twisted round so that she could look up at them both. Richard had not seen such a look on her face before. It was a startled look, alert, a little defiant, and fascinated as if she looked because she must, but there was also, perhaps in her bright eyes or in some almost insensible softening of the lines of her face, a suggestion that she liked looking. She liked looking, at Gerald! Is it possible? thought Blunt, who much disliked looking at Gerald.

Thus did Richard for the moment forget his distress at the grievous and bitter trials that lay ahead for Corys and think only of the most unexpected discomfort that he now experienced on his own account. 'Thank you so much, Cory. Will you have lunch with me or go home?' said Richard.

- 73 -

Corys said she must go home. She turned on her thin red cushion and faced the stern.

'Shove off!' said Corys, in her deep voice.

Gerald shoved. For a moment he and Richard stood, watching her back and then turn and row out into the turmoil of wind and waves upon the lake.

'Queer stick of a kid, isn't she?' said Gerald, a little patronizingly because he, being young, must understand her better than could any middle-aged hero like Blunt.

'Is it possible, it can't be possible, that I am jealous,' thought Blunt, following Gerald along the boat-landing, and still more astonished at himself because the sudden recollection of Miss Ozzard brought him an uncomfortable kind of relief. He did not want Miss Ozzard. He never wished to see her again. But she had appeared to love him and had certainly wished to marry him. Somehow, this thought gave Blunt reassurance in face of young Mr. Lovely's cock-sure immaturity.

'I really believe it must be a Helm Wind,' said Blunt, ignoring the young bounder's rhetorical question about Miss de Bainriggs.

Later that day Richard had his friend, Corys, to comfort again and knew that there was then no thought of Gerald in her mind. From the end of the Island Richard had seen her row across to Penny Rock. There, no doubt by appointment, she met Mr. Lovely. They talked and walked within Richard's view, passed out of sight and after a long interval reappeared again. They shook hands on the rocky shore and then Mr. Lovely's head and grey-green shoulders could be seen over the wall as he walked back along the road to the hotel. But Corys disappeared. She had stood a moment, looking after Mr. Lovely, and had then walked away among the trees and not come back to her boat.

The sun had set and black-out curtains were being drawn over lighted windows all over the valley when Blunt, by now seriously uneasy, got into his boat and rowed across to Penny Rock. For some time he had had an odd feeling about Corys: he seemed to have developed a sensitive perception that told him when she needed help and that there was some sort of affinity between them was proved, he thought, by the fact that she had always, when he had felt this, accepted him and his help as if she had known that he would come. This evening it was silent on Penny Rock. Behind the dark bulk of Silver How the sky was bright with that colourless glow which gives a northern austerity to some mountain sunsets. Yet the water at this lower end of the lake was entirely shadowed by reflections of fell and woodlands so that it lay, dead calm and black, a witch water, touched here and there by brilliant silvery sparks of light where perhaps a fish rose or some unseen water bird stirred the smooth surface. There was a smell of water and dead leaves and mildew on Penny Rock, and the dead leaves, decaying into mould though they were, gave a tawny warmth of colour to the ground that seemed exotic, beneath the shadowy dusk of the branches and beside that unlit lake.

'Cory!' called Richard, but gently because of the silent fall of night.

There was no answer and he did not call again. Instead, he searched for her, walking fast and yet looking into every fold and hollow of the rocky ground and down among the reeds by the lake. It was dusk when he found her. She was lying on her face, but she had chosen a sensible place on which to lie, where a ledge of grey rock jutted out above a marshy hollow. There was lichen and moss on the rock and as she lay one hand was tearing up little sheets of it and breaking them into dry and hoary fragments. Her forehead was supported on her other wrist. She was trembling with cold, or misery, or both, and now and then she gave a hushed whimper, like a dog that is wretched but dare not cry aloud.

'Cory! Cory, darling!' said Richard, and knelt beside her.

Corys rolled on to her side and looked up at his face, vaguely outlined against the black tree trunks and the bright, wild sky.

'Oh! Richard!' said Corys, and suddenly clung to him and hid her face against his shoulder. 'Oh! Richard! What shall I do if I can't bear it?'

CHAPTER IX

Late that night Grandy de Bainriggs and Blodwen stood at their front door before going to bed. Corys was in bed and for the last hour had been asleep. Mr. Blunt had gone back to his Island after a thoughtful period in the long parlour when he and Grandy had smoked, and Blodwen had knitted, mostly in silence. There was calm about Bonfire Hall though a gust of wind could be heard, roaring as it went, in the Bainriggs woods across the lake. It was so dark that Grandy's cigarette glowed bright as a red lamp.

'How far can a German airman see a cigarette?' asked Grandy, but not as if she expected an answer.

Blodwen stood, staring at the vague pallor that was the lake, and thinking of London and her husband. What was happening beyond this black silence of the clouded, mountain night? How much longer could she bear to be shut in here, imagining but never knowing what went on the other side of the veil of distance and the censorship?

'I am pleased with Corys,' said Grandy, after a while. 'I can't conceive, of course, how she manages to be so completely immature at seventeen. When I was seventeen I was in love. I forget who he was, but it wasn't the first time. However, immature or not, Cory has the power to attract men.' Corys' mother, greatly disliking such talk, gave a disapproving sort of murmur.

'I can just hear you saying God forbid! in your head,' said Grandy amusedly and turning to look at her shadowy daughter-in-law. 'You're quite Victorian, Blodwen. To attract men is a gift, like another. If a girl has it well and good; if she hasn't she can do very well without it. But I am glad Corys has the gift, though I am sorry for Richard. He's come too soon, or so I fear.'

Poor Blodwen felt as if Grandy were ruthlessly unwrapping a cocoon long, much too long, before its owner, sheltering within, was ready to be exposed.

'Oh, don't, please, Grandy,' said Blodwen, with a shudder of distaste that was perfectly perceptible to Grandy beside her. 'Listen! Isn't that a Jerry, a great way off?'

They both listened but it seemed that nowhere in the hidden immensities of the dark sky was there any Jerry and Grandy laughed, but gently.

'You're hopeless, Blodwen,' said she.

Next day Corys got up early as usual. She rowed across to see Blunt and asked him to meet her and the builder later in the morning at Old John's ruined cottage. 'Old John is coming too; it will be the first time he has been back since the fire,' said Corys. 'I was sorry about your kippers yesterday, Richard. I asked Mummie and she said not more than three minutes in the pan. Has it spoiled your pan? Because you can't buy one just now she says.'

'Oh, it didn't matter a bit, I had a good lunch at the Prince,' answered Richard, not thinking of what he said.

He thought instead of Corys as he had last seen her, dragging herself up to bed at Bonfire Hall, with her mother hovering anxiously just above. He thought of how he had rowed her over the dark lake and how her boat had tugged at his stern with queer, rippling, gurgling noises and how Corys, before that, after weeping herself into a most forlorn state, had had to be almost carried on board. The short row had revived her and she had walked up to the Hall and spoken in a boisterous kind of shout to her mother and Grandy in the long parlour, but then, at sight of the anxiety and pity on their faces, her tears had begun again, streaming from her eyes quietly without any sobbing or twisting of her distressed face.

'I'm so sorry,' had said Corys, weeping. 'But I absolutely can't help it. I am all aching with tears and I can't stop them coming. My throat aches so, Mummie, and my head feels so queer.'

Her mother had taken her away and she had not looked back at Richard. And now, here she was, talking about Old John and kippers.

'Do you want me to come now, Corys?' asked Richard, not looking at her because he saw she did not want him to. She was very pale and her eyelids were red and her quick, abashed glances at him had a defiance in them that meant that if he were sympathetic she would weep again.

'At eleven, please,' said Corys, and went quickly away.

Corys looked exhausted, but the looks of Old John made it clear that her exhaustion was to some purpose. Life had come back into him since yesterday. Like water after long thirst the good news of his cottage had revived him. The flagging of his vitality had begun to make him fail and Corys was right when she said there had been that in his face which spoke of death. Now, that look was gone.

'Miss Cory, see here,' said Old John, peevishly, in the burnt-out cottage. 'If so be you are going to rebuild this spot, do it proper, like. Put window back, same size, same place, where it's always been. And as to a watter-tap, I don't want watter. I'se got it up in coppice. If so be you put watter in cottage it'll freeze i' winter, and I don't hold with watter from tap any road.'

Old John knew his mind. The builder, whose family had lived in Grasmere since before the thirteenth century, had the same kind of mind. Matters were soon settled. Oak How was to be rebuilt so that it should be exactly the same as before the fire, and as Miss Corys would let them have the seasoned oak trunk they would be able to get to work at once.

'Do try and get it ready for him by Christmas, Robert,' said Corys, to the builder.

Corys had been polite to Richard and had included him in the conversation and even asked his approval of their decisions, but she had not asked his advice and he surmised that she had wanted him there as a kind of refuge in case the two old men had wanted something done she did not want.

'Not that I could have made them alter their minds,' thought Richard, regarding them.

'You are very lucky to have your house rebuilt for you,' said Richard, with some emphasis, to Old John.

'Ay,' said Old John, without perceptible emotion. 'I was never one to hold with insurance,' he added, pensively, 'and it's come all right for me, without, and that's saved me a bit, quite a tidy bit, to be sure.'

Old John, musing on this tidy bit, slowly rubbed one thin hand over the other and stared placidly at the bright lake.

'Miss Cory, tell Robert he's to put them wrestler slates back on roof top—I'll have none of them new-fangled riggin' tiles,' said Old John, emerging suddenly from his satisfied meditation.

Mr. Lovely had gone to the village that morning, seeking the builder. He had not found him and now, full of energy, he came hunting Robert the builder Back o' Lake and appeared in due course outside Oak How.

'Morning!' said Mr. Lovely, to all of them as they came out of Oak How. 'I'm going to want all your men and all the stuff you can let me have,' added Mr. Lovely to the builder.

'Ay?' said the builder, regarding Mr. Lovely cautiously. It appeared that Mr. Lovely had planned, long ago, what he would do if the young Miss let him have a bit of building land. He was going to buy wooden houses, bungalows, sheds, and garages, wherever he could get them. He was going to have them taken to pieces, sent to Grasmere, and put together again to form a kind of house.

'I want six rooms. They may all finally be under one roof, or there may be a roof of its own to each room,' said Mr. Lovely. 'I don't care what kind of plan it has or what it looks like. But there's bound to be a lot of waste, taking down old wooden buildings, and I shall want some extra wood, no doubt, and slates would come in handy for the roof, or bits of it, and where can I get a bath and lavatory fitments? And have you lead piping? Probably I shan't want much. Is there main water along that road by the bye?'

Corys and Old John and Richard left the others talking and went down to the lake.

'Him that buys him for a fule won't sell him for one,' said Old John, with a backward jerk of his head that meant he referred to Mr. Lovely.

'I hope Robert won't work for him instead of at Oak How,' said Corys, anxiously. 'I do want you to be settled in again before Christmas, John.'

'Ay,' said Old John. 'To be sure you will. We all wants that. Good day, Miss Cory, and good day, sir.'

Old John went on along the lake to his work in Bainriggs wood and Corys and Richard got back into her boat.

'Isn't it queer to have Grasmere full of strangers in November?' said Corys, in a bright and conversational manner. 'Did you hear about Rudie Sweeting finding a water rat in their well?'

It seemed that either the war or, perhaps, the evacuees had upset the Lakes weather that November. Instead of westerly winds and rain there blew, day after day, a cold wind from the east. It brought a moving sea of cloud that drove, dull with the faintly brassy gloom that tinges easterly airs, constantly above the valley. It brought, also, rheumatism, sciatica, neuralgia and discontent to the inhabitants of Grasmere and the natives said it was the Helm Wind and that it would last three, six or nine days. Thus the wind resembled the Bise, which vexes Geneva, and other mountain winds, most of which seem to be unpleasant, but it lasted more than nine days. It was welcomed only by Mr. Lovely and by Corys. He welcomed it because this easterly weather was not the type of weather to interfere with the building of houses, and she for the same reason. Old John should have welcomed it, but did not. It was impossible for so true a son of Grasmere as he was to welcome the Helm Wind and, though the rebuilding of Oak How proceeded unhindered by rain, frost or snow, he grumbled unceasingly at the cold.

It had not been possible to prove that Jownie Wife had set Oak How on fire. A stack of yard wood, carefully built against the north wall of the house, had been entirely consumed and some people said that this seemed to show that it had been set alight and had fired the overhanging eaves above. Other people pointed out that burning eaves might have fired the stack beneath them. Meanwhile, Jownie Wife did nothing objectionable and stayed hidden in the woods most of the time so that, what with the war and the evacuees, the talk about her died down very soon.

'She did it, all right,' said old Miss Trusty, in Bonfire Hall. Miss Trusty had come over from her Hen House above Chapel Style and was having tea with the de Bainriggs.

'I met her, soon after the fire, up by the tarn,' said Miss Trusty, 'and I said to her, "Jownie Wife, you fired Oak How and you are a bad old woman." She just blinked at me in her sly way and said nothing. But we understood each other. Corys, you haven't a bit of wood about that I could take for my Hen House door, have you? There is a crack down it, an inch wide.'

The dry weather agreed with Miss Trusty because the walls of her dwelling-place got damp inside when it rained for more than a week. She named it The Hen House, though the addition some years ago of a fireplace and chimney had made it a somewhat more elaborate structure than those still occupied by hens in the vicinity. Corys had often gone over Red Bank with an armful of fire-logs for Miss Trusty and the old lady and the young were friends.

'Come to-morrow and have tea with me, Cory,' said Miss Trusty, on this November afternoon, with her keen little eyes noting every sign of some sorrowful burden, the weight of which Corys was barely able to sustain.

Mr. Lovely had borrowed Old John from Miss de Bainriggs. On the afternoon of the day when Old John began to fell the beeches on Penny Rock to make room for Mr. Lovely's wooden house Corys set out for The Hen House. She met Richard, wandering uneasily toward Bonfire Hall, for the thought of Corys' grief haunted him and he felt he could not keep away from her till it should begin to lighten.

'Come with me to The Hen House?' said Corys with that note of gaiety in her voice which made the solemn shadow in her eyes seem the more marked.

So Richard went with her. The Island was helping Richard; he could now walk up Red Bank without feeling the world go dim about him. His heart must be stronger, he thought, and his long, solitary meditations were beginning to make him conscious of some things he had not thought much about before. On such things as strength and harmony and patience brooded Richard and began to think them so threaded through the foundations of life that no blow at the structure of life could finally destroy them. Yet, Corys was so young; could she hold firm, like a sapling willow, in the wind of misery that now blew upon her?

'I'm morbid about the child. It's silly to imagine and perhaps exaggerate other people's feelings,' thought Richard, glancing at Corys' serious profile as they came to the top of the hill and knowing, too well, that he did not exaggerate.

They had a peaceful tea at The Hen House. Miss Trusty, though fierce, was peaceful. Griefs and joys had come to Miss Trusty, stayed with her a little while and sunk into the past. Yet, here she was, going on undaunted and still quite uncertain where she was going to, which, after all, made things interesting as she drew nearer that unknown goal. Miss Trusty had come, though slowly, and after nearly eighty years of going to church, to believe in God and thus she had few anxieties save about such things as her hair coming out and her chimney-stack, which, like Fold-in-the-Wood, was built of water-worn stones and liable to fall down.

The east wind did not blow upon The Hen House but, with curious roarings and rushings, over the crags far above it. Thus, they sat with the door open and watched dusk come to the miles of country below. When the wooded and rocky slopes from the hollow of Elterwater to the top of Wetherlam were all grown dim together beneath the darkening sky Corys spoke, out of her shadowy corner.

'Miss Trusty, do you think it is possible for any one to have a trouble so bad that they cannot bear it?'

Miss Trusty had been talking, dreamily, of the death of her kitten when she herself had been six years old. That great grief had set a barrier, said Miss Trusty, between her days before the kitten's death and what came after.

'For a long time it seemed that Kitty's death had divided my life into two,' had said Miss Trusty, who loved to talk of her youth, 'as perhaps it did.'

Now, she looked quickly at Corys and then away again, far down to where the little pool of Elterwater seemed to shine more brightly as the dusk shadowed all about it.

'Whether or not a trouble can be borne is nothing to do with the trouble,' said Miss Trusty. 'All troubles can be borne if the person troubled is spiritually in good health. And if they are not, they can become so. Ask and it shall be given unto you,' said Miss Trusty, in the quiet voice of one who states a truth well proved.

Corys made no reply to this and it was Miss Trusty who eventually broke the silence and told them to get away before it grew any darker.

'There's no moon and you'll soon not be able to see your feet,' said Miss Trusty.

Richard and Corys walked back almost in silence. When they got near Fold-in-the-Wood Corys said something about Miss Trusty and what a horrid hut The Hen House was, and what a dear she was, and then the door of Fold-in-the-Wood just below them was opened widely and a dim but illegal glare of light shone out. In the glare, which was not so very illegal since the Sweetings had perforce to use Miss Trusty's old oil lamp, stood Mr. Gerald Lovely, surrounded by the pale heads of the Sweeting sisters. There was a clamour of talk. Then he moved away, the door was shut and the darkness, but not the quietness of the night, returned, for Gerald, as he walked, sang. He sang invisible, like a nightingale though there were no leaves to hide him in November. He sang in a pure tenor and the music of his voice rose as if the dark air hid a fountain of sound as bright as it was clear.

Corys stood still, and Richard with her, till Gerald's song faded to an elfin whisper, like a distant echo of itself.

'Did you know he sang, and like that?' said Corys, then, in an awe-struck voice.

'No,' said Richard. He was not musical and he thought bitterly that it was just like Gerald to have a voice and go shouting about the woods. 'I wonder if the Sweetings sing as sweetly,' added he, trying to be more amiable.

When Corys got home it was dark. She had glanced back as she walked and had been able to see Blunt's boat, moving, dark upon the dim lake, to the Island. Then she looked ahead, expecting to meet Jet. Jet knew when Corys was coming and always met her at the last bend in the homeward track, met her in a humble ecstasy, thankful for her safe return. This evening there was no Jet. Through the silent night Corys went on, anxious and puzzled.

'Where is Jet?' said Corys, directly she entered Bonfire Hall. No one knew. No one could remember when they had last seen Jet, but Jane Peascod said that Jownie Wife had come and begged for scraps and that Jet had barked at her, some time in the afternoon.

'I sharpened her off,' said Jane, with satisfaction, 'and off she went. Jet? She barked, and Jownie Wife cursed her, but I know nowt else. Miss Cory, there's been a ewe in cabbage patch. I chased her out but she's brought down a lot of wall. Will you tell Old John to put it up again to-morrow?'

CHAPTER X

Towards evening on the next day the Sweetings caught Jownie Wife. Corys had come early and told them she wanted Jownie Wife, and all that day the Sweetings and Richard Blunt and Corys had hunted her up and down the fells and through the woods and had not seen a glimpse of her apron. That the Sweetings got her in the end was due to luck and muscle rather than to any particular intelligence on their part. Returning to Fold-in-the-Wood after having hung about the grocer's in the hope that Jownie Wife would be making her usual Friday purchases, they had seen her scuttling away into the fern and undergrowth above the road. So they had caught her and held her, since six arms, young and vigorous if not really so very muscular, were at last too much for two, wiry and tough but old.

Corys and Richard Blunt were, the Sweetings knew, lurking about in the Bainriggs woods in the hope of intercepting Jownie Wife as she returned to her shack near the quarry. So they took their capture to Bonfire Hall, having every confidence in the ability of Grandy de Bainriggs to deal with her.

'Here she is, but she won't say a word,' said the Sweetings, in the long parlour.

Grandy de Bainriggs looked over the top of her cheap, steel-framed spectacles at Jownie Wife, who was firmly held by Essie on one side of her and Mag on the other, while Rudie hovered behind, ready to clutch at any outlying portion of her meagre garments.

'Jownie Wife, I'm ashamed of you. Where is that dog?' said Grandy, in her deep, melodious voice.

However, it was not one of Grandy's good days. She had not many bad ones but this was one of them. Many years ago she had got some kind of low fever when she had been tipped into the Niger, quite by mistake.

She always declared that the fever came back now and again, and though Blodwen could never discover any rise of temperature certainly Grandy sometimes went all limp and depressed and said she felt much more hollow inside than appeared justified by what she knew of the size of the legitimate hollows within the human frame. To-day she had declared quite early that her Niger fever was upon her again and now, confronted with Jownie Wife, she knew there was not the virtue in her to quell the resistance of the weasel-like lady.

Jownie Wife knew this too and, though there was no expression in her black beads of eyes, there was triumph behind them as she looked at Grandy.

'Where did you put that dog, you wretched little stoat of a creature?' said Grandy, though perfectly aware that Jownie Wife was silently trying to make her lose her temper.

'What dog?' said Jownie Wife. 'I kna' nowt about any dog.'

Grandy gave a grunt, which was a mistake, for Jownie Wife correctly interpreted it to mean despair, irritation and contempt. Contempt! Girt, fat, off-come woman, who was here only because she had had the luck to marry into a family better than her own, who was Grandy de Bainriggs to feel contempt for Jownie Wife?

'We may as well come to it early as late,' said Grandy, after her grunt, and in that flat voice which meant she was trying to be sarcastic like.

She took five shillings from her little green bag and held it out to Jownie Wife.

'Now, where's Jet?' said Grandy, in a flatter voice than ever.

'Thank you kindly,' said Jownie Wife, quickly taking it, 'but that don't pay me for being turned out of my own spot on Island.'

Fortunately, for her Niger fever was liable to make Grandy use language but little suited to the pink, shell-like ears of the sweet Sweetings, Blodwen came in at this point. She saw at once that Grandy was on the verge of a tantrum and that Jownie Wife, though in an evil temper also, was half-starved and feeling exhausted. Somehow, she got Jownie Wife detached from the anxious clutches of Essie and Mag, out of the room and into the kitchen.

'Is the wood split for to-morrow's kindling, Jane?' said Blodwen, thus sending Jane, much injured in her feelings, out to the shed.

'Teapot's on fire; kettle's boiling,' said Jownie Wife, much gratified, and she sank into Jane's warm, cushioned chair.

So she and that young Mrs. de Bainriggs, who might be a foreigner, but was worth two of them stiff-necked Bonfire Hall folk, had a nice cup of tea, well brewed, together, and young Mrs. de Bainriggs nivver said a word about dog, Jet or anudder, but wished Jownie Wife well when she got up to go.

'Tse thankful to you, ma'am,' said Jownie Wife, who had not said that to anybody for twenty-five years. 'And if so be you should ever be gaan along Thirlmere way, there's an auld barn Armboth way, and I did hear tell, from a tramping kind of fellow, there was a dog, tied up there and hardly treated. He heard it crying, he said.'

'You know the old Armboth barn?' said Blodwen, placidly, as she came back to the long parlour. 'Jet is there, tied up. Children, do you think your father would let you borrow his car so that we can go and fetch her?'

The Sweetings had been listening with discomfort to Grandy, who had been telling them more than was good for them about Jownie Wife's past, or what was supposed to have been her past.

'Oh, rather!' said they, all leaping together towards the door. 'Shall we get it now?'

When the rescue party finally set off, which was at ten o'clock next morning, Grandy and Richard and Blodwen were left behind. Mr. Sweeting's little car, which was the only one he would lend his daughters, held four people. When Essie and Rudie and Mag had got in, and then Corys, it was, obviously, full, but the Sweetings cried out that it always held one, and sometimes two, more. Gerald Lovely and his sister, having heard overnight from Mag of what was toward, had come to Fold-in-the-Wood to see the rescue party well away, or so they said. Really, they had not known what else to do. Until they appeared Richard had taken it for granted that he would go but now he hesitated. Certainly the little car could not hold more than one extra adult and that young Gerald was as fit as a Martindale stag.

'You'd better go with them, Lovely,' said Richard, stepping back. 'Oh, but won't you go, sir?' said Gerald, but so perfunctorily that his foot was already on the running board.

'Too bad,' said Grandy, glancing at Richard as the car drove off, and the disappointed faces of the Sweeting sisters, looking back, silently said the same, though Rudie, at the wheel, nearly upset the car in doing so.

By now the dreadful scars made at Penny Rock by Old John were clearly visible from across the lake and Corys, wedged in the back seat between Gerald and Mag, felt that sharp pang of utter misery that comes when a grief has been half forgotten and then suddenly confronted again. Gerald, too, looked over the rippled water, and saw the white tree stumps that were a sign of his father's wealth.

'He's going to call his new mansion Lake View,' said Gerald, 'my old dad, I mean. Odd thing, but he's as excited over the conglomeration of wooden shacks he's going to put up over there as he was when he built High Castle, outside St. Helens. He's worrying the life out of that old chap of yours to get every bit of tree root out; says beeches will sprout up through our floors if he doesn't.'

'Oh!' said Corys, and wished to say more but could not, because that ache in her throat had come again.

Richard went back to his Island and told himself that he must not keep on forgetting that, at thirty-five, he was already a crock, and must always be something of an invalid. Self-pity so absorbed him that he had little thought to spare for Corys, though the heavy thuds of Old John's axe travelled across the lake a perceptible time after the flash of it showed, bright in the dull light.

Grandy and Blodwen went back into the Hall. 'Jownie Wife will get the better of you yet, tea or no tea,' said Grandy, with a chuckle.

When the car came back, just before lunch-time, it seemed that she was probably right. They had driven as near the Thirlmere dam as war-time regulations allowed and then walked along the road on the west of the lake to the site of the vanished Armboth Hall. The road was closed to all traffic but they met no one and were not stopped. When they got to the barn they found the door unlatched and, within it, signs that a dog or dogs had been kept there. But no dog was there then and when Corys called 'Jet! Jet! Where are you?' they heard nothing but the faint whisper of Launchy Gill, rushing down through the woods nearly a mile away.

'Oh, dear!' said Blodwen, much vexed. 'And I am sure Jownie Wife meant to be kind last night.'

'She must have got over that quite soon,' said Grandy. 'And then she'd nip over the Raise and have Jet out and hide her somewhere else before day. So, she'll expect to get another five shillings and more stewed tea, and when she's played this trick once or twice more she'll get a shilling from Jos Blaine for telling him where Jet is, by then.'

Blodwen looked at her daughter and could not understand what she saw. Corys was terribly white but, though she had what Blodwen vaguely thought of as the foundation of a tragic expression, there was a kind of superficial restlessness in her eyes and a look of expectation that seemed odd. With Penny Rock gone, and Jet gone, what thing, disturbing, perhaps, but not altogether unpleasant, did Corys expect?

That afternoon Richard, listening beside his hogg-house fire to Corys, was aware, as Blodwen had been, that she had something on her mind other than her preoccupation about Jet.

'Jos Blaine used that barn at one time,' said Corys, with more vitality in her voice than he had expected. 'And, once, we thought we saw him coming along the road, but it was the top of a sheep. Do you know what Gerald did? He picked up an old fence stake and said he would knock Jos out with it. He would, too, I think, but, of course, it wasn't Jos.'

Under a high and clouded sky, the fells were clear with a sombre clarity that showed every crag and gill, each green intack and patch of russet bracken, and the high, pale grass slopes, in detail that would have been vivid had not all been shadowed. Yet, there was colour in the clearness of the cloud shadow and whether from this shadow or themselves the fells seemed to draw a rich, deep purple gloom or a sepia tinge, transparent as a peat stream. Remote above the valley in these dim, clear hues of distance, stood Seat Sandal, and Rydal Fell and, between them, the still, upturned face of Stone Arthur, and out upon these lonely slopes looked Corys, from the hogg-house, and felt herself troubled for the first time with a trouble that seemed beyond their reach.

She sat with her face turned from Penny Rock so that Richard saw her outlined against the open doorway, the lake, and the dusky woodlands of Bainriggs. Motionless, on a stool, with her tall back bent and her chin propped on one hand, she looked to Richard like a statue in bronze, for she wore her green corduroys to-day. The sculptor, had one modelled her, would have called her Expectation, for that air of waiting which so often was associated with Corys was very marked just now.

'Richard,' said Corys, hesitatingly. 'Richard, do you think it a mistake for a girl to dress and act like a boy?'

Mr. Blunt was startled. What, in the midst of all her troubles, was making Corys ask herself, rather than him, this question? He thought he knew, and cursed Gerald Lovely afresh. Not by an immature lad, neither boy nor man, and heartless with his immaturity, should the first doubts of herself have been stirred in Corys. But perhaps it was the Sweetings. He gave a little sigh of relief. No doubt, it was the girlish Sweetings who had been teasing Corys and making her wonder could they be more right than she, after all?

'A mistake?' said Richard, slowly, with these thoughts weighing on his words. 'I don't know, Cory. I rather think it doesn't matter very much, either way.'

'Not matter? I think it might matter a great deal,' said Corys, turning her face so that he saw it dimly lit by the fire into which she seemed to be gazing. 'Sometimes, Richard, little things settle big ones. Couldn't a girl who had always acted like a boy miss things, some kinds of things, before she had time to change?'

'If, under her boy's clothes, she was a normal girl, growing into normal womanhood, I doubt it,' said Richard, becoming increasingly alarmed. Who was he to blunder in among the delicacies of adolescent girlhood? 'Breeches don't stifle womanhood, Cory, any more than they stifle breathing.'

'Then why have women always dressed differently from men?' asked Corys, 'except a few odd ones, and they, Rudie says, look ridiculous—'

Corys stopped suddenly here, remembering, and leaving unsaid that word 'behind' which Rudie had added so devastatingly to her criticism.

'The better to attract men,' said Richard, suddenly light-hearted. Certainly, it must have been the Sweeting sisters who had set these ideas whirling about in Corys' mind.

At this, the child looked quickly at him and Richard felt ashamed.

'I am sorry, Cory,' he said hastily. 'I did not mean to be flippant. But I think I am as bewildered as you are about—breeches—' Here, a sort of hysteria and an excessive nervousness about saying the right thing gave a tone to Richard's voice that was almost like a giggle.

'If an Englishman is terribly in earnest about anything he tries to dodge round it by being flippant,' explained Richard, perfectly aware that he was failing Corys, just when she needed help.

'And are you terribly in earnest about woman's dress?' said Corys, astonished and suspicious.

'About you in it, or not in it, I certainly am,' said he, grave again, but impelled to speak with an apparent lightness for fear that Corys' womanhood, however little developed, might otherwise divine how truthfully he spoke.

'Oh, well!' said Corys, looking out again at a swan that moved, spectral pale in the dusk, silently upon the dark lake. She gave a scarcely audible sigh and Richard knew that she was drawing back into herself those problems which she had, with the difficulty of the young, made articulate for his resolving.

'I shall have to ask Mummie,' said Corys, and got up to go. He stood listening till the sound of her oars, gently scrooping on the rowlocks, died away. By now there was dusk in the valley but on the upper slopes of Rydal Fell and high in the bare trough of Greenhead Gill there lay a dim glow, so dim it cast no shadows, but warm with the hidden sunset.

'Poor Cory,' thought Richard, half amused, 'and poor me,' he added, ruefully, looking up at the sunset glow and thinking how high above him were the bright slopes of a heavenly resignation.

CHAPTER XI

A week before Christmas the barometer began to fall. The weather had been unusually dry at the Lakes ever since the outbreak of war, so that imaginative people and the despondent wondered what would happen if a shower of incendiaries fell in the woods. The drought suited Mr. Lovely in one way since it made building possible all and every day, but it also exasperated him because the builder's men refused to let the weather affect their proceedings. If it had rained they would have worked as much as they thought right for Mr. Lovely without any regard for the rain; if it was dry, they would work no more. So, many quiet, rainless days went by without any work being done on the frightful mass of wooden partitions, sections of roofs, doors, floorboards, worn joists, matchboard linings and window-frames that Mr. Lovely had accumulated from his purchases of wooden houses, bungalows, garages and garden huts. He had advertised his wants in a dozen or so of local weekly newspapers, spread over rural England, and one tall, pale, wooden house had come from Dungeness and a brown bungalow from a Cornish beach, while he had drawn a supply of more or less dilapidated garages from all along the Welsh border. Naturally, the various parts of the various erections had got a bit mixed up, on the journey, or as they were unpacked, or on the Penny Rock site. The L.M.S. van came nearly every day for some weeks, bringing a fresh lot of more or less mangled portions of what had been buildings, and these fragments were cast down on top of each other till the extraction of any particular bit involved the playing of a giant and rather dangerous game of Spillikins. Also, as the days went by Mr. Lovely became increasingly haunted by the fear of fire. Old John quietly persisted in carrying on his brushwood burning in Bainriggs wood as soon as he had cut down fifteen beautiful beeches on Penny Rock, and Mr. Lovely felt convinced that sparks would settle on his precious, dry dump which was the dishevelled but pleasantly bulky embryo of his even more precious Lake View.

If Mr. Lovely were dissatisfied so was Corys, but she had not expected to be anything else. Well she knew that one individual could never be the only pebble on the builder's beach. Even if Old John developed shingles, as do most Grasmere men who take to the wilds, the builder could not be expected to neglect all the rest of the valley in order to get Oak How completed. It was particularly galling to Corys, of course, that most of the time when nothing was done at Oak How something was being done at Lake View, but she knew that a builder, like a dressmaker, must inevitably keep all his customers strongly irritated but let none of them become desperate.

During these weeks Corys grew thinner than ever. She never talked of Lake View or of Jet and, to Richard Blunt anyhow, she never mentioned Gerald Lovely, who had gone back to Cambridge and then to London to do fire watching for an aunt. Always rather silent, she now talked less than ever and Grandy said that this lack of talk, combined with the dark shadows under Corys' eyes, signified that her liver was out of order or that she was in love.

'You cheapen things so,' said Blodwen, angrily flushed, one afternoon when Richard had come to tea.

'A lot of what is called love is what I call cheap,' said Grandy. 'If Cory is in love at the moment it'll be with a cheap love, a twopence coloured, quickly faded, leave no mark behind it love.'

Corys was out. They had told Richard she had gone on her bicycle to St. John's Vale to get a hundred larches from the forestry place there.

'On her bicycle!' exclaimed Richard.

'A hundred larches, young enough, will go in her bicycle basket,' Blodwen had told him, smiling.

Now, she turned to him, as to a refuge.

'Don't believe a word that Grandy says,' said she. 'Cory is a child still. Grandy shouldn't talk as she does.'

'And Blodwen shouldn't walk so head-in-air,' said Grandy, not offended. 'She'll come down with a wallop some day.'

The larches were, they said, to be planted all together in a little wood which, when they grew up to be about twenty feet high, would hide Penny Rock from the Hall.

'Cory will never get over the sale of Penny Rock,' said Blodwen, looking out of the window to where the light coloured reflection of the fragmentary Lake View lay, blurred by faint ripples, amid the dark reflections of wood and fell. 'By that I mean that her grief at its loss will affect her growth, mentally and spiritually. It will become a part of her as a bit of metal railing sometimes becomes part of a tree trunk, that grows around it and hides it, but it is there all the time.'

'We all have bits of that kind of metal in our make-up,' said Grandy briskly, but a little sadly too. Her face brightened again. 'A beautiful Arab I met in 1900 is one of my bits. The loss of him is in me somewhere, no doubt, but I've taken no harm from it. Nor him, neither,' she ended, with another chuckle.

As before remarked the barometer began to fall a week before Christmas and Grasmere residents thought that, at last, their normal weather was to return and hover, damp, fitful, but always beautiful, over vale and hills. However, though the barometer continued to fall, day after day, the weather became not wet but even drier, as so often happens at the Lakes. There was frost every night. When dawn came it glowed cloudless above the Rydal gap and, one after the other, the snow-covered tops of the fells were lit with a rosy light that changed to gold so that they shone like lamps above the shadowed lake. By the time the snows were white in full sunshine the golden light lay here and there in the valley, bright as a jewel in the grey haze of frost and shadow, and then the sun rose clear of the fell tops and shone all day so that the slopes of russet bracken were red as a fox beneath the snowy heights and the long shadows of walls and trees, shifting moment by moment on the valley pastures, told the time of day to those who could read so astronomical a message.

Corys' father came home before Christmas and Richard Blunt, who had wondered so often what kind of man he was, grew friendly with him in a day. Miles de Bainriggs was a little stout, pale from busy days and nights in London, and so out of training that Richard could walk faster and farther than he. Shrewd, kindly, humorous and with the manner of a tolerant man of the world, he looked observantly at his daughter and remarked, dispassionately, that she had been foolish to sell Penny Rock if she was going to break her heart about it.

'Presumably you wanted to rebuild Old John's cottage; certainly you could have got the money to do it only by selling land. So now, you've done what you wanted and felt you ought to do, and you've necessarily lost Penny Rock. You can't have your cake and eat it,' said Mr. de Bainriggs, lazily stretched out by the fire in the long parlour with his wife knitting khaki gloves very close beside him. 'It would have upset you more, I dare say, if Old John had fretted himself into his grave for want of his home. And as he told me to-day he has left Oak How to you in the will he made last week it won't have been a bad investment for you.'

Corys gave a wriggle of discomfort. She hated it when her father's common sense thrust itself in among her dreams and cherished sorrows, but she felt it bracing, too. Richard, listening and watching, from the chair in the long parlour that was now called Richard's Chair, thought how safe a thing was common sense, and how uncommon. What with the war, and his heart, his horrid feeling about Miss Ozzard, his feeling for Corys and the unusualness of his solitary life upon the Island he had thought himself in some danger of passing into that state of mind when every trifle assumes significance, everything seems fraught with some hidden meaning and the mystery of life becomes tangible as a morning haze that might, at any moment, part and disclose to human faculties something beyond their apprehension. To think thus may be true but, as Richard well knew, it is difficult to sustain and, probably, not very practical. He was glad now to hear Corys' father talking with what is generally supposed to be sound and practical sense; he felt that, after these months of brooding in the uncanny peace of Grasmere, he welcomed the rough and ready way in which the other man solved difficulties that he did not really understand. After all, however delicately difficulties were approached there was no hope of fathoming them; better to butt a way through life, thought Richard, and probably less harm done.

Just before Christmas Gerald Lovely returned to Grasmere, having put out five incendiary bombs and rescued his aunt, upon whom a wardrobe had fallen owing to blast. Finding the Sweetings out when he called at Fold-in-the-Wood he went idly on and was given tea at Bonfire Hall, where he told stories of London under fire and Corys, listening, and watching him, felt the strong call of his youth to her youth as well as that queer, vague stirring of an emotion that was not unpleasant, though scarcely pleasant. Between the elderly bodies of her mother, and Grandy, and her polite but obviously uninterested father, Corys looked at Gerald and felt a sense of comfort in his presence, because he was young. Gerald, who had plenty of young companions in his life, looked now and then at Corys and thought her an awkward bean-pole of a creature and scarcely out of the nursery, but, just as he was leaving, he asked her to a tea-party at Ambleside.

'The Sweeting kids and Myra are coming,' said Gerald, 'and I'm sure we would all be pleased if you would come too.'

The three elder de Bainriggs thought his manner patronizing and almost fatherly, but Corys accepted the invitation with a humble alacrity.

'Heaven help the young,' thought Grandy, as Mr. Gerald Lovely made his rather off-hand farewells, 'for nothing else can.'

Pride and shyness prevented Corys from wearing, for the tea-party, her one feminine costume, a frock and overcoat of soft green cloth that she had not worn for two years. 'Anyhow, it must be far too short for her, by now,' said Blodwen, resignedly, watching her daughter stride away, in her green corduroy jacket and slacks and with the green band round her stiff, thick dark hair.

The Sweeting sisters were delightful to behold in new blue coats with a silvery fur at neck and wrists and Myra Lovely looked distinguished if grumpy, with her dark hair brushed straight back from her forehead and a leopard-skin coat hiding the more bony angles of her figure. However, Corys, in her green slacks, made no heads turn in Ambleside, for the townsfolk were by now well accustomed to the sight of art students, evacuated from London, whose sex was indeterminate, though by now most were female since all the men fit enough to do so had gone away to fight, long ago.

Their party attracted some attention even in the crowded hotel lounge where they had tea and Gerald was complacently aware that the pale, gold, silky heads of the Sweetings, of so unusual a colour and three of them all together, drew glances and even stares from the hotel guests, who were, no doubt, artists themselves. He did not realize that some of the glances were for Corys. It was known that a very young, male violinist was visiting, or about to visit, Ambleside, and most of the people thought Corys must be he.

Essie and Rudie and Mag did their best at first to include Corys in the tea-table talk, but directly they let go their verbal hold on her she sank again into speechlessness. Corys could talk about the wintering of Herdwick hoggs, the use of poultry manure in vegetable gardens, the intolerable nuisance of dry larch needles blown, in autumn, under the edges of roofing slates so that rain came through; she could discuss Shakespeare and the poems of T. S. Eliot and Dorothy Wordsworth's Journals and the probable sites of vanished fulling mills in Grasmere. Of all these things were the Sweetings, Myra and Gerald completely ignorant. They spoke of dances, cocktail parties, plays, the cinema, the petrol shortage and what to do with car batteries that did not get charged because the cars did not run fast or far enough to charge them. Thus, the conversation resolved itself into Corys de Bainriggs speaking with the accompaniment of a polite silence from the others, or to three Sweetings, and two Lovelys speaking, mostly together, while Miss de Bainriggs listened and made no comments. And, after this, a thing happened that everybody felt afterwards to have been regrettable. Corys was forgotten by the rest of the party and then lost, so that they had to drive home without her.

As soon as tea was over they had all strolled out and down to Waterhead to see the sunset on Windermere. Looking at it and talking, now, of Bridge, the three Sweetings and two Lovelys wandered up and down and then more up than down and then back to Gerald's car. Corys had regarded their backs, as they went, and had decided she had had enough of them and they of her. So she had hidden near a boat-house and when, after five minutes, Gerald came running back to look for her he naturally did not see her and, after waiting by the car for nearly half an hour, he drove the others home.

Meanwhile, Corys went out to the end of a boat-landing and perched herself, insecurely enough, on its railing. There, she looked at the sunset but, like the others, thought little about it though it undoubtedly sobered her meditations and gave to them that semblance of a solemn clarity which is easily acquired by thinkers of seventeen. Here, thought Corys, she was at the parting of the ways. Was she to be man or woman? Was she to go on, dressing as a boy, doing work a boy would do, getting daily tougher, more weather-beaten, healthier, until perhaps one day she would win a Guides' Race? Or was she to change, now that she was seventeen, and consent to be a girl?

'Detestable apes,' thought Corys of girls in general and the Sweetings in particular. 'Silly, self-conscious dolls, all painted and powdered, tied up in idiotic clothes, wearing ridiculous curls, going out to tea-parties, and work parties, and thinking about young men all the time.'

Corys knew something about herself that she thought was odd. She liked children, when they were good and clean. She very much liked to have a child slip its hand into hers and walk like that, but this liking did not account, she thought, for the strange feeling that came deep in her chest when she sat in the bus near a woman holding a baby. She longed, on these occasions, to snatch the baby and hold it herself and she knew, though without knowing how she knew it, that, if she did so, that queer feeling like an ache would be satisfied.

'If I let myself grow all manly I shan't ever have a baby,' thought Corys, 'for no man would want to marry me. Gerald doesn't care a scrap about me but he's off the deep end over those pinky-white Sweetings.'

It was nearly six o'clock but the sunset, owing to Summer Time, still made of the bay a sea of gold. There was no wind, but, somewhere out where leafless trees showed dusky beyond the golden water, the river Rothay entered the lake and perhaps its current caused the long, faint undulations that seemed to flow, as if the lake flowed, towards the south. This noiseless, golden pulsation of the water, as if the evening breathed in the peace of quiet surrender to the coming night, deflected Corys' thoughts from babies. She stared at it and at the clear edges of the Langdale fells beyond, a far, dark wall against the west.

'How I do fuss!' thought Corys, and her mind seemed to stand still and let itself be filled with calm.

As she went home along the right bank of the Rothay and the Loughrigg Terrace Walk it occurred to Corys that her thoughts of babies and her thoughts of Gerald had remained quite separate. She had no idea of marrying any one for many years and years; she had never had any idea of marrying Gerald or, indeed, of doing anything with him, beyond adoring contemplation. For her, babies still hovered in a soft, pink haze beyond her reach, quite detached from any thoughts of man.

'Yet, there must be somebody some day, if I am to have any,' thought Corys, of men and babies, and suddenly conceived a bright idea about Gerald. 'Yes, I'll do that, and, if it works with him, it'll show I can get a husband some day or other,' said Corys out loud beside the Rothay. The Rothay, flowing rosy with sunset through the wan and dusky grasslands, went on quietly rushing and shining as it had done since the Ice Age, but knowing it, she felt that it agreed with her.

CHAPTER XII

Another war time Christmas now came to Grasmere. With three times as many people in the valley as there were normally in winter the shops were always full; a clutter of alert, well-dressed babies in their prams obstructed with their nurses the letter-box in Red Lion Square, it being the habit of prams to congregate outside the post office; strangers asked peculiar questions, at all times and of all persons. 'Is that Scafell Pike?' would say an elderly pedestrian, waving vaguely towards those slopes of Silver-how that look so immense from the village roads. 'Oh, is there a post office in Grasmere?' and 'Which is the church, please?' The *Westmorland Gazette* got itself mixed up over its statement of times for the black-out and the red mail-van made its one delivery of letters in the middle of lunch. Another test was made of the local air-raid siren, which was tootled by hand, but no one, fortunately, was able to hear it except two households on the same side of the valley who thought it was a bus changing gear on the Raise.

Neither Lake View nor Oak How was finished before Christmas and so Old John continued to live up on the fell and took no harm owing to the dry weather, and the Lovelys, perforce, went on making themselves an intolerable nuisance to the elderly Grasmere lady who had, in one of those moments of compunction which unfortunately come to every one, offered them what she described as the shelter of her roof. They were not inconsiderate guests for, like every one else from the Prince, except the Sweetings, they were too terrified of being turned out to do anything but grovel to their new hostess. However, by doing nothing but grovel and move, inert as saccharin, about her house, they plagued the old lady until after a week she felt she would scream if they did not at once go away.

An old resident of Grasmere gave, according to custom, mince pies and sixpences to Grasmere children on New Year's Day and this ceremony seemed to bring the Christmas season to an end. It had been remarkable for the wonderful weather, which continued to be dry and sunny whether the barometer went up or down, and for the immense number of frugal, war-time tea-parties at which Grasmere householders entertained as many of the vale's war guests as could be accommodated in their drawing-rooms. The result of all this hospitality was that a large number of people were in doubt whether or not they were expected to bow to each other and few hostesses could remember the unfamiliar names of their guests or guests those of their hostesses; thus, a descriptive method was adopted for identifying strangers and The Green Lady, The Distraught Gentleman, Girl-from-Score-Crag, Woman-in-Goloshes and similar titles passed usefully into the local vocabulary and became as non-transferable as railway tickets.

Richard Blunt had spent Christmas Day at Bonfire Hall. For some time letters for him had been directed there, so that he had only to row across a short stretch of lake to get them instead of going to the crowded post office. The mail arrived after Mr. de Bainriggs had gone off, up Helm Crag. It was late, even for Christmas Day, because the van had been attacked by a ram as it stood outside Fold-in-the-Wood and the driver, as a result, had to keep stopping to fill his leaking radiator from the lake. He brought many cards and letters for Richard, but the biggest and most expensive card of them all was from Miss Ozzard. It was a woodcut of the old street in Chelsea where she lived and she had written on the blank inner page: 'My good wishes, always. Maimie.'

Observing that the eyes of Grandy and Corys, at least, had noted his look of disorder and the way he stuffed the card in its thick envelope into his pocket, Richard spoke impulsively.

'It's a card from the young woman I was engaged to,' said he. 'Should she be allowed to go on sending me cards? She's not well off, and it worries me and impoverishes her.'

'I'd forgotten. So you were engaged,' said Corys, profoundly interested. 'What was it like?'

'If she is not well off, you may be sure it means she still thinks she has a sporting chance,' said Grandy. 'Has she?'

'No, she has none,' said Richard, thoughtfully looking at Corys, though his words were for Grandy.

'Ha! What did I say about Cory?' said Grandy, silently and inside her head, to the unheeding Blodwen, who was wondering if the fish van would have enough fish to get along to the Hall on Friday.

This card from Miss Ozzard, his increasing weariness at being shut up in Grasmere and some perception that Corys' obviously uneasy state of mind was not entirely due to her loss of Penny Rock and Jet, all made Richard suddenly think of that modern cure for so many troubles, a cure so commonly resorted to that it is called simply a change. Other kinds of change had been going on inside him, of which he was only partially aware. He could walk and even climb more easily than had been possible. Sometimes, for perhaps two or even three hours, he forgot that he had an injured heart. The sense of furious, bewildered misery which had so heavily oppressed him when he was first invalided had begun to pass. The long, wakeful nights on his Island when he lay listening to the passage of aeroplanes overhead and knew, too well, what must be happening in other parts of the country, had led him, at last, to grope towards a sense of something that was less resignation than acceptance. Where life was, suffering was, as mysterious as life. Who was man to say there should be none?

These spiritual consolations, though they began to alter Richard's outlook upon all things, by no means shielded him from irritation and despondency when what he thought of as essentially trifling matters went wrong. And now this Christmas card from Maimie Ozzard; Corys' wan looks; the hideous appearance of Lake View, daily growing bigger and more grotesque across the lake; his growing sense of being shut in among the fells while all the war thundered by outside, these things weighed upon his mind and so, in a sudden rebellion, he suggested to the others in the long parlour on that Christmas Day that he, and some of them, should have a change.

'I've saved a bit while I have been here. There's nothing to spend money on in Grasmere except gifts at the Gift Shop and books at the Book Shop and I've bought a lot of those,' said Richard, apologetically. 'And so I have enough saved to treat myself to a long change. But I would rather have a short one and, say, two of you with me. Where shall we go?'

Corys at once suggested Carlisle. No one could think of anywhere else to go. Blodwen said she would go nowhere, but stay at the Hall. Miles was returning to London in a day or two and she knew she would be uneasy away from his official home address. If he were injured and a wire was sent what delay there would be in forwarding it to Carlisle! Grandy said London would be more interesting but she would be willing to go anywhere in order to get away from Grasmere, as long as Richard chose a comfortable hotel, where they did not switch off the lights every time an enemy plane went by ten miles away.

'There are some good shops in Carlisle,' said Corys, thoughtfully. 'Are you sure you can afford it, Richard?' she added, but without anxiety.

Thus, at the end of the first week in January, Richard, carrying two suit-cases, Corys, carrying one, and Grandy, burdened with nothing but her generous figure and vague fears of an attack of her Niger fever, all walked into Red Lion Square to await the Windermere bus.

'Red warning on,' said P.C. Smith, officially, but with enjoyment. 'Take cover.'

P.C. Smith had his tin hat slung behind him and stood in Red Lion Square, warning people. In front of the post office were grouped A.R.P. and First Aid workers, each in a tin hat and all looking hopeful, for it was hard to keep in training without some practice.

Richard hesitated, the shadow of R.A.F. discipline still heavy upon him, but Grandy said: 'Nonsense, we're going to take the bus, not cover. Don't be silly, Smith.'

A seagull screamed from the quiet sky; Stone Arthur lay, high in the east, with light mist drifting about his still face as if he breathed at last; people who had been hustled by P.C. Smith and the A.R.P. workers into shops began to come out, laughing. Then the great bus rolled in from Keswick, was immediately filled, as were all buses in Grasmere this winter, and Richard's holiday had begun.

Carlisle may be old but, to Lake District visitors at least, it is gay. It may be small but it is crowded. There is a Woolworth's there. There are Belisha crossings, but these are no disadvantage since there are so many people that they are obliged, and prefer to, walk, all over, all the streets, and the buses, of which countless droves move ceaselessly in and out of the town, must find their way among the people just like any old horse and trap. In Carlisle Richard, from his Island, and Grandy, from her unwelcome seclusion at Bonfire Hall, were vividly aware of that curious lightening of the heart that comes to country dwellers when they go to town. A sense of ease and opulence softened and gilded their thoughts. There was a kind of triumph in walking forth, down unfamiliar streets, meeting endless strangers, staring in the shops, hearing the roar of traffic and feeling that they, themselves, had achieved something in coming to share these urban activities.

They stayed at the Crown and Mitre. Their bedrooms looked over the Market Place at the demure gaiety of the miniature Town Hall. After dark Corys turned off the light and looked out. There was but a new moon, long set. The nights were quite dark and the Market Place was dark as they, save for the creeping within it of those monsters that were buses. Lit within by dim lights, their glass windows stained dark blue, two pin-points like candles where side lights should have shone and red lights behind that, though half obscured, cast a glow like blood upon the smooth tarmac of the roadway, these buses moved with what seemed an incredible perception of the world about them. All the evening they rolled in, circled in the blackness of the Market Place and moved off again, almost silently, and as if they felt their way by some sense of touch in the wheels which invisibly sustained the bulk of their dim, blue glass bodies. Corys thought of them, finding their way out of the dark ditches of Carlisle streets into the country lanes and so to Longtown and Burgh-by-Sands and Brampton, setting down farm folk after a day's shopping and swinging slowly on again through the unlit, silent night.

'Once, a Carlisle man got drunk,' said Grandy, as Corys emerged from the window curtains and turned up the bedroom light. 'He was found trying to push in the front of a bus. He said the blank thing had been following him about all evening.'

Grandy enjoyed the Mitre; her private bathroom; the sound of traffic and footsteps and voices under her window; the lit show-cases in the hall where silk scarves and coloured umbrellas and woollen jumpers and tartan kilts glowed scarlet and gold and green; the officers from the Castle in the lounge; the good meals, and the waiters.

'So he didn't marry you? Too bad,' said Grandy, one morning, helping the chambermaid to make her bed, for all the chambermaids but two had gone away to fill shells. 'There are too many girls about, and that's a fact.'

Corys, sitting by the open window, staring at the people in the top of a bus just outside who stared straight back at her, wondered what girls did when there were too many of them. Too many for the work girls had to do, or too many for each of them to have a young man? A pity, perhaps, there could not be a girl epidemic, or some definite destruction of girls, such as periodically reduced the numbers of surplus rabbits.

'If the Sweetings were destroyed Gerald might begin to think about me,' reflected Corys. 'Grandy, don't forget my hair is to be done at eleven, sharp.'

Grandy had interfered very little with Corys' shopping and had made no inquiry as to why she was buying girls' clothes. Corys knew what she could afford to spend; it would do her no harm to try and hold to her own opinions against the soft, scented opposition of the elegant saleswomen. But to the hairdresser's Grandy went with Corys.

'No curls,' said Grandy, to the girl in the white coat. 'Shorten it here, and here. Get it to lie back with a kind of ripple each side. Get it to do what it wants, in reason, but tidily. Hair falls into forms that suit the face below, and I don't want my granddaughter to look like Miss de Bainriggs wearing a wig.'

The result of all this business of adorning Corys appeared on their last night at the Mitre. In the intervals when Corys had not been darting in and out, between the hotel and this shop and that, they had gone about in buses and on their feet, and had been to Bowness-on-Solway, and Wetheral and Lanercost and Canonbie and even Caldbeck. It was on their last day that they went to Lanercost and saw the pale red Priory in its green valley, quiet as if the Scots had never come to break into its holy places, throw out the vessels of the temple, smash the doors and reduce all to nothingness, as the old chronicle recounts.

They got back at the edge of dark, seeing the squat tower of the cathedral outlined black against the glow of a stormy sunset. A little tired, a little dreamy with thoughts of Lanercost, they had tea in the gaily lit lounge and then sat, talking little, at ease in the big arm-chairs. Corys moved first. Rather reluctantly she got up, gave her grandmother a look that meant she wanted neither advice nor assistance in the enterprise now at hand, and left the lounge with a dour look of resolution on her rather elfin face.

'She's an interesting child,' said Grandy, looking at Richard through the smoke of her cigarette. 'But astonishingly immature and full of inhibitions. Where she got them from I don't know. Not from me, that is certain. I believe she has theories about love and marriage but I don't think she ever applies them to herself. I think she regards herself as untouchable and there's a danger, or so it appears to me, that Cory may dream of a possible lover round the next corner until she herself has rounded her last one.'

'Ah! Well, we'll hope not,' said Richard, vaguely, and feeling nearly as uncomfortable as did Blodwen when Grandy talked about Corys as she might of any other young animal.

Grandy and Richard were punctual at dinner because they were both hungry. Neither of them had seen Corys since she left the lounge. Just after they had ordered their soup Corys appeared in the doorway. Every other evening she had worn her green corduroy jacket and a plain, very short tweed skirt.

Now, the head waiter, who had become quite a friend of Corys during their week's stay, looking at her, did not hear a stout gentleman in evening dress say that he must have a large raw onion because he was on a diet. 'Yes, sir,' said the head waiter, writing onion on his note pad though well he knew, in sane moments, that no one had had an onion, large or small, for seven months.

Corys wore what she had chosen as an evening frock. It was of a dark blue velvet, the colour of her eyes, without trimming and most simply cut. It reached her ankles and hung about her in folds that had the simplicity of linen fold panelling and that shifted as she moved with a shimmering softness. This dress, in its richness of colour and texture, emphasized the natural austerity of Corys' youth, an effect heightened by a silver arrow, fastened just below the square-cut neck line. Her hair, thought Richard, looked now as young hair should, soft and smooth and yet with wavings in it, and it gleamed, as she turned her head, like a bird's dark wing. Her eyes seemed darker than usual and wider open, and there was still a look of dogged resolution on her face. She came threading her way between the crowded little tables with her watchful gaze fixed on her grandmother, and only when that lady had given her a quick, approving nod and Corys had slid into her chair next his did Richard realize that she was breathing hard, so that the silver arrow rose and fell with little quick movements.

'All this floppy stuff round my ankles,' said Corys, breathless, but speaking in her usual deep tones, 'is absurd. It tickles.'

CHAPTER XIII

Lake View was finished on February the seventh and Oak How on the eighth so nicely had the builder, as by a farthing damages against Old John, recognized the prior claim of wealth. Lake View had six rooms and one bathroom, because not enough lead piping could be got for more. It was painted green outside because the painters wished it to be this colour, though Mrs. Lovely had had thoughts of a yellow house, shining like a patch of sunlight in the lakeside woods. The parlour and kitchen were under one roof but each of the other rooms had a roof to itself, an arrangement, said the builder, that might work all right till heavy snow came. Then the snow would lie in the little valleys formed between each separate roof and as it melted soak through and wet all the partition walls. This, said Mr. Lovely, could not be helped and every one must remember there was a war on. For a long time he had had some of his furniture from High Castle, St. Helens, stored in the village, so all that remained to be done was to decorate Lake View inside and then have the furniture put in.

From Oak How could be seen Lake View, like a large, confused café that had prospered and been added to, room by room. On February the ninth Old John moved back into Oak How. Corys had had all his furniture that was not completely burned repaired and stored at the Hall. She had added to it a few things bought at what was locally described as a cheap sale in the village, which meant a sale at which but low prices were obtained. On the morning of the ninth Corys lit his kitchen fire, put on a kettle, set his old arm-chair beside it and the little round table that had been made when there was oak to spare in Grasmere so that it weighed half a hundredweight. Milk, cup and saucer, bread and even a little of her own ration of butter and sugar did Corys set on the table, while upstairs she made up his ancient double bed with bedclothes that had been kept well aired at the Hall. Then, at the end of his day's work, for he would not stop before the end, she went with him to his old home, gave him the door key and followed him into the kitchen.

'Ay!' said Old John, slowly rubbing his hands together and looking observantly about him. 'Ay! There's chair and table, and kettle on fire and all. It leuks about the seam to me but I doubt there'll be things wanting here and there. Ay, there's sure to be things amiss, some-wheres.'

Still looking about he let himself down into his chair, with the caution of one who had not done so for many weary months. He settled himself on the worn cushion, rested his stick against the arm and sat, leaning a little forward with his hands hanging between his knees.

'Ay, there's teapot, too, and I can see Robert's patched that settle wi' a nice bit o' Bainriggs oak, but where's my little stool, Miss Cory? Where's the little stool at, my grandfather made the year they cut walnut tree down at the Rectory?'

Old John turned his eyes, now distressed, upon Corys, but he did not get up and Corys knew, with feelings of despair, that he relied wholly upon her to produce the little stool.

'It was burnt, John, and I meant to try and get you another but I forgot,' said Corys, her voice low and full of shame and misery.

'Burnt! My little stool!' said Old John. 'And you forgot about it, Miss Cory! Where do I put my pipe down then?'

After this, Old John began to see faults almost everywhere. The new window-frame was not of Bainriggs oak but some of that rubbishy unseasoned stuff Robert had had by him for no more than a year or so. There was a silly, new-fangled latch on the kitchen door. The stairs sounded hollow: hadn't Robert made the steps of solid oak as Old John had told him? Window-sill in bedroom didn't look, to him, the same width; it wasn't! See, Miss Cory, bed always stood so, back to wall by window and now it won't fit. Robert's put in window-sill all hapsha-rapsha, not caring what he did. The bedroom floor didn't slope and Old John nearly fell down, adjusting his steps to the slope that was no longer there. His little pick-hammer was gone from cupboard by bed; cupboard hadn't been burnt but pick-hammer was gone. Robert's men had pinched it, o' course. Corys found the pick-hammer down in the woodshed but for Old John's other woes she could devise no remedy. Greatly depressed they looked at each other, down in the kitchen again. Old John's hands had begun to shake and he looked white and exhausted. Corys made him tea and after a scalding cup the colour began to come back into his thin cheeks and light into his eyes.

'Ah, well, it was bound to be a hard home-coming after such a misfortune,' said he, 'but I must just put up with it. One thing, Miss Cory, I hadn't noticed till just now. Do you see how well I see the new gentleman's house across lake? Lake View he told me it was to be called. Come close beside chair and look. See? Ay, there 'tis, all green and as big as the Hall a'most. Ay, now I shall have sumat to look at.'

A week after the Lovelys had moved into Lake View they gave a party that they called a house-warming. Certainly, Lake View was in need of warming for Mr. Lovely had not been able to have central heating put in, and though the outer walls were double cold came, he said, in through the various roofs.

'All our rooms, do y'see, are attics, up in the roof, as you might say,' Mr. Lovely did say to Blunt on the evening of the house-warming.

It was now early March and the first snow of the winter had fallen the day before. It had followed some nights of frost and it lay unmelted on the dry, cold ground so that, for once, the fell summits, their bare slopes and the flats of the valley bottom were alike and only the walls, the dusky patches of woodland and the becks, as yet unfrozen, showed dark on the white country-side. On the day of the house-warming it did not snow at first but the sharp frost overnight had covered the lake with a sheet of thin ice so that Corys chose to walk to the party and Blunt found it a tiring job to row himself across to what had been the Bainriggs boat-landing and was now the Lovely one. It did not thaw all day and by four o'clock it had grown much colder and there were fifteen degrees of frost, so that the narrow lane of water that Richard had broken open with his bow and oars froze again almost at once. He arrived at Lake View five minutes late and Corys, wandering along the road and watching his slow progress, met him as he came ashore. There had been no sunshine but now there came a dim, tawny glow in the formless mists that had hung pale above the fells all day. This sunset light shone from the frozen lake with the dull lustre of pewter and Blunt's boat moved black across it and the crunching sound of the ice he broke seemed to fill the silent dusk.

'Let's go in together,' said Corys, as he stepped on shore and tied his boat to the railing.

The snow covered Penny Rock and hid Mr. Lovely's new path of white stone chippings; it lay thick on all his five roofs; even the new-cut beech stumps, capped with snow, had reverted to the wild into which Lake View had thrust its offensive but, it was to be expected, not very lasting wooden walls. The windows, heavily curtained, hid all lights within, and the only colour in the arctic austerity of the landscape came from the painted wood, green as moss amid the snow, and from an ancient thorn tree that stood close beside the front door. Its twisted trunk was white on one side, its thin branches snow laden, but in the midst of it sat three cock chaffinches, each on a snowy twig, one above the other, and their rosy breasts showed vivid as Chinese lanterns in the intricate network of black and white.

From out of this frozen wilderness Corys and Richard passed with an almost bewildering suddenness into the full glare of the Lovely hospitality. There were huge log fires; where there were no fires there were oil heaters, each with one red glass eye; every room and passage was lit with brilliant electric lights, the parchment shades of which were each of a different colour or shade of colour. Green, orange, blue, red, yellow, indigo and violet shone the shaded bulbs, gay as the colours of the spectrum. All the doors were wide open so that the gaiety of bedspreads, bright as the lamp-shades, of many coloured curtains, and the expensive Turkey rugs and velvet hangings in the lounge, mingled, as the guests roamed the house, like the colours in a kaleidoscope and emphasized the workmanlike austerity of the blue and white kitchen and green and white bathroom. There were tea and coffee; there were cakes and sandwiches and hot sausages and cocktails; biscuits and Grasmere gingerbread; there was dance music from an immense gramophone; there was room for a couple or two to dance from the middle of the lounge along a passage and turn in the kitchen and back again. Gerald and Myra had come for the house-warming. Mr. Lovely's two maids, when not serving the guests with food and drink, sat close against the red fire in the Aga Cooker and watched, calm but well amused.

Corys wore her Carlisle frock of blue velvet with the silver arrow and her hair still gleamed, well brushed, but its Carlisle wavings were softened by more natural rumplings that well suited the flushed excitement of her look. She had drunk black coffee and eaten all kinds of things, sardines, and chocolate creams and cheese straws and cakes. She had been into every room. She had danced with Myra and Essie Sweeting and her friend Richard. All the Sweetings were there, in green and silver like snowdrops, but their noses kept on going shiny, owing to a war-time shortage of cosmetics.

Was it this that made Gerald suddenly drop Rudie's arm and come to Corys and ask her would she dance with him? Gerald looked most beautiful, with his brown face browner than ever above his white shirt front. He danced well but he held her roughly, with a sort of hard, careless, yet peremptory hold that made her feel uncomfortable. After a few short turns, like this, up and down through the house, he caught at a coat that hung beside the front door, pulled it about Corys and drew her out, into the white stillness of the evening.

'There's no room in there,' said Gerald. 'Let's—let's do a turn out here. Can you dance in snow, my Boy Blue?'

A snow shower was just coming to an end. Gerald laughed as the flakes fell on his face, upturned to see if there was a moon. He had his arm still about Corys, and though she wished he would take it away she did not quite know what to do about it. Perhaps it was the custom at dances for men to keep their arms round their partners' waists; Corys had never been to a dance before and felt herself painfully ignorant.

'Come on,' said Gerald, boisterously, and they tried to dance, along the front of the house where the snow had only sprinkled the ground.

'No,' said Corys, and suddenly tried to stand still. 'Gerald, you're drunk. Stop it, I tell you.'

For Gerald, unabashed, continued to try and dance though she would not stir. She had realized by now that he smelt of the cocktails he had drunk, too many cocktails, and like other country girls she was familiar enough with drunkenness to regard it with an amused kind of contempt.

'Stop it!' said Corys again, and almost violently, for Gerald was now trying to sway her back and forth as she stood, sturdily resisting.

So far, the cocktails had made Gerald feel more amiable than usual. He allowed her to slip from his grasp and he followed her through the front door and closed it quickly behind him, because of the black-out. The heated air, scented, full of coloured light and the sounds of the gramophone, felt like some bright solid after the scentless, thin, snow-lit air outside. Gerald looked down at Corys and saw her, in the glare, with melting snow-flakes on her dark head and a startled, defiant look on her flushed face. He drew her behind the hat-rack and put a finger under her chin. Corys looked intently up into his face: it had a silly look, she thought, half grinning, half wild, and there was an odd glow in his eyes. 'Ouch!' said Corys, as she had said on the Raise to his father. 'Get away!'

For Gerald had tried to kiss her; whereupon Corys had suffered what seemed to them both from some kind of explosive outbreak. She had hit him on the face, wriggled out of his arms, kicked him, given him a stinging slap on the ear and turned her back and walked away, all, it seemed, in the one moment.

'Gosh!' said Gerald, fingering his scarlet ear, and looking after her with an expression that now had nothing but silliness in it.

'Do you think we could go home now?' said Corys, to Richard Blunt. 'Gerald is drunk and I've kicked him.'

Richard had been sitting on the lowest step of the stairs that had come from Dungeness, for that tall little house had been incorporated like a pele tower in the middle of Lake View. He was talking to Myra Lovely about Harlech and the evacuation to that romantic spot of part of the University of Liverpool.

'In the Mabinogion it says they feasted seven years in Harlech and the three birds of Rhiannon sang unto them, and all the songs they had ever heard were unpleasant compared thereto,' said Myra Lovely. Myra had a small handsome face with neat features and her hair looked as immovable and solid as her brother's, but when she talked of the three birds of Rhiannon her eyes shone, bright and wild, from her neat face. She wished to go on telling Mr. Blunt about how the lovely birds had seemed to be at a great distance over the sea and yet appeared as distinct as if they were close by but that queer child, Corys de Bainriggs, came along, looking all worked up and saying Gerald was drunk.

'Oh, not drunk,' said Myra, reluctantly abandoning the birds of Rhiannon, and casting an observant glance down the passage at her brother. 'Not drunk, just lit up a bit. You kicked him, you say? Good for you. Oh! don't go yet,' added Myra to Mr. Blunt, beseechingly, 'You're the only sensible person I've ever met, out of Wales, who could talk about Wales.'

Mr. Blunt, however, would not be dissuaded from carrying off that silly kid in blue velvet, who had probably egged Gerald on, anyway. So Myra got listlessly up and went and told her brother that he should have known Corys was much too young and schoolgirlish to understand his silly games.

'After three cocktails you're not safe with any woman under thirty,' said Myra.

Richard and Corys walked silently away from Lake View. The icy stillness of the night closed about them as if they had stepped from the heat and glare indoors into water, deep and cold. The snow shower was over. The frozen lake was now snow covered, a white surface flat as a floor in the white slopes.

'It looks as if our horrible experiences at the party had blanched the lake with terror,' said Blunt, flippant as usual when an uncomfortable turmoil of emotion was making any speech but invective difficult to him.

'You can't row back,' said Corys. 'You must come to us for the night.'

In Bonfire Hall no one said anything about Gerald Lovely that night. Corys appeared in the long parlour wearing her old green jacket and trousers; she looked as pale as she had been flushed; she talked little and went early to bed.

'Something has upset our young person,' said Grandy, 'and she wanted to shake it off with the velvet frock. Have you been trying to make love to her, Richard? If you have, she'll probably go all mannish again and Carlisle will be wasted.'

However, up at her open window, Corys thought otherwise.

'Gerald certainly hugged me,' reflected Corys. 'But not because it was me. He hugged me because he was drunk; men do, I know.'

Staring at the white lake Corys remembered how she had met a drunk man driving a cart some months ago. He had looked down at her, grinned idiotically, given a kind of loving howl and held out his arms, longingly and so enthusiastically that he had nearly fallen off his cart. Just so, thought Corys, had Gerald clutched at her.

'It hasn't proved anything,' thought Corys, but now of Gerald's embrace. 'I must just go on wearing girls' clothes and fussing with my hair till I see whether or not he gets interested. If he does, it'll show I can get a husband some day if I'm girlish. If he doesn't, I can let myself be comfortable again as probably I couldn't get one, anyway. So that's that. I wonder if Richard will be able to row himself home to-morrow.'

A sudden gust made a curious metallic noise in the snowy branches of an oak by Corys' window and shook down a powdery shower of snow. She stretched herself, gave a sigh, and went to bed.

CHAPTER XIV

On the day after the house-warming at Lake View Gerald and Myra Lovely returned, he to Cambridge and she to Coleg Harlech where, under the direction of the geography staff, she helped to dig holes in the Morfa so as to try and find out how long it had been there. Left alone, Mr. Lovely, save for an occasional visit to his ancestral factory at St. Helens, consoled himself by extending his path of white chippings from Lake View to the lake edge, chopping down a Scots pine, and beginning to build what he called an arbour from the least gnarled of its branches. Mrs. Lovely, who liked something lively and was surprisingly fond of fresh air, sat all day by an open window making gloves for mine sweepers, with the wireless blaring out, in a lipless bellow, music, speeches, news, warnings, instructions and cookery recipes, all adapted to listeners who were at war. These sounds were transmuted by their transit across the lake into a formless and brassy outcry which soon began to drive Grandy de Bainriggs quite frantic. By now the snow and frost had gone, though the east wind had come back, which was worse, so Grandy rowed herself across to the Bainriggs boat-landing one day. Mrs. Lovely sat by her window, as usual, almost buried in gloves and with the wireless close beside her chair telling her some of the virtues of the carrot.

'Good morning. I can't stand that devilish row you're making,' said Grandy, and switched off the melodious voice that seemed to have the sweetness of grated carrot in it.

Mrs. Lovely shrieked, in reply to Grandy's greeting and in a justified astonishment.

'Row? What row?' said Mrs. Lovely, really not understanding for the moment. 'Do you mean the wireless? Had I got it on? I was thinking about Myra, that's my daughter, and her summer outfit. What will she need to wear in Wales? Do you know Wales at all?'

Grandy did know Wales and so they talked and Mrs. Lovely said, after a while, that she supposed it must seem strange at Grasmere to hear any noise at all and she would try to remember about the wireless but it always seemed lonesome to her without it when Myra was away.

'Doesn't hearing nothing make you want to scream?' said Mrs. Lovely, and Grandy found this horror of silence very interesting and comparable to some tendency she had observed among the wilder tribes on the upper Congo.

Thus, Grandy and Mrs. Lovely became friendly, being honest and well-meaning women though rather difficult to live with because Grandy was too vigorous and Mrs. Lovely too inert. Mrs. Lovely did try to remember about the wireless and Grandy, while making no attempt to tolerate its now intermittent blarings, yet admitted the possibility of the human body becoming so inured to loud noise as not to be aware of it.

'It may act as a stimulus on some forms of life,' said Grandy, of noise, 'particularly when at all rhythmic in quality. The natives on the Zambesi had drums—'

At this time Mr. Blunt found himself made uneasy, perhaps by the advent of spring. His mother had had the roof blown off her house, which she found justly irritating since it was in the depths of the country and only extreme stupidity or carelessness in the Hun pilot could have induced him to drop such a large bomb so near it. She wrote to Richard that repairs were already in hand and she was getting along pretty well under the part that was covered by a tarpaulin. There was no need at all, she said, for him to come and do anything about it and, indeed, there was room only for herself and her maid under the tarpaulin. Her letters made Richard still more keenly aware of that horrid feeling as of living in the bright, still air bubble that was Grasmere suspended in the midst of murky and troubled waters. Then, he could not readily recover from his sense of outrage at that young Gerald having done something that had made it necessary for Corys to kick him. Corys herself did not seem at all outraged. She never referred to any untoward happenings at the house-warming but she talked without embarrassment of Gerald, and Richard could only suppose that Corys was still too much a child fully to be sensible of insult, in which he was right. Discomfort, anger, and a faint, bewildering sense of shame oppressed Corys whenever she remembered Gerald by the hat-rack, but to her the whole affair seemed quite outside herself. It could not be she, Corys de Bainriggs, whom this young man had consciously hugged; he had been drunk, otherwise he could not have done such a thing. No man could. So Corys went her way, untroubled, but still taking some pains about her hair, and about washing several times a day, and wearing girls' frocks at frequent intervals so that, when Gerald came back for Easter, she might observe what effects a girlish Corys had upon him.

Richard's uneasiness drove him to books. He began to read about the Bainriggs estate as he had said, long ago, he would do. He borrowed books from that library in Ambleside, founded by the late Miss Armitt, which is one of the not too frequent glories of that ancient little town. He took notes of what he read and discussed them with Corys by the Hall fire in the long evenings.

'But, look here, there was a Henry de Banrige who held of the lord a tenement in Gresmyer by fealty and ½ lb. of cumin or 2d. in the fourteenth century,' said Richard, 'and there was also a Richard de Baynbrig who held a tenement which rendered per annum 30/6 and a pound of cumin. And in 1615 somebody paid one pound of cumin for ten acres, nigh unto Grasmere Tarne, held by an ancient charter, and it is called Bainriggs. But Bainriggs is more like a hundred acres, isn't it?'

Arguments on matters such as these kept Richard and Corys happily occupied for many an hour and Grandy, benevolently regarding them, cocked an eyebrow at Blodwen over their bent heads. Blodwen, terrified lest spoken comment should supplement the cock of the eyebrow, scowled and bent her own head over her endless knitting. If only Corys could be sheltered from that observation of Grandy which was without illusions! Observation so without illusion was as likely to lead to wrong conclusions as was the most sentimental gaze of a sentimental spinster, thought Blodwen, longing for the old-fashioned reticence about what used to be called affairs of the heart.

'Cory has no heart, of that sort, and won't have for years, probably,' said Blodwen, to herself. 'I suppose Grandy would describe her as a person of immature glandular development. I don't know about Richard, and I don't want to know, but however he may feel about Cory I know he can be trusted.'

Corys' growing up was complicated by her two griefs. Old John was all right and now comfortably settled down again in his cottage, but Corys' grief for the loss of Penny Rock, and the loss of Jet, persisted and she could as yet find no comfort except in periods of forgetfulness and, after these, the painful load seemed the heavier when she was conscious of it again. Jet, with her sensitive, timid, loving ways might be suffering the extremity of anguish that a dog could suffer and, thinking of this in bed, Corys twisted about in misery and felt she simply could not bear to think of Jet, and yet could not stop thinking.

'I can't do her any good by tormenting myself like this,' Corys argued with herself one night. 'And she may be well and happy.'

And yet Corys went on bearing Jet's burden as, she thought, Jet would have borne hers if she, Corys, had suffered and Jet had known it.

The loss of Penny Rock and its violation by Mr. Lovely with his wooden villa were not much easier to bear; the harm was done; nothing that she could do would alter that. Jet might, one day, be found and rescued, but not so Penny Rock. Penny Rock had been sold into bondage and must now bear the horrid green house and white path and crooked arbour and bear them, presumably, for ever, since if they fell down or were torn up successive generations of men could build them up again.

'Probably Lake View in the long run may change less than the rock itself,' thought Corys, one dismal evening as she looked in the dusk across the lake. 'The rock has no one to renew it; as the ages go by it will be worn away and altered. But I dare say there will always be some one ghastly enough to rebuild Lake View or build something even worse. Oh! Gosh! What was I about to sell that land and betray my own Penny Rock? Probably, Old John wouldn't have died after all and he's always grumbling, now.'

Spring came slowly that year and Gerald Lovely went to Devon for

Easter. In the middle of May, when the Sweetings gave a party, the fell tops were, yet again, white with snow. The dry weather had continued, with frost at night, so that there was scarcely any growth of new grass and the farmers were getting desperate; they had very little hay left from the previous year, the ewes and lambs were weak after the long winter and there was nothing for the dairy cows to eat in the bare valley pastures. Those residents who depended on the fell streams for their water-supply were miserable, since the smaller becks were all dry, and Sour Milk Gill, up Easedale, showed but as one or two pale threads upon the wintry hillside. Snow had never ceased to hover about the valley and on the day of the Sweetings' party it whitened even Silver How and Helm Crag and Loughrigg, those lower heights that remain free when Fairfield and Seat Sandal are smooth with an unbroken whiteness.

The Sweetings' party was an odd one. Mrs. Sweeting had always paid some one else to run her house for her and she did not propose to begin housekeeping, she said, at this time of day. So the Misses Sweeting were told that they could stop talking about joining the army, the navy or the air force and get to work at Fold-in-the-Wood. Essie said to Richard that once things were working smoothly at home she and Rudie were off to be Wrens and when Mag was old enough she would follow them.

'Then the parents must scrape along by themselves,' said Essie, at the tea-party, her face flushed and her eyes anxious because father would eat more than his share of the sandwiches.

Mr. and Mrs. Lovely were at the party and Miss Trusty and all the three de Bainriggs and, of course, the adored Mr. Blunt. There was not enough room for twelve people on the ground floor of Fold-in-the-Wood, but the Sweeting girls had no time to sit down, and Richard, Corys and her mother sat on the stairs. It was soon evident that the guests were going to eat more than had been thought possible by the Misses Sweeting and a number of domestic catastrophes marked the efforts of these ladies to supply more sandwiches and more plates of bread and margarine. A crash, followed by a pouring sound, was obscurely explained by Mag. 'Rudie has kicked to-night's soup,' said Mag, from behind the half-open scullery door. 'The floor is the only cool place in there, when the oil stove is going,' added Essie, handing tea to Miss Trusty.

Another and very heavy crash came shortly after.

'A bomb,' said Grandy, resignedly. 'Well, it was not to be supposed that Grasmere would escape for ever.'

But it was not a bomb. The oven, said Rudie, had fallen off the stove, owing, no doubt, to Mag having put a heavy stack of pie dishes on the end of it. 'There was nowhere else to put them, and the oven was endways on, to make more room,' said Mag.

After this, Mrs. Sweeting became tiresome because her pince-nez were lost and then because she wanted permission to gather firewood on the Bonfire Hall land. 'You must have such lovely views and it looks so peaceful along there,' said she to Blodwen, who did not know what to do but agree.

'Yes, of course, but don't forget the bull, Blodwen,' said Grandy's robust voice, her watchful eyes admonishingly upon her daughter-in-law. 'Old Wilson's bull that gets out of the bull field more often than not,' she added, to Mrs. Sweeting. 'He loves to roam about the Hall woods and Cory doesn't make enough fuss about it, to my mind. But she is so good at quickly going up trees.'

That put an end to Mrs. Sweeting's yearning for her neighbour's wood but her pince-nez were still lost and she continued loudly to grumble till Rudie, by now so exhausted that she was nearly weeping, found them in the bath. When tidying the parlour the Sweeting sisters were in the habit of flinging all the things that normally were piled on chairs and sofa into the bath, from which they were removed in armfuls when the party was over. Their mother's pince-nez were, unfortunately, at the bottom of the bathful.

'There you are, you devils,' said Rudie, to the pince-nez in their blue case.

A smell, that reminded Grandy, or so she said, of burning horses, now began to penetrate, visible as a faint blue haze, through all the little rooms. Before its cause was discovered half the handle of a stainless steel knife was charred quietly into nothingness; Mag had propped it against the door of the little oil stove because otherwise the door might have burst itself open, unnoticed in the stress of the party, and then the little stove would have flared flame and smoke all over everything. Immediately after the rescue of half the knife handle the butcher's boy came and thrust a limp, horrible something in a brown-paper bag into Mr. Lovely's hands, Mr. Lovely being at that time the nearest person to the front door. Oozy, tragic looking stains on the paper bag made Mr. Lovely thrust it hurriedly away from him; with some vague idea about the washable qualities of leather he put it down on a leather covered *pouf* and there Miss Trusty, shortly afterwards, sat on it.

Essie had only just finished coping with the five shillings worth of stewing steak that represented the family joint for the week, and with those marks upon and behind Miss Trusty that are bound to occur when steak is sat upon, when the fish van called. Not with the voice as of a fish called the fish van, for, to human ears at least, fish do not call, but in a brisk, human voice sounded the chant: 'What'll you have to-day? I've cod.'

'Oh, what have you got?' said Mag, according to her usual flustered habit.

'Cod,' said the fish man, twiddling his big knife.

'Oh, I don't want the flappy part,' said Mag, blushing at even this elusive reference to the stomach of a cod in the genteel presence of the tea-party, all of whom could hear all that was said.

Mag was destined to take, throughout her life, what tradesmen chose to give her. The fish man now turned his back, did things with his knife and some string and gave her the flappy part, disguised as a solid, tied up, steak.

'Oh, thank you so much!' said Mag, with misplaced gratitude. The fish man looked at Grandy. 'I'm going on to your place now,' said he, with a faint lift of one eyebrow and a look that told Grandy that he had a baby halibut, six oranges and a pound of sausages hidden away for Bonfire Hall.

As everybody was wishing to leave they all did so together, eagerly grasping at the opportunity for escape afforded by Mrs. Lovely's strength of mind. Mrs. Lovely was tired and hungry and her eyes were watering with the wood-smoke from the Sweetings' fire. If it was all right for Mrs. Lovely to get up and go it must be equally so for the others. As the seven of them streamed forth into the cold May evening the greengrocer's van arrived, and they heard his voice. 'No onions; no oranges; no apples; no, miss, I've no tinned fruit to-day. Carrots, miss? Thank you, a quarter of carrots.' He looked at Grandy. 'I'll be getting along to you,' said he, with a droop of one eyelid that told Grandy he had, hidden like the baby halibut, treasures for her.

'It is very hard for all these newcomers,' said Blodwen, who had understood the looks of both fish man and greengrocer man. 'They get only what is left over when all of us have had what we want.'

'Self-preservation, that is,' said Grandy, striding along with her fine head held high to meet the breeze. 'The tradespeople do the best for those of us who will be still here after the war—why bother about the others whom they may never see again?'

Richard said good-bye and went away to his boat; Corys, who had been attentively studying the girlish accoutrements and ways of the Sweeting sisters, went away too, but up the fell, to gather young bracken. If Grandy would not eat it that could not be helped. Up on the fell, in a marshy flat that had once been a tarn, Corys met Old John, gathering whatever was necessary to make himself what he called bog bean tea.

'Jownie Wife came by just now,' said Old John, slowly straightening his bent back. 'She said that bitch Jet had been moved from Armboth barn, stolen she said, before you got there that day. She said she had heard tell there was a black and white bitch working for Dixon, up Langdale, not so long back, and that Jos Blaine got to hear of it and came over and made a disturbance and Dixon had to let him have the bitch. It's my opinion, Miss Cory, that Jownie Wife took her from Armboth and sold her up Langdale, but I'll be seeing Dixon and I'll find out.'

Forsythia bloomed, leafless and golden, over the garden walls of Grasmere. Larch woods looked like green mist; then the daffodils were over; wild hyacinths began to show at the top of their green stems; wood anemones turned their white faces away from every breeze; the beeches were sunny with little leaves, airy as green butterflies, and even the oaks showed a dim gold tinge as their buds swelled. Willow warblers sang; spotted flycatchers and pied flycatchers caught flies; whitethroats stuck up their little crests at Corys; the cuckoo called across the lake and the blue tits were building again in their nest box at Bonfire Hall. All day the sun shone and the vale of Grasmere was like a green basin, full of peace and bird songs, and at dusk the May moon shone and the sound of the low streams, unheard by day, rose like a whisper into the silent night.

Not so, in London. There, the May moon brought fire and bombs, to Chelsea as elsewhere. The house in which the Ozzard family rented three rooms received a direct hit. The Ozzard family was killed save for the only daughter, Maimie, who had gone to an evening party at the home of a young accountant who, she had hoped, might marry her one day. Somehow, the fact that Miss Ozzard's family and all her possessions had been bombed made the young accountant like her less than he had thought he did. He was of little help to her in the hours that immediately followed the catastrophe. The late Mr. and Mrs. Ozzard had quarrelled, he with all her relatives, she with all of his. Thus, there were no relations to whom Maimie could think of appealing for advice and, perhaps, food and clothing. In her pretty pale blue evening frock, her imitation leopard-skin coat, hatless, and with three pounds in her blue georgette hand-bag that the accountant's mother had, though grudgingly, lent her, Maimie went to Euston and bought a ticket for Windermere.

'Even if I can't get Richard back again I may find some sort of job up there, with children or old ladies,' thought Maimie, sitting still and staring out at England as the train ran north. So much unbombed England! Which was real, this, or what she had left behind in Chelsea?

'Perhaps Richard will help me,' thought Maimie, if the vague impulses and feelings that now determined her actions could be termed thought.

CHAPTER XV

Naturally, the Euston train, being affected like everything else by the war, was three hours late at Windermere. Fellow passengers who were also going to Grasmere gave Maimie a lift in their car and set her down in Red Lion Square. There, she did not know what to do. It was now late and it seemed that everybody must be abed though it was still bright daylight, since by now the sun set two hours later than it should according to war-time clocks. The silence and loneliness of the square under the bright sky gave Maimie an uneasy feeling, as if some disaster that yet left the houses standing had stricken Grasmere. She had only half a crown left in her blue bag. She dared not knock on any of the closed doors; who knew what sleep, or what death, might lie behind the dark curtained windows? She must go to Richard. She had heard from his mother, who had regretted the end of their engagement, that he lived on the Island. Walking with an odd feeling as if her head had but little relation to the uncertain movements of her feet she went back to the Prince's boat-landings, where there were still a few boats though the hotel was no longer one. She had spent many a summer holiday at Bowness so she untied a boat and easily rowed herself to the Island, where she carefully tied its bow to a young birch that grew close beside the calm water. Holding to the slender, silver stem Maimie looked about her. The fading but still bright sky, the quiet, shining waters, the delicate green of the wooded slopes and the remote peace of the hill edges against the fading glow in the west, all these frightened her. They could not possibly be like that; there must be some horror behind them, a horror the worse because it was silent and invisible. She recalled a dream she had dreamt once, about a fire in a house. Every one had known the fire was there, burning so that soon the house would be consumed, but no one saw or heard it. Now, she felt herself in some such frightening dream, for shock and emptiness were making her light-headed.

'Richard must be in there,' thought Maimie, and looked vaguely at the hogg-house. Could she walk so far? She let go of the little birch and stumbled forward, staring at the ground. When she reached the door she clung to the wall with one hand and with the other knocked, hurting her bare knuckles on the rough oak planks.

Richard was sitting with Miss Armitt's treatise on *The Fullers and Freeholders of Grasmere* open upon his knee and his gaze on the dying fire. Corys had told him of Old John's story of Jet and her possible capture by Jos Blaine. How could he get Jet back again for Corys?

'I believe soon I could give Blaine one on the chin,' mused Richard, who had been examined by no doctor since he came to Grasmere but knew himself to be gaining strength, day by day.

And then, he heard Maimie's gentle rapping on his door and, much surprised, went to open it.

'Oh, Richard, Mummie and Daddy are bombed and I've nowhere to go,' said Maimie, suddenly weeping a little and collapsing into his arms.

Reflecting afterwards on his behaviour under this severe trial Richard could not see what else he could have done but comfort and feed Miss Ozzard and then let her lie on his bed, profoundly asleep beneath the gay eiderdown that had been a Christmas present from the three adoring Sweetings.

Sitting once again beside his fire, now with fresh logs on it, Richard felt all the worse because he was shocked at himself for feeling anything at all beyond pity for poor Maimie. Poor Maimie! Little, soft creature, with her fair curls and her china blue eyes and her maddening, childish manner, what sights that even a seasoned soldier would view with horror, must she have seen! What fearful sounds of fire and bomb, crashing walls and human agony, must those ears, which Richard had always thought rather a silly shape, have heard! Richard felt a deep sense of shame that she should have undergone this fiery trial while he idled at Grasmere, sleeping through the quiet nights, renewing his strength, dreaming of

Corys who had, it seemed, become as much a part of his healing as had the winds and the waters and the cheerful silence of the fells.

And yet, other thoughts would insist on being considered. There was Maimie, asleep; here was he, beside his fire. Would people talk? Should he have put her, half fainting as she was, into his boat and taken her to Bonfire Hall? 'Fool,' said Richard, to himself. 'Let them talk, if they want to. Every one would have been asleep at the Hall and there would have been endless delays in getting her to bed. The poor thing was about dead to the world, and I don't wonder. The real point is, what next?'

However, this difficulty seemed to disappear next day. In the morning Richard had comforted Maimie when she woke, late, after a sleep that had seemed more like unconsciousness than normal slumber, and then fed her and then taken her across to Bonfire Hall. There, Blodwen welcomed her with an almost awestruck gratitude. Blodwen had been getting thin and sallow, losing sleep, losing appetite, because of the suffering in bombed cities.

Behind the green fells, under the same night sky that stood harmless over Grasmere were done things of which she read and heard, things she could not bear to think of, and, like Richard, she held herself guilty that she did not share the sufferings and the grim, gay endurance of those in raided areas. And now, here was some one who had lost everything because of a German bomb; some one left alone, quite alone, and with what must be the most frightful memories behind her sad, bewildered blue eyes. In one of those two empty bedrooms did Blodwen most joyfully instal Miss Ozzard; perhaps the other might be made, later on, into a little sitting-room for the girl, and so would Blodwen be eased of her burden, the burden of other's suffering and the burden of those rooms that Corys and Grandy would not let her offer for the sheltering of the homeless.

'They are not rooms, but lofts,' Grandy had said, often, but still patiently, 'and we are told to clear out our lofts because of incendiary bombs. No billeting officer would put any one in a loft and, anyway, Bonfire Hall is too far out in the wild, and Jane Peascod would give notice at once and then where should we be?'

That neither Grandy nor Corys made any objection to Maimie

Ozzard being housed in a loft made Blodwen fear their motives in being so scrupulous about the A.R.P. instructions had been wholly selfish. Furniture was soon collected for the bigger room from all over the Hall, blackout curtains put up and a fire lit in the little fireplace that stuck out almost into the centre of the room because the chimney-stack, up here under the slates, was full of flues from lower rooms. Then Blodwen put Maimie to bed and kept her there for some days, writing the while to good shops in Carlisle for pretty clothes to take the place of those lost in Chelsea and cooking at frequent intervals delicate, feathery, spongy, creamy foods and drinks, made of milk and eggs and sugar, Trinidad arrowroot and Benger's food and calves' foot jelly, and feeding the patient with them, a little at a time. Blodwen mothered Maimie as she had never mothered Corys and found, in doing so, that her anxiety for Miles in London was changing its character. From a numb and haunted sense of dread, helpless and oppressive, began to develop something very different, a sturdy hopefulness and an almost sudden conviction that even for Miles himself suffering and death, if they came, must be better than any shirking of his job.

'I was getting morbid and you've helped me not to be,' said Blodwen, to Maimie, and Maimie smiled her rather sweet smile but did not understand Blodwen at all.

The advent of Miss Ozzard made Richard very uncomfortable. He did not think himself responsible for her well-being but he felt himself so. He knew that she had no money. Her parents had lived, since her father's retirement, on the small pension that he drew; it had been thought, vaguely, that if Maimie married she would be able to look after her mother, should her father die first. If she did not marry she must earn her own living and be prepared later on to keep her mother as well. She had had six months' training as a children's nurse but she was not very efficient, and though her bright looks might get her a job what would she do when she was older? Middle-aged nannies must be outstandingly efficient or, naturally, young and cheerful ones will get all the jobs. There seemed nothing ahead for Maimie except, if she lived long enough, a room some day in a Home for Decayed Gentlewomen, and, after a period of that, a lonely death and pauper's funeral. Was it surprising that she appeared willing to marry Richard, or the accountant, or the next man who might come along? Was it even blameworthy?

'It seems pretty frightful that a girl should be willing to give herself to any chap with a little money, just for money,' thought Richard, uneasily but almost continuously reflecting upon Maimie, and then blamed himself for superficial thinking. Not just for money would Maimie sell herself but to save her life. A little home of her own, a very little money and a sense of modest security for the future would mean life to Maimie; without these there might be existence, but nothing more. If he were in such a situation, he, Richard Blunt, would he not marry Myra Lovely or her mother, or even Miss Trusty to escape from it?

One June afternoon Richard was doing gymnastic exercises, more or less hidden from boats on the lake by the little crag of the Island and its pines and firs. He did them every day now and, every day, felt that more strength and elasticity had come back to his muscles. As he worked and bent and swung himself about he thought that Miss Ozzard was like a mountain beck, a pretty, shallow, babbling thing, but Corys was like the lower end of her beloved Grasmere lake, deep, cool, hiding who knew what in its silent depths?

'Richard!' said Blodwen's voice, through the shadow of the trees. And there was Blodwen, in a boat, and agitated. It seemed that Corys had met Jownie Wife on the previous evening. 'As a matter of fact she chased Jownie Wife and caught her, somewhere on White Moss,' said Blodwen, 'and Cory asked about Jet and Jownie Wife seems to have convinced Cory that Blaine has her again. And this morning Cory went out, much as usual, but she didn't come home for lunch and then Jane Peascod told us Cory had gone to get Jet and we weren't to worry if she was a bit late. Jane was not to tell us this till after lunch. What can we do, Richard, and should we do anything? Cory is very capable. I don't feel I can leave Maimie yet, or perhaps I would go after her myself.'

It seemed to Richard that Corys' mother, though agitated, was not agitated enough. He said at once that he would go after Corys. He went with Blodwen to the Hall, greeted Maimie, who sat huddled becomingly in a Shetland shawl by the parlour fire, and studied the map that Blodwen spread on the round table.

'Take the bus to there,' said Blodwen, her long, slim finger on a road-junction. 'Walk up that road and then turn right, by a cart-track up that dale. Blaine's is the only house in sight once you are through the narrow part. But are you really wise to go? It seems to me you may easily miss Cory, and she may get home before you do. I am not at all afraid of any one being really bad to Cory; even Blaine would not dare to be, unless he was drunk.'

'It is market day at Keswick; probably all the Blaine household will be there,' said Grandy and at the same moment Maimie spoke, in her soft, weak voice that was as sweet as meringue compared to the crisp clarity of Grandy's words.

'Oh, Richard, do go. I think you ought to,' said Maimie, watching his face.

'I'm going,' said Richard and he went, taking the map and striding off as if he were as fit as he had been when first he met Miss Ozzard.

Maimie sat, when he had gone, remembering that first meeting. He had been home on leave, after months of danger, overwork and lack of sufficient sleep. There had been danger everywhere; it was no good thinking of the future. Even Maimie had forgotten her own future and thought only of Richard when they got engaged. After six days of frequent meetings, for they had mutual friends in London, they had got engaged and then Richard had gone back to his flying. There had followed his crash; his V.C.; his terrible illness; his marvellous, even if partial, recovery, and then his jilting of Maimie.

'Of course, I wasn't good enough for him; I knew that, always,' thought Maimie. 'But this strange child is too young, and she doesn't care for him at all, not in that way. Poor Richard.'

Meanwhile, Richard walked fast to the village and there, not waiting for any bus as Blodwen had supposed he would, he hired the one car available in war-time Grasmere and was driven off, by Miss Wilson, who owned it, over the Raise. He had hastily looked at the bus time-table in Red Lion Square and had seen that no bus came from the north for the next two hours; thus, he knew he could not miss Corys for even if she were to follow fell tracks for a mile or so from Blaine's farm she must then take to the main road. He left the car eventually at this point on the road and asked Miss Wilson to look out for Corys and, if she came, to keep her till he, Richard, returned. Then, he hurried off, up the narrow dale where cart-track and stream ran together between steep slopes of bracken and, in the June sunshine, hot, sweet scents of fern and bog land filled the air. Above this, the dale widened into a miniature hollow, with green meadows in the flat and the white farm-house and grey outbuildings of Blaine's set just above flood level at the upper end. There was no sound save the murmur of the stream, here flowing quietly through banks of peat, and when Blunt reached the farm it seemed deserted. He stood a moment, in the cobbled yard, listening, and vaguely watching steam drift up from the sunlit heap of manure. Where was Corys? Had she passed him, somewhere on the slopes, following some sheep track, sunk deep in the tall bracken?

A moment later Corys appeared. She had watched him, coming through the meadows, but had been baffled by the quickness of his walk. He had looked like Richard, but Richard never walked so fast. So she had hidden herself and observed him through the holes in an old fence wall Now, she came forward, glad to see him but greatly preoccupied.

'Jet is shut in that old barn,' said Corys. 'We must get her out before the people get back from Keswick. I'm glad you've come, but why did you?

Richard looked at her. Corys was as tall as he was now and still too thin. She wore her old grey shorts and silver-grey pullover; her face was tanned an even, beautiful brown that made her eyes look an unusually vivid blue and her hair, soft and bright, showed that she still took care of it though Gerald Lovely was back at Cambridge. There was something wild and taut and hawk-like about Corys, there in the sunny farm yard, and any one who sought the woman in her would have a far chase and, perhaps, but little profit of his labours at the end. Yet, Richard looked, and looked at her again, and for that moment was conscious of nothing but Corys.

'Why did you come?' repeated Corys, but absently, for she thought of something else. 'Look here, come and help me, if you can. I must get her free soon or they'll be back. If you help me with the first stone I can probably do the rest.'

The heavy oak door of the barn was locked but at one end an earlier doorway had been roughly built up, without mortar. Many of the stones were water worn and one or two little ones had already fallen out, leaving hollows in the surface of the two feet thick wall.

'Look,' said Corys, wondering, but without interest, why Richard was so silent. 'Look, if we make a hole under that big flat stone all the top ones won't fall in on us. But they're wedged so tight I can't get any of them out, by myself. I was looking for some kind of crowbar when you came.'

As they worked and Corys talked to Jet, who whimpered in reply from within, Richard realized how ruthless was Corys. Single-minded, absolutely determined and without fear, or sense of fatigue or discouragement was Corys. She worked with a furious energy, cutting and bruising and scraping her hands and arms on the stones, pushing back her hair with a bloody hand, straddling her thin legs, bending her back, heaving, pulling, lifting with little panting sounds and involuntary grunts. She dropped a heavy stone on her foot, straightened sharply and caught her head a nasty blow on the flat stone that bridged their hole, crushed her left hand under a sliding boulder and got a bit of slate grit in her eye.

'It'll do no harm if I don't rub it,' said Corys, screwing up the eye and blinking down the dale with the other one. 'Keep a look out, Richard, those brutes must be coming along soon.'

Richard had suffered a good deal of violence, too, in the breaking of the wall, but he had been less wild and careless than Corys in his movements and had found time to feel surprise at the comparative ease with which he worked. Unless his muscles were entirely galvanized by Corys, toiling there beside him, they and his tiresome heart must be much stronger than he had suspected.

'One more stone, and then I can crawl in,' said Corys, gasping. They both tugged at it and it fell, with a thud that shook the ground.

'Keep a look out down the dale,' said Corys, breathlessly, and she crept in to what looked a cavern, darker than any night beyond the sun's glare.

Out from the hole came the voice of Corys, murmuring to Jet, and a musty scent of old hay, and mildew, of rats and cobwebs and oak beams, three hundred years old, and a coolness, like the coolness of a vault beneath a grating in a sunny street.

'She's chained,' said Corys, within, in a muffled and struggling voice, 'but I'm pulling out the staple from the beam. Oh, I can't do it. Oh, I can—the wood must be rotten. Come, darling, come, my pet. You're safe now.'

'Cory, they're coming,' said Richard, urgently. 'I can see three people in a cart. Be quick. Which way shall we go?'

Corys grinned as she crept forth, with Jet hugged against her thin chest. It was a boyish grin that oddly stirred the blood smears on her cheeks.

'That's easy,' said Corys. 'Come after me.'

She darted through the farm yard and out at a gate on to the fell slope. There, she kept on the far side of an intack wall and then plunged into the bracken. Richard, closely following, found that if they stooped a little the waving green fronds closed above their heads.

'I'll find a sheep trod directly,' said Corys, panting, 'and then it'll be easier. Don't try and go quickly or they'll see the fern waving.'

That was a curious walk. For nearly half a mile they went slowly, stooping down, hidden in the slender forest of the bracken stems. They walked in a green dimness, but it was hot and airless and the smell of sunlit fern and crushed fern was so strong that it gave a suffocating quality to the heat. Corys found a sheep track but soon a dead sheep blocked it; hidden by the bracken it had died alone, as it had wished to do.

'The farmers hate bracken, partly because a sick sheep can't be found in it,' said Corys. 'Probably this silly thing could have been cured. I'm going to peep out, Richard, to make sure where we are.'

Corys' small brown face among the great fronds, that seemed to Richard luxuriant as those of any Amazon forest, was not likely to be perceived from Blaine's, the buildings of which looked already small below.

'Jos is shouting. He's drunk, I think,' said Corys, with enjoyment, 'but he must have seen the hole we made for he's dancing in the yard, with fury I mean. Odd, isn't it, why that kind of person wants to dance when he is annoyed? We're on the right way, Richard. Once over this ridge and we can come out in the open, and a good thing, too, for the bracken fades out, a bit farther on.'

There had been no chance to tell Corys of the car he had hired. He thought her prepared to walk all the way to Grasmere and she showed great surprise when she saw the car, waiting far below, and realized he had come in it.

'How frightfully extravagant,' said Corys, 'and Miss Wilson won't be best pleased to have me, like this, and Jet in her fine new car. Why on earth did you come by car, Richard? Wasn't there a bus?'

'The car was quicker,' said Richard, gloomily.

Richard was tired. The excitement; his exertions in making the hole in the barn; the slow, tedious, stooping walk in the close, green heat of the bracken; above all, a most curious feeling about Corys; all these had made him feel that kind of fatigue that is usually accompanied by ill temper. What business had Corys to have those eyes, and those slim brown hands, and that remote and waiting look if she lingered so intolerably on the edge of womanhood? For the first time he felt impatient with Corys; savagely breaking holes in walls, getting herself into such a scratched and battered mess, behaving illegally and so entirely and abominably like a boy, how could any man get at the real Corys, through those defences of hers that were impregnable because she had no idea as yet what they defended?

Miss Wilson looked at Corys with disgust.

'I took you for a gipsy lad,' she said. 'Has that dog fleas?'

CHAPTER XVI

At the end of the summer term Mr. Gerald Lovely suffered a curious misfortune. There came a bomb, late one night, near his college and so the window of Gerald's room fell out and the electric light went out. When he got back to his room with a lighted candle he resumed preparations to make himself a cup of tea. His kettle was a whistling one and by now it emitted an unusual and strangled kind of hiss. Gerald vaguely put this down to some more subtle effect of the bomb, but he was wrong. The whistle had been partly choked by an earwig so that but little steam could escape, and when he carelessly jerked the kettle the stopper with the whistle in it blew off and hit him in the mouth with such violence that one of his front teeth was broken off and fell into his little green teapot.

'Oh, heaventh! What thall I do now?' lisped Gerald, bleeding and much agitated.

All the dentists in Cambridge had appointments for every working minute of the next three weeks and to treat disorders much more urgent than was his, so Gerald had to arrive in Grasmere a week after his misfortune, no longer bleeding, but terribly conscious of the dark gap in his beautiful row of teeth and of his lisp.

Corys knew on which day he was expected at Lake View. She sometimes forced herself to go and see Mrs. Lovely because, sitting in Mrs. Lovely's lounge, it was, naturally, possible to look out over lake and fells without seeing Lake View. From nowhere else round the lake was this possible. When June was drawing to an end she called on Mrs. Lovely again, but this time in order to find out when Gerald was due home. She found this out easily since Mrs. Lovely spoke of nothing else save a few words of Myra, who was not coming home but was going to continue investigations into the age of Harlech Morfa and the question of how boats got to the Castle rock before the Morfa was there.

'Yes, Gerald is due next Wednesday,' said Mrs. Lovely. 'How do you think the war is going, Miss de Bainriggs? I do hope it is going well because, if not, Gerald will have to join something a year from now when he has his degree.'

In spite of all the agitation about Jet and her perpetual, miserable feeling that she had betrayed Penny Rock, Corys had been thinking a great deal about Gerald. She pictured herself meeting Gerald in the sunlit woods, rescuing Gerald from danger, though she could imagine none in the vale of Grasmere except, perhaps, a ram, irritable in autumn; seeing, from Bonfire Hall, Gerald walking on the main road and hearing him sing, though that would scarcely be possible on account of the traffic. In all her thoughts of Gerald it was she who helped or saved or admired Gerald; in all her dreaming of him it seemed she wanted nothing from him but friendly recognition and, at the most, a glance of approval. One glance of approval from Gerald, from a Gerald sober and preferably out of doors, and she knew that she would have achieved her whole heart's desire and satisfied herself, as well, that some day, some where, she could get herself a husband and some babies, three babies, thought Corys, would be nice, with, perhaps, one or two more later on.

When he had been in Grasmere before, Gerald, with all his teeth and able to speak clearly, had been attracted by the pretty Sweetings. They, still, with faithful persistence, adoring Richard Blunt, in much the same impersonal manner as Corys felt that she adored Gerald, had not been interested in Gerald, who they found commonplace. They were too well accustomed to people like Gerald, running after their fair heads, large blue eyes and sweet, tinkling voices. However, now that Gerald was back again at Lake View, he seemed to have forgotten the Sweetings and, after a period of moroseness, when he wandered about the valley with his mouth tight shut upon his gap, he began to hover around Bonfire Hall.

'There is that young Lovely again,' said Grandy, looking from the window of the long parlour one hot July morning. 'I verily believe he is going to go after sphagnum with Cory. I had not supposed a young fellow would be interested in Cory; the young are so conventional.'

'How good-looking he is!' said Maimie, who had risen listlessly from her long chair.

Maimie seemed to have recovered from the Chelsea bomb. Homeless and alone, she had now to decide how to earn a living, but she could not. Her recovery had not given her what had always been lacking, energy, perseverance and grit. That these were lacking may have been Maimie's fault or not, but certainly it was her misfortune. How was such a girl, a girl rather delicate, too pretty, inefficient, rather attractive but quite without the vitality to be a charmer of men, to keep herself in an acquisitive and selfish world? Maimie did not know, and she was beginning to fret herself thin and pale again. Blodwen did not know, and though she would most willingly have kept Maimie, as a pet for ever, she knew that Miles would not approve of her doing so and could not afford it, anyhow. Grandy did not know or care. She rather disliked Maimie and wished she would go away and earn a miserable pittance or die, somewhere out of sight.

'What does a girl do, whose parents have left no money and who cannot earn a decent living?' said Blodwen periodically, to Richard Blunt.

'Not earn a decent one, I suppose,' said Blunt, openly irritated at last by this aggravating query. Did young Mrs. de Bainriggs think he was responsible for Miss Ozzard? If so, she thought wrong.

Now that Gerald was back in Grasmere Corys was wearing, every day, the well-cut short skirt and plain silk sports blouse that she had bought in Carlisle. They were both blue, of a shade lighter than her eyes. A dark brown tie was the same colour as her hair. Not yet was Corys beautiful, or even pretty, but there was a distinction and promise and vitality about her that made the three Sweetings, when the four girls were together, look like delicately tinted blancmange. Up on the fell slopes, looking for sphagnum moss on the morning when Grandy had seen Gerald join Corys as she set forth, Gerald found himself rather fascinated by this tall, silent, lissom creature who looked at him with so odd a gravity in her deep blue eyes.

'Quite jolly up here, ithn't it?' said Gerald, lisping, for though the dentist at Windermere was to make him a new tooth it would not be ready for a month because the dentist, like the Cambridge one, had too many patients.

Corys was thinking of a number of things at once. They were now high above the valley, which was hidden by a ridge of waste grassland, still bleached with winter though green blades began to show. There had been a little tarn in the hollow behind the ridge and the sphagnum moss and juniper bushes grew about the marshy borders of the bog that had filled the tarn and extinguished its lonely shining. There were heavenly smells up here, wild and hot; the ground felt warm as they sank their fingers in amongst the moss; it was so silent they could hear the wind in the grasses and, in a moment, as Corys knew, they would move, picking moss as they went, to where they would see westwards over ridge after ridge of fells, each gleaming with the dim, olive-tinted sheen of sunlit bent grass. Here, Corys felt herself at home and had need of none beside her. Here, the curious way she thought about Gerald in the valley seemed trifling and rather absurd. Which was real, those heavenly fell slopes and her joy in them, or the restless, uneasy longing for something from Gerald, but what she was not sure? With every need satisfied by the fells and the sunshine what did she want more? And then, Gerald lisped, and every time he spoke there was that hideous gap in his teeth. He should hide it, somehow. It was awful of him, to go about like that.

'Yes, it's nice up here,' said Corys, abstractedly. 'Here! Stop it! You're getting a lot of juniper needles in your moss. And aren't you ever going to get your tooth put right? It makes you look so idiotic.'

It seemed unreasonable but this disfigurement of Gerald greatly offended Corys. Indeed, as the hot summer days went by and Grasmere grew fuller of visitors than ever, owing to many coming on holiday and a few because of bombs, she began to try and elude Gerald, for the reason, which seemed odd to her, that she did not know what to do with him now that, apparently, she had got him.

Gerald, finding Corys increasingly unresponsive, naturally began to think the more of her. He was supposed to study a good deal but between his spells of reading and his visits to Windermere to see the dentist, he began to pursue Corys, and Corys, still dressed as a girl and soberly gratified at this proof of her power when in girls' clothes, yet began to treat him with a blunt carelessness of manner.

Still, Gerald persisted and continued all through August to visit frequently at Bonfire Hall.

'I almost had hopes for a rich son-in-law for you,' said Grandy to Blodwen one day. 'But not much hope. I felt pretty sure that Corys would go on in her usual no-man-may-look-at-me manner, and so she is. But if she wasn't after Gerald, I still don't understand what made the child willing to be a girl. I don't imagine she is thinking of Blunt, do you?'

'No,' said Blodwen, and hesitated. 'She talked to me about girls' clothes, and behaving like a girl before you went to Carlisle,' she added, in an uncertain manner. 'I am sure she had no thoughts of Richard in her mind then. But I rather imagine she had become afraid that she might lose something if she went on trying to suppress her girlhood and she knows quite well, for she told me so, that she could never do a real man's work.'

'Afraid of falling between two stools; she's right in that,' said Grandy, musingly. 'But the quickest cure for all her troubles would be to fall in love.'

'But not yet,' said Blodwen, quickly. 'Cory is half child still, Grandy, as you know as well as I do. She is not ready for that kind of love, and she won't be, perhaps for some years. I wasn't, when I was her age. I grew up slowly; you, I know, were the opposite.'

'Thank the Lord, yes,' said Grandy. 'A hang-over from childhood is a dangerous thing, Blodwen; before you're quit of it your youth, and its chances, may be over.'

Autumn came early that year. There had been abnormally dry weather at the Lakes ever since the war began, but at the end of this August there began a rainy period and the vale was dark, day and night, with cloud and the dense shade of wet trees in full leaf. Corys' triumph at the rescue of Jet had by now been almost forgotten. Jet had been nursed and petted until she had recovered from the hardships she had suffered and Corys had then sent her to a farmer friend, far off by the shores of Morecambe Bay where she would be active, useful and happy and safe from Jownie Wife and Blaine. Now that she was gone and Old John content, though always grumbling, in his cottage, Corys felt renewed despair at the awful spectacle of Lake View where there should have been nothing but the sunny green of the beech trees above the grey rock and their reflection in the lake in that bright, inverted world into which she had loved as a child to stare. Her awkwardness in dealing with Gerald also depressed her at this time. True, he had deserted the pretty Sweetings to come tramping about, all over the fells and through the woods, after her, but she still did not know what to do with him and she felt sure that any of the Sweetings would have known. Would she have to ask Mummie about it, and would Mummie know?

During the last week of August it rained every day. Grasmere's wartime guests, who had seen it only when dry, could not at first believe their eyes and thought some kind of catastrophe must have overtaken the climate, perhaps owing to the bombs and gunfire that seemed to them to encircle the Lake District. Instead of sunny skies, shining in the lake and all through the leafy woods, slowly shifting glooms moved shapelessly overhead, engulfing now one fell and now another in a deep shadow, leaden or purple-dark. Out of one part or another of this sullen sky rain fell; there was no wind and the pallor of rain dwelt on Helm Crag, or Rydal Fell, and cleared again or spread, as if by contagion in the sky, over the valley which then seemed to become one, for the moment, with the waters that filled the firmament. The silence of long drought was now broken and sounds of rushing streams filled the whole valley so that it was no longer possible, as in ordinarily rainy weather, to walk from the clamour of Tongue Gill through a quiet space to the outermost whisper of Sour Milk Gill. The natives of Grasmere, though once more carrying umbrellas and wearing rubber boots, took no other heed of the rain, but the war guests stayed indoors, hoping it would stop.

When the rain had lasted a week Corys came to the Island one day, immediately after lunch.

'I can't chop wood and I can't cut bracken, and Grandy is cross,' said Corys, restlessly, in the hogg-house. 'She ate eight red herrings for breakfast. Mummie and I cooked them because Jane feels woffy. They were awful queer, Richard, kind of stiff and poky, and they slithered about in the wash-basin and looked at us with horrid, dead eyes. Grandy said they were all bones and scales but I think eight was too many. What shall we do, Richard? Oh, Gerald has got his new tooth, and he says it's too big and too white but the dentist has screwed it into him so he doesn't know what to do about it. Can I clean your fireplace, Richard, or make your bed, or do something?'

'I think we'd better go to Ambleside,' said Richard, after a moment's pause. 'I've a book that is due back at the Armitt Library, and we could have tea at Dodd's.'

They waited in the rain and a queue for a bus. When it came the conductor let them in and then ordered them out again and they had to wait for another, why they did not know, but, as Corys said, it must be owing to the war. At the Armitt Library they found a good fire, because though it was August it was also wet, and they sat by it, thus drying their legs, and, meanwhile, looking up facts about Bainriggs in immense reference books.

'If I could only find the site of the capital messuage!' said Corys, her brown cheeks glowing with warmth and excitement.

'What does goldarr mean?' said Richard. 'Look: "the farm of Gresmere with a moiety of the mill and fulling mill, goldarr of sheep, moors, fishings and a brew house, is worth £7 17s. 3d."That was in 1274. Do you know what goldarr was?'

'Dunno,' said Corys, reading over his shoulder and mumbling part of what she read, aloud. '"Hamlet of Gressmere, in 1324, the forest there is worth nothing; in the said hamlet there were II tenements in the lord's hands ... the forest there ... and a brewery house there, but now they render nothing for default of tenants." Why default of tenants, Richard? Was it the Scots? Oh, look, there ahead: "1390, decay of a tenement which Richard Baynerigh held." Why do they spell Bainrigg differently every time?'

The fire flickered with a drowsy, cosy, flapping sound. They could hear the rain, drumming down outside. It was so dark that Richard switched on the table lamp; in its rosy pool of light they sat and read and passed, as they read, into that enchantment which is created by thoughts of familiar places as they were, very long ago.

"'To the Sate Sandall, as heaven water deals, and so to the Grene Tofot at the head of Sandall,'" read Richard, of a watershed boundary, as if it was poetry. 'Cory, what is a Tofot?'

After tea they missed the five o'clock bus and began to walk home, up the right bank of the Rothay. It was now raining as heavily as it had done that day, just a year ago, when Mr. Blunt walked the same way on the other side of the river. Memories of that day brought him uneasily out from the glow of feeling that had come with him from Ambleside. Then, a year ago, he had just jilted Maimie and had been unrepentant and rejoicing in his freedom. That freedom had been easily won. Then, he had not met Corys; now, he had, and could a free heart ever be his again?

As he mused, unprofitably and even dangerously, for depression of spirit in such a downpour might surely induce a chill, that meteorological violence popularly known as a cloud-burst was being prepared, by appropriate movements and temperature changes, in the lower sky just ahead of them.

'It really is a bit dampish, isn't it?' said Corys, happily, and with a shake of her wet head that sent bright drops flying like a momentary halo.

CHAPTER XVII

On this wet afternoon Maimie Ozzard had a short rest after lunch and then set forth to the village because her kind hostess, Corys' mother, wanted to cash a cheque and was not anxious to go to the Bank herself. Grandy was still not fully recovered from the eight red herrings and Jane Peascod, who was seventy-seven and hence entitled, she felt, to feel woffy sometimes, still experienced the mysterious symptoms associated with woffiness. Thus, Blodwen did not care to go out and, besides, there had been another raid on London and she felt uneasy when she was out of hearing of the telephone.

In Grasmere cheques are not to be lightly cashed. By now, Maimie was familiar with the ritual surrounding visits to the Bank. If a customer was in the Bank, a fact easily ascertained through the ground glass of the door, no one might enter till he, or more probably she, came out. The rigours of this unwritten law were mitigated by the fact that the Bank had a porch, in which some generous and thoughtful person had caused a broad wooden bench to be placed. Yet, even so, considerable hardship had to be supported in bad weather, for the Bank, now it was war time, opened for only a few hours twice a week, and the war guests, being wealthy, were for ever wanting to do things in a Bank and thus outnumbered the natives who found themselves, quite often, crowded out of the porch.

On this wet afternoon Maimie found the porch full of two Jews, from who knew where, a Londoner and a stout lady from Liverpool. She, with several others, stood against the house wall, trying to get some shelter from the eaves, while a jay screamed at them all from a tree across the road. In time, as more people gathered, a kind of sideways queue developed, flattened against the wall but retaining a vivid sense of whose turn came next. Proceedings were slowed down by the Liverpool lady, who wished to change her investments because she had been feeling dull in Grasmere. Shut in, dry and warm behind the glass door, she discussed finance while the bank clerk's sandwiches, which he never had time to eat in Grasmere, grew a little drier and more curled up at the corners.

'Hullo!' said Gerald, grinning at Maimie. He had found himself with only ten pounds in his pocket-book so he had had to come and get some more, wet though it was. He had been to call at Bonfire Hall that morning and had seen Corys, darting into the wet woods as he approached. Why did she do that, wondered Gerald, much interested?

'How are you getting on with all our odd friends at the Hall?' said Gerald, leaning against the wall beside Maimie and thinking that her blue oilsilk hood made her look rather pleasant.

Maimie was three years older than Gerald. She had been engaged. She had suffered. She thought him a charming boy and had given him good advice now and then, about too many cigarettes and getting his head so wet.

When Maimie had penetrated to the porch and then, after another ten minutes, into the Bank and there cashed Blodwen's cheque and got two pounds for it, she came out to the street again looking quite pale and Gerald said he would not wait to get any money himself that day as there were no cigarettes to be bought, anyway.

'I think I will go a walk before I go back,' said Maimie, uncertainly. She felt very tired but she knew it was not a real kind of tiredness and that probably she would feel less so after a walk, if only the walk could be interesting and enjoyable.

'Come on, then,' said Gerald. 'Take my arm? You look a bit played out and I'm not shy. Are you?'

They walked past the Prince and on, past Lake View, to the footbridge over the Rothay that led to the Loughrigg Terrace Walk and Bonfire Hall. There Gerald said he must turn back.

'Rain is coming through three of our roofs,' said he, 'and I promised my Mamma to crawl about and tack bits of tarred felt on them. But the snag is that it never comes through at the spot you think it does, and once you have put a nail through tarred felt you mustn't take it out again. Bye-bye, my child; be good.'

– 144 –

Thus, by now tired of walking with Maimie in the rain, Gerald returned home and lay on his bed, reading what has been described as modern poetry.

Some quarter of an hour after this the cloud burst. In other words, a thundery up-rush of heated air over Loughrigg became so violent, though imperceptible to an observer on the ground, as to prevent drops of water falling for an appreciable time. Then, the drops having accumulated sufficiently to overcome the upward current, they overcame it and fell earthwards in so concentrated a downpour that an inch of rain came down in the first ten minutes. By now Corys and Richard had left Rydal Water behind them, and were walking towards Bonfire Hall by the low path along the river, some way behind Maimie, who had taken the Terrace Walk. They had come out of the wood and the bare, steep slope of Loughrigg rose above them for a thousand feet.

'This is rather fierce, isn't it?' said Richard, but doubtfully, for Corys might say otherwise.

'Yes,' said Corys, a little anxiously, and indistinctly because of the rain. 'I don't think I like it, just here, under that slope—'

Her words were drowned in the roar of the rain that now began to be a cloud-burst. They were enclosed by rain, for there was darkness in the rain so that they could see but a few feet through it. The river to their right was hidden but they still heard its roar, though faintly through that of the rain. The slopes that tilted up on their left were hidden too and now water began to flow down them as if a dam had burst somewhere up on the fell. Like a shallow stream it poured down, but everywhere at once, rippled round their ankles and passed on, unseen again, and rushing with the sound of rapids heard on a still day. They could not see their path, and it was difficult to feel it underfoot because of the water that soon began to bring with it stones, rolled headlong in the flood. It began to seem that even so shallow a sweep of water might knock them off their feet, as rushes of wet earth not more than a foot deep may, in Switzerland, carry away, and then bury, cattle and even men.

'Is it a cloud-burst?' shouted Richard, idiotically, for what did it matter what it was? 'Cory, is it a cloudburst?'

It comforted him to hear his voice but she could not hear it. She was listening for what she knew lay ahead, that steep and stony beck which comes down Loughrigg and enters the river near the outlet of Grasmere. She began to hear it as he spoke, a harsh uproar muffled by the deluge so that it was but a menacing whisper.

'We must go back,' shouted Corys, her lips almost against Richard's wet face.

She was not sure that he heard her, so she took his arm and turned him, facing up the slope for a moment. And it was then that she saw Maimie, as a dim, pale bundle that seemed to crawl, and then slide, and then check, as if it dug its hands into the sodden slope, and then move hopelessly down again, impelled by the rushing sheets of water, mud, stones and torn masses of bracken.

Corys shook Richard, who had not looked up as had she, being too intent on his right ankle which had just been painfully struck by a sliding stone. She shook him and, with a hand under his chin, turned his face up so that he saw the bundle, too.

'A woman!' said Richard, without surprise. With all the world, and the heavens above it, dissolved into the fluid darkness that raged about them, mobile as whirling vapour, he could feel surprise no more.

He went a few steps upwards, scarcely able to keep his feet, and, tottering, bent over the limp, soaking woman.

Maimie had been overwhelmed by the deluge and had stepped, unseeing, over the edge of the path. Thus she had fallen and had been unable, on the steep slope, to save herself from being washed down it and she was but half conscious.

'Maimie!' thought Richard and, grasping the shoulder of her coat, tried to lower her down so that Corys should get firm hold of her before she could be washed and rolled into the unseen Rothay.

There was a moment when it seemed that Corys would be knocked off her feet by Maimie and Richard, without conscious thought, gave Maimie a sideways push so that Corys was saved, but Maimie very nearly carried away. After this he sat on the slope, slipping down and grasping Maimie closely so that she should not be swept against Corys. Between them, they got Maimie on to the level path where the impulse of the rush of water was less. By now the first, fearful intensity of the rain was over; it still roared down, blotting out everything save a little space about their feet, but it was now possible to breathe more easily and to stand upright. With this slight lessening of the turmoil the sound of the Loughrigg beck became louder; down it boulders, that had moved but a few inches in a generation, were now being hurtled and the roar and crash of their passage, heard more clearly every moment, made Richard think some frightful violence moved unseen and from all sides towards them. Then, Corys' gestures made him realize that the danger lay on the way they had been going and his wits, working more normally, recalled the Loughrigg beck.

'We must go back!' shouted Corys, again, and Richard, nodding, silently cursed Maimie and seized her shoulders.

Corys, her back to Maimie and one of that now unconscious lady's feet in each hand, began to stumble along the path, back towards the footbridge.

'Gosh! She's heavy!' thought Richard of Maimie, and wondered if her wet, limp, dead weight would injure Corys. Could not a girl be too easily injured by carrying even half of a sodden, sagging, full-grown woman?

'Go easy, Cory!' shouted Richard, and wobbled Maimie's shoulders to draw the child's attention.

All the land at the head of Rydal Water was flooded. The rain, though it still fell thickly and with violence, had less darkness above it and they could see, when they had laboriously waded to the footbridge, that everything between them and the main road, high on its retaining wall, was under water. The footbridge was an island and under it the Rothay roared, over its banks, over the meadow that was the only fertile part of Bainriggs, and rushing, fierce, and rippled into a great arrow head, towards the right-angled bend where it turns to Rydal lake. It was when they were getting off the bridge that Corys slipped and then Richard frightened her. It had been difficult to carry Maimie across the bridge, which is only one person wide and, of late years, has had a railing on either side. Scrambling down the steps on the farther side into water, the depth of which she did not know, Corys slipped on a submerged stone and for an awful moment Richard thought Maimie's body would override her and push her aside and into the dark, glassy sweep of the main current. Thinking this, Richard let Maimie's shoulders down on the top step with something of a bump and, somehow leaping past her, he seized Corys and stood, waist deep, clutching her and looking distraught.

'Lord! Richard! What's up?' said Corys, panting, and trying to free her hands so that she could catch hold of some part of Maimie, who was slowly subsiding in the oddest manner and sagging together as she sank, very slowly, down the steps, with the water already rising in a little wave against each ankle.

Corys could not free her hands. Richard had them both in one of his, his left arm was round her shoulders and she felt suffocated by the violence with which he pressed her against him.

'Richard! Let go! What are you about?' said Corys, feeling the rain run down her neck as she looked angrily up into his face.

'You'd have been dead in another two minutes,' said Richard, as if he was in a savage temper.

He looked savage, with a black, furious look made more remarkable by the water that streamed continuously over his face from his soaking hair. But as Corys, still struggling, looked up at him this look altered.

'Richard! Please!' said Corys, suddenly ceasing to struggle and standing still within his arm.

It was the first time she had seen in any man's the look that came to Richard's eyes now; she never forgot it and she never forgave it, though, later, she came to understand it. Richard had been tired out and over-wrought by danger and exertion. He had had a terrible, though she considered quite unnecessary, fright about her safety. He had sprung to her rescue and held her, in thankfulness and triumph. And then he had spoilt so much, so very much, by letting that look shine in his eyes.

'Oh, please!' said Corys, trying to back away from him and bending her face down so that he saw only her wet hair.

But Richard had seen her face before she hid it and knew that Corys, child though she might still be, had realized aright what she had seen in his. She had realized it and had been revolted, with a revulsion wild and fierce and powerful as the flooded river. He let her go at once and, looking vaguely down to see what had struck against his leg, saw Maimie, half submerged. Maimie! He had forgotten her. Wearily he stooped and grasped, once again, those wet, slippery shoulders.

'If anything, she's a bit wetter and heavier than before,' said Richard, in almost his ordinary voice. 'Can you manage her feet again, Cory? We've not got far to go to the road, now.'

The heavy sound of the river was behind them as they waded towards the main road, like a burden that could not be escaped, and the chill of the rain and the flood, soaking through clothes already soaked, was as cold, Richard thought, and as heavy as the abominable Miss Ozzard.

'Wretched girl!' thought Richard, well aware that the unconscious Maimie, sagging and sliding herself between Corys and him, had left a less tangible barrier between them that he did not know how to move.

CHAPTER XVIII

Miss Ozzard lay in bed at Lake View. Gerald had spoken truly about the roofs, but that over Myra's bedroom had not as yet leaked and she lay in Myra's bed, looking through the open window at the Island. She had lain there for two days and nights by now and Richard had not been to see her. The housemaid had met him, coming to inquire, but as she had been able to tell him how Maimie was he had not come farther. Certainly, it had been raining at the time. Corys had been once. Richard had sent flowers, with a hurried scrawl: 'Hard luck. I hope you'll soon be fit again. Richard.' The grocer's boy had brought them, with the bread. Maimie felt utterly alone, as she lay, looking at the Island and felt, at last, that she had really lost Richard and would never get him again.

'Anyhow, there is Blodwen,' thought Maimie. Blodwen had been to see her, each day, and had brought eggs, which even the Lovelys' money could not buy at this time. 'But I can't live on Corys' mother, or on anybody. I must try and keep myself. If only I could get worse and die now! How much easier it would be!' thought Maimie, quite ignorant of whether it would be easier or, perhaps, less easy.

Mrs. Lovely had told her that Richard and Corys had carried her to the main road on the afternoon of the cloudburst and that then, most miraculously, a bus had come along and, still more miraculously, it had not been full. The bus had taken them to Lake View and there, fearing that Maimie was dead or dying, Richard and Corys had staggered along Mr. Lovely's path of white chippings, carrying her, and had besought shelter for their prostrated burden.

'It would have taken too long to get you all the way round to Bonfire Hall,' had said Mrs. Lovely, 'and, besides, Miss de Bainriggs knew Miss Wilson had gone to Liverpool with some people who have a house there and wanted to know if it was bombed. So there was no taxi and they couldn't have carried you from the Square. They both looked pretty done in, as it was.'

Mrs. Lovely was kind but impersonal. Mr. Lovely was kind but worried. He began to fear that Lake View might be damp, if it were not already so. Not only the rain through the three roofs worried Mr. Lovely but the lake being so close beside his door. He had thought that he wanted a lake frontage and now he began to wonder if he did. At mother's age, and his age, it would never do to develop rheumatism and there certainly seemed a something that came from the lake, a kind of breath off the water, sometimes chill and sometimes warm, but that must, always, be damp.

'Well, how are you to-day, my young lady?' said Mr. Lovely, but not really wanting an answer. He brought Maimie some gingerbread, for he had just been to the village, and she was glad to have some one to talk to who stood, literally and metaphorically, between her and the Island of her lost hopes. 'That cloud-burst of yours has played the dickens with the lake. In my opinion the lake outlet has wanted a good clearing ever since we came, and now that blessed stream from Loughrigg has chucked masses of stones and mess into it and the lake is backing up. They'll feel it in the village, and so I told them this morning. Not that the lake will get into the village, but what comes from the village, if you take me,' said Mr. Lovely, thus delicately alluding to what comes out of drain pipes, 'won't come so easily. And I'm anxious about Lake View. The lake could never rise so high as we are, of course, but it'll come nearer and I don't want it nearer. Well, feeling better, are you? That's good,' said Mr. Lovely, to whom Maimie had had no chance to reply.

However, Gerald was kind, and in a way that showed he thought Maimie a distinct personality and not just a poor creature one had to be kind to. The sight of Maimie, fainting, half drowned, so helpless that, when he stumbled a little in helping to carry her, her wet, golden head wobbled against his chest, had given Gerald sensations that he felt to be remarkable and curious. And now that she was getting well but was still so weak that she could not even stand, or so the housemaid said, he liked to take her a newspaper or a couple of precious cigarettes and see her smile, with such gratitude and pleasure as made her little white face look quite different. She, a woman of experience, who had loved and lost, and been bombed and, no doubt, suffered other agitations more mysterious to Gerald because she was so poor, she seemed really to appreciate him. Now, Corys de Bainriggs, who had looked like a wild, tall rat when she and that Blunt fellow had come staggering into Lake View with Maimie, on the cloud-burst day, Corys didn't seem in the least like a woman. She wasn't such a freak to look at since she took to wearing decent clothes, but there was something wanting there, thought Gerald, mentally shaking a solemn young head. Weren't there people who never grew up?

'Don't you think it would be better if that Cory kid went right out of Grasmere and did something ordinary, like munitions, or Wrens or Waafs, or something?' said Gerald, restlessly staring out of Maimie's window at the north-east corner of Bonfire Hall, which was all of it he could see.

'Much better,' said Maimie, in her quiet, but assured manner. 'She needs to mix with other girls. Now, when I was her age, there was a boy, down our street, and would you believe it,' asked Maimie, who did not do so herself, 'I was almost engaged to him! Such a nice lad, but of course we were babes and the parents ... well, there was trouble, one way and another. Do you like Cory, Gerald? You know her so much better than I do.'

On other occasions Gerald and Maimie discussed the Sweeting girls.

'Very pretty, and nice, good-tempered little things,' said Gerald. 'But childish, don't you think? There seems to be something, something they haven't got, if you know what I mean. Now, Cory, of course, one never knows what she is, or isn't, though I think it is mostly isn't, but she's more interesting, in a way, than the Sweeting kids. Don't you think so?'

Maimie went back to Bonfire Hall as soon as the doctor said that she would not get pneumonia or rheumatic fever, both of which complaints he had rather expected to develop. Gerald found that he much missed her womanly sympathy and worldly wise comprehension, and, above all, her appreciation of himself. However, shortly after this he went back to Cambridge from where he began a correspondence with her that lasted nearly a month and then died out, spasmodically but eventually completely because other people took her place in his mind.

Maimie spent the autumn in reading to old war-guest ladies, taking war-guest children for walks, acting as secretary to a war-guest financier, and helping in the Gift Shop, all of which jobs brought her in a little money, which she was able to save since Blodwen de Bainriggs insisted on keeping her at Bonfire Hall.

Mr. Sweeting bought, by telephone, a garden hut that was advertised in the *Westmorland Gazette* and immediately he had done so nineteen other offers were received for it. In this hut, re-erected behind Fold-in-the-Wood, were stored two tons of coal, in case of shortage, or deep snow, and on the coal the Sweeting sisters piled, temporarily, superfluous objects of all kinds, from wicker chairs to tins of soup. Busy all day long in cleaning, tidying and warming Fold-in-the-Wood and inventing strange meals made of sausages and cheese, or tinned beans and frozen cod, the three girls continued faithfully to adore Richard Blunt. There was, indeed, no other man in the valley that it was any use to adore, since the men war guests were old and if there had, at any time, been any young Grasmere men, they were all gone to the war. An interest secondary only to their worship of Richard was Corys de Bainriggs, whose periodic attempts at being a girl amused them a good deal. There was, however, something besides amusement in the feeling they had, when they were with Corys in the village or other public places, and Corys was wearing her new tweed overcoat with that hand-woven scarf Richard had given her on her seventeenth birthday. People always stared at the three Sweetings but it seemed they looked at Corys differently, at first casually, but then with an attention which the Sweetings felt was lacking in the amiable, admiring glances cast so universally upon them. And so Essie and Rudie and Mag told each other what a scream Corys was, a boy one day and a girl the next, and how no one could take her seriously, but they felt jealous.

All through the autumn things seemed to go on the same as usual at Bonfire Hall. Richard came as often. Maimie was in and out. Blodwen was more cheerful, to be sure, but that was because of Maimie. Grandy had two attacks of Niger fever and became friendly with three war-guest ladies whom she had rescued at different times, one from being benighted in the woods behind the Hall, one from Jownie Wife who was swearing at her in the road Back o' Lake and one from a nervous breakdown. This last lady had burst into tears in Red Lion Square one day when the grocer had said, 'No honey, no oranges, no tinned tongue.' The real cause of her tears was a bomb, in London, a month previously, and Grandy, who was in the Square when she began to weep, divined that the grocer was only one of those cumulative burdens that are described as last straws. Grandy had dried the lady's tears and told her there was nothing to be ashamed of in tears and so they became friends. These rescued three spent much of their time at the Hall, worshipping Grandy and being jealous of each other, and it was they who told Grandy that Miss Corys was looking ill.

'I know it,' said Grandy.

'Can't her mother—?' said the benighted lady.

'No,' said Grandy.

'How sad,' said the sworn-at lady. 'I mean, how sad to be so young and yet look ill,' she added hastily, fearing she might have seemed to criticize Corys' mother.

'She's too young,' said Grandy, 'too young to be well, at her age.'

Naturally, this mystified all three ladies and they began, after an uncertain pause, to talk about what Miss Jones had said at the last work party. 'Can she be a spy?' said they, unconsciously wishing she might be.

Christmas came and, as necessarily, went. Myra Lovely came home spotty with chicken-pox, so Gerald went to friends in Hampshire. There were air-raids, elsewhere. There was fighting, far away. The newspapers got smaller and smaller and the eight o'clock News lasted only four and a half minutes, for which the B.B.C. announcer seemed to apologize. Every one at the work parties said something extra warlike was going to happen, somewhere, at any time. But in January, as peacefully as it might have done eighty-five years ago (when it last happened) there began the great frost and snow at Grasmere.

This arctic period came on gradually. There were frosts at night and, on some days, snow showers. It thawed during the day and there was a good deal of sunshine. After about a week Rydal Water was frozen all over, and looked black, like black glass, save at the lower end where there was dead white ice on which the first skaters of that winter glided, moving, it seemed, aimlessly as little flies circling in summer sunshine. Grasmere by this time was partly frozen so that the tawny brilliance of the frosty sunset behind Silverhow was reflected, as bright, from the open lanes of dark water, and shone as but a diffused glow from the large spaces of ice.

'You'll have to get off your precious Island,' said Grandy to Richard as he said good night on one of these frosty evenings. 'Or else you'll have to wait, on it, till the lake really freezes or the thaw comes.'

'On Derwentwater they have an ice-breaker,' said Corys, from her corner by the fire, 'for the people on Lord's Island. But we've nothing here.'

Corys had taken to sitting in the corner of the oak settle that was out of the direct light of both fire and lamp. There she sat knitting while Richard and the others chatted. Staring thoughtfully into the fire she wondered at the apparent ease with which Maimie, who had been engaged to Richard, spoke, and even drew his attention to her by making bright little remarks which were often amusing, but silly, Corys thought. How had she been able to let herself get engaged, to begin with? It seemed queer to Corys. No doubt she had been kissed by Richard, and perhaps Richard had looked at her as he had done, in the cloudburst, at Corys. Corys tried to stop herself thinking before she got as far as this, but she did not always succeed.

'I don't believe this weather will last; it never does,' said Richard, speaking to no one in particular. 'But I dare say I had better get in some more fire-logs and some tins of food; I've let my stores go down lately.'

Naturally, or so everybody felt it to be, Richard was marooned on the Island after this. By the next morning the lake was frozen hard enough to prevent the movement of any boat but not hard enough to be walked upon. This tiresome condition lasted for two nights and three days, the lake freezing at night and getting partially thawed during the sunny noon hours. In the middle of the third night Richard walked ashore. There was a clear moon and a frost of such severity that water froze in his bucket in the hogg-house though he had set it near the small fire. His logs were nearly all burnt, his food store alarmingly low and thus, cold and hungry, Richard made his cautious way over the thickening ice at midnight for fear that further thaw next day might make the passage once more impossible. He woke Old John and spent the rest of the night beside the smouldering fire in the kitchen of Oak How.

After this, there came an inch or two of snow that melted in the sunshine but lay all day, white and wan in shadow. More snow fell and now it covered the valley and the fells and lay, about three inches deep, and apparently unaffected by the clear sunlight that, day after day, made the weather more remarkable. Intense frost followed. The temperature on two nights dropped to below zero. Countless houses in Grasmere were without water, for the pipes, if they did not freeze in the walls, froze outside, in the ground. In some cases water mains in the road were frozen. Windows were covered with a sheet of thick ice that, in fireless rooms, remained unmelted all day. At Bonfire Hall the light of sunrise shone against the ice-covered glass so that it seemed the windows were hidden by a sheet of some rosy, opaque material. Corys breathed holes in this ice, until it grew so thick that she had to scrape it away, and looked out every morning on the lake, dead white in the snowy hollow, and up to where the dim rose of dawn shone behind the pure, white slopes of Nab Scar and filled the space of sky between them and the arctic wastes of Loughrigg. Still, the sun shone daily, but there was no thaw and unmelted hoar frost made every twig, and branch, and dead leaf, feathery white so that the woods looked like dim, grey clouds on the white slopes.

There came an evening in the third week of January with a falling glass and a hazy dullness in the sky. The temperature rose to freezing-point. Icicles, hanging in a deep fringe from the gutters, began to drip, one slow drop after another that froze and formed an upward pointing icicle below. Next morning there was a faint dust of minute particles of ice that showed only on door-steps and flagged paths. The sky was covered by a white and formless obscurity that darkened as if it was being thickened from above; then snow began to fall, in small flakes, drifting upon an air, otherwise imperceptible, from the south-east. It lay, soft, unstirred, thickening with what seemed an incredible quickness. The air was so dense with the fall of it that rooms were dark at midday and out of doors people moved uncertainly with that sense of being muffled in a suffocating obscurity that is felt in thick fog. By next morning the snow lay two feet deep on fells and valley alike; on the frozen lake; covering frozen streams; piled so high on tree branches that all trees, whatever their normal habit of growth, were bowed alike into grotesque, crouching shapes. Every wall and fence top was capped with perhaps a foot of snow. Bushes of holly, brambles and wild roses were roofed over so that they became smooth domes of unbroken snow, and in the narrower lanes snow curved from the wall tops on either side to form a slightly cup-shaped surface high above the buried roadway. In the village the snow-plough, going round twice in the day, pushed most of the snow aside, leaving a track covered with an inch or two of compact and icy substance, as slippery as it was hard. But the Raise was blocked and the road to Ambleside was blocked and Grasmere was isolated, the more so since the telegraph and telephone wires were down, broken by the weight of windless snow.

'Thou mun bide here,' Old John had said to Richard, on the morning after Richard had escaped from the Island. 'There's worse to come yet.' But Richard was obstinate. He dragged supplies on a sledge across the ice to the Island and hoped to settle down again, reading about Bainriggs, cooking his queer meals and watching sunrise and sunset move, above the valley, rosy-gold, with their remote, orderly brightening and fading on the snowy fell tops. His hopes were disappointed. The hogg-house was too cold. With temperatures four and five degrees below zero outside he found he could not warm it, however big his fire. Also, his loved solitude was temporarily at an end. Until the snow too deeply covered it crowds walked upon the lake. Dogs raced, perambulators were pushed, on a Sunday family parties sauntered, skaters cut intricate figures, on the ice. Voices sounded, echoing from the fell slopes, out on what were normally the lonely spaces of the lake. Boys played hockey; children played ball, on the ice. Daily, numbers of people came on the Island, walked about the hogg-house, and, peering in through the loop-lights wondered, audibly, how any one could live in it these days. It became apparent to Richard that no one could. He bought a thermometer and found it registered twenty degrees of frost in the hogg-house at night and could not be made to rise above twenty-five degrees Fahrenheit during the day. Old John told him that even Jownie Wife had left the Island during a severe cold spell one winter.

Richard's decision to go and live with Old John, until the great frost and snows ended, was made the easier because the Island had not helped him, since the cloud-burst, as it had before. He had thought that, on it, he might get the better of his distress at having frightened Corys. He had tried to get the better of it; he had listened to the lonely sounds of wind and waters; he had told himself it was not his fault if men loved and women were afraid of their love; he tried to think of those who must have loved, and made a mess of loving, on the banks of this enchanted lake and how they lay now, none the less restfully, in the churchyard above the murmuring Rothay. And then he would check his thoughts, which had become woolly. How did he know their rest, if they did rest, was not affected by their muddled love affairs? How did he, or any one, know anything at all about the dalesmen who were dead? The sense of mystery in all things that had soothed Richard on his first days of true convalescence on the Island did not sooth him now, strongly though it affected him.

'Certainly, everything is mysterious, but one can't go on staring at mystery and getting hypnotized as if it were a candle flame,' thought Richard, shuddering on his last night in the icy hogg-house. 'I want Cory; there is mystery enough in that, no doubt. And if I can't have Cory I must get something else, a job perhaps.'

On the next day when he was settled, warm and comfortable, in Old John's best bedroom, with permission to sit, and cook, in the kitchen as much as he chose, Richard suddenly determined to see a doctor. He went to Bonfire Hall that evening, laboriously, through a foot of undisturbed snow.

'What doctor do you have?' said he, in the long parlour.

'We don't have one; it is sometimes safer not,' said Grandy. 'When I was in Hong Kong a doctor wanted to have my leg taken off.' Corys spoke at the same time.

'Oh, Richard! Are you ill?' said Corys. 'And do you know Mr. Lovely has bought Grey Craggs on White Moss and that he says he hates Lake View?'

CHAPTER XIX

Now that everything which could freeze was frozen and, as well, buried in snow that varied in depth from two feet to three feet, according to situation and the severity of the latest snow-storms, it might have been thought that Mr. Lovely would have ceased to worry about Lake View being damp. He had plenty of other worries, all of a meteorological character except for mother's left big toe, which looked as usual but gave her pain. Doctors, said Mr. Lovely, know nothing about two things, human feet and human diet. Mother must go to a fully qualified chiropodist, not to some delightful young lady who would curl her hair and cut her toe-nails with equal enthusiasm. However, the nearest fully qualified chiropodist, at this time, lived at Morecambe and since nobody could get even to Ambleside in this weather, mother had to go on suffering from whatever big toe disease it was which made her toe feel, but not look, bright red and sharply pointed.

Since the frost set in there had been no damp to soak into the valleys between Mr. Lovely's five roofs but he feared the future extremely. Each valley was now filled with compact snow that had been partly frozen and was as hard as ice. The gutters all round the house supported about nine inches of ice, in a solid block, the product of dribbles of snow water from the roofs above them. Soon, the weight of ice would bear them down and then they would fall off and probably kill some one in doing so. They had had no water-supply in the house for three weeks. For a time water had been fetched from the nearest house, that called Bainriggs on the main road to Grasmere, but now they were frozen up, too, and so Mr. Lovely did not know what to do, and the maids both gave notice when asked to melt snow and blocks of ice that Mr. Lovely dug for them. Fortunately he found it possible to use his smaller car after a time. Its tyres were frozen to the garage floor and, though the anti-freeze mixture had behaved as it should in the radiator, the oil in those parts of the car that held oil was stiff and hindered, instead of lubricating, the poor thing's movements. When the snow-plough had been along Miss Wilson brought her taxi to as near the gate of Lake View as she could get. Then she and Mr. Lovely dug a passage one car wide through the massive wall of snow the plough had cast aside and she fastened a rope to the frost-bound car and started her own engine. Mr. Lovely pushed behind. Miss Wilson's taxi pulled. The little car, suddenly detaching itself from the icy floor, moved forward so that Mr. Lovely fell across its luggage-rack. After Miss Wilson had towed it about the village, and up the Raise and back, it was all thawed out and ran quite well. Thus, when the snow-plough had been along fairly recently Mr. Lovely was able to fetch water from the Flax Home Industry house till that froze up, and then from the schoolmaster's, and eventually from the house in the village that remained miraculously unfrozen and supplied water all day long to endless people, who tramped ceaselessly in and out of its kitchen, slopping water on the floor as they left.

Early in February Mr. Lovely felt hardy and adventurous one morning and so he walked up the White Moss road, thinking of Lake View. When the thaw came, what would happen to Lake View? All that snow in the roof valleys, where would it go as it melted? The builder had warned him where it would go, but in the frenzy of having some kind of roof put up, to shelter mother and the kids, Mr. Lovely in the dry, open weather of autumn had paid but little attention to talk of deep snow. Also, the lake was too near Lake View; he had been saying that for some time but nobody could do anything about it apparently. He had told the local Surveyor that a few handy, hefty men with spades could clear the lake outlet and so cause the water-level to drop quite a number of inches, which would be more hygienic for the whole village and make him feel less watery at Lake View. But the Surveyor said any men that were handy and hefty were either gone to the war, or on war work, or else run off their stout legs with too much to do at home.

'That pain in mother's toe, probably it is due to the lake,' thought Mr. Lovely, despondently staring at a Herdwick sheep that, even more despondent than he, was perched with its match-stick hind legs on a snow-drift and its fore legs on a wall top, trying to reach a ragged bit of moss that showed beneath the edge of the snow that capped the wall. 'And when the snow melts and comes streaming down into Gerald's room and the maids' room and the kitchen, what shall we do then? And if this snow gets away, there may be more, and next winter more still.'

There had been no snow-plough up here on White Moss and at the top of the hill Mr. Lovely felt exhausted and stood still, up to his knees in snow. There was no sunshine; the sky was paper white and yet darker than the fells, which stood with their snowy edges delicately outlined against it. There was no wind and the silence was unbroken, save by the faint thud as snow slipped, now and then, from some overloaded branch in Bainriggs wood. The air was cold, and pure with the scentless purity of snow that lies deep upon the good earth scents of moss and leaf-mould and wet grassland. In spite of the misty sky there was a painful glare and Mr. Lovely looked from the white road and over the snowy woods up to the white fells, against the white sky, and felt his eyes ache and a kind of dizziness assail him. Then he heard the sounds of some one digging snow and groaning, and he went on to a gateway and saw an elderly gentleman, flinging snow on a great, flat shovel from his buried path and over a wall. Each time he flung it over he groaned, swore, and scooped up another shovelful.

'Can I help?' said Mr. Lovely, still out of breath himself. Thus, they became friendly. The old gentleman explained that he had burst a muscle in his chest, shovelling and flinging snow on the previous day, and that he found it exquisitely painful to shovel and fling snow to-day.

'But my chauffeur has gone to the war, and the maids resent being asked to dig snow, and my wife fell down the front steps this morning and injured the bottom of her back, and we expect the doctor, and I must clear a path for him,' said the suffering gentleman.

This gentleman had, within his gate and at the end of the buried path, an immense house, called Grey Craggs. He had lived in it for thirty years but, even before the snow came, he had been beginning to feel that he and his wife were getting too old for White Moss.

'And maids don't like it, they don't indeed,' said he, thankfully watching Mr. Lovely shovel and fling snow. 'I have a little place down in Devon and, when this damned snow is gone and people can get about again, I think I shall take advantage of the war demand for houses and sell Grey Craggs.'

'Ho!' said Mr. Lovely, forgetting in his excitement that he was in Grasmere and not St. Helens. 'Ho! Will you indeed? Now, I am looking for a place, somewhere well up above the lake, if you know what I mean. How high are you, and what are you thinking of asking for the property, just between ourselves as you might say?'

As a result of this meeting and his charitable action in helping to dig a two-foot deep trench along the old gentleman's path, which they completed just as the doctor arrived, on ski so that their labour was wasted, Mr. Lovely bought Grey Craggs. Before any of their several circles of friends and acquaintances knew of this transaction the village knew of it. The village knew the price that Mr. Lovely had been induced to pay and commended the business capacity of the old gentleman. The village would be sorry to lose the old gentleman, with whom they were fairly familiar by now, but they had been thinking for some time past that he would die soon as, indeed, he did a month after getting settled in at his little place in Devon.

Thus was Corys able to tell Richard that Mr. Lovely had bought Grey Craggs before anybody but the village and herself knew of it, since from Old John or Jane Peascod she heard everything the village heard, even though neither of these ancient retainers set foot off the Bainriggs estate.

'Miss Cory was mortal interested when I told her about Mr. Lovely buying Grey Craggs,' said Old John, later in that evening when Richard had been to Bonfire Hall to ask them about a doctor. 'She'll have it in mind to buy back Penny Rock, to be sure, but she'll not be able to do it. He'd ask a fancy price for it, and that house of his they call Lake View. It's the rich men, like him, as asks fancy prices, and gets them too. Nay, Miss Corys' had her money for Penny Rock and spent it on this spot, at her own wish, and now she'll git nea more money. She mun just mak' the best o' it, as we all must as life goes on. Ay, to be sure, so we must.'

'Thankless old ruffian,' thought Richard, of Old John, but knew he was wrong in thinking so.

The weather went on being arctic. Every few days it snowed again, heavily and for hours at a time. The temperature fell, once more, to below zero, and the snow, by now so deep that walls and rocks showed as shapeless mounds of white, had the light, dry quality of icing sugar. Where it thawed on the surface and then froze again it glittered in sunshine like the snow fields of the Engadine. Where the snow-plough could not penetrate people trod themselves troughs to walk in and householders, like the old gentleman on White Moss, cut and dug vertical walled gorges a foot wide down their garden paths. Each time it snowed these troughs and gorges were filled again, level with the white surface. For a week Corys could not collect eggs from her hens because of the great drift against the hen-house door. There were few cars to be seen on the roads and these only pottered about the village and then had an awful time meeting the mail-van on the narrower roads that led to their respective homes, for the walls of snow on either side of the snow-plough's track made passing impossible. Every day some one fell down, walking on the roads, and those living on the flat felt themselves lucky, for hills were often so slippery, owing to the snow-plough and alternate thawings and freezings, that it was possible to walk only on the edge of the frozen mass of snow at the sides.

One day Richard went with Corys to look for Jownie Wife, who had not been seen for some days so that P.C. Smith thought she must be dead. He had sprained an ankle, falling on the icy road opposite the Book Shop, so he could not look for her himself. Richard and Corys went across the lake. Sheep had been wandering over it that morning, their backs and breasts white with frost and snow-dust, and Corys had observed they did not sink in the deep snow upon the ice.

'If their little hoofs don't sink in we can probably walk on the frozen surface,' said Corys, and she succeeded in doing so, though Richard went in to his knees now and then.

They went up the White Moss road and stood at the top, looking at the country-side. In the windy sunshine, crystal clear, clouds of snow were blown like smoke from Loughrigg. Jackdaws waddled in the snow, near by, now one foot sinking, now another. A farmer tucked bunches of hay among the bushes for the sheep that streamed, at his call, up over the snow slopes, their woolly bodies flat with hunger.

'Oh! Richard!' said Corys, forgetting her troubles and clutching his arm for a jay, perhaps ten yards away, had alighted on a great snow-drift. For an instant, before it saw them, it sat in the smooth, white curve of the drift, vivid as a jewel with its fierce crest, its brilliant eye, blue and pink and white feathers, looking as exotic in the frozen whiteness as some tropical flower. Then it saw them and flew, dodging behind the snowy tree branches.

'Oh! Lovely!' said Corys, blinking her eyes, for now the north easterly air was drifting a cloud of fine snow crystals, sharp and icy, upwards over the roadside wall.

'Richard, do you think it is possible that Mr. Lovely may be willing to sell Penny Rock now that he has bought Grey Craggs?' said Corys, as they began to stumble towards Jownie Wife's shack.

'I suppose so,' said Richard, as unsympathetically as possible. 'But he'd want a big price for it, and the house.'

'There are some things it seems impossible to do without, whatever they cost,' said Corys, in a low voice.

Jownie Wife's shack was buried in snow, but she had dug her doorway clear and wanted no help from anybody.

'T'se food and yard wood in plenty,' said she, resenting their inquiries, 'and I'm warmer here nor you in your old hogg'us, or you in the Hall,' she added, looking bitterly at them in turn.

As they left Jownie Wife Corys walked out on a tree-grown ridge on her own Bainriggs land that commanded a view down to the lake. Through the white woodlands she could see Penny Rock, as white. All the roofs of Lake View were a foot deep in snow; this side of its walls was plastered white with the last fall, that had frozen on the painted weather boarding. Only the smoke from its chimneys, grey as mist, and the sharp slopes and ridges of its roofs distinguished it from the white plain of the lake, the shapeless, muffled trees and the buried land, that had high drifts where once were hollows and hollows where the wind had swept ridges and rocks almost clear.

'If Mr. Lovely decides to sell Penny Rock I shall feel like that,' said Corys, waving an arm vaguely towards the baffling snows, 'all kind of extraordinary and confused. I don't think I shall be able to bear it, if he says he will sell. It will be too exciting. I couldn't sleep last night, thinking of Penny Rock. There are some things one wants so frightfully it seems one must have them. I shall tell Mummie and Daddy they must let me sell out a chunk of something; grandfather left me a little money. After all, it's my money, but I can't sell any out till I am twenty-one, unless they consent.'

Corys seemed to be talking as much to herself as to Richard. He thought she had forgotten by now that he had ever frightened her but, a moment later, he knew he was mistaken.

'Cory, if you want so frightfully badly to buy Penny Rock back I'll see if I can lend you the money, and you can pay me back, any time, little by little,' said Richard, surprised to find his voice rather breathless and this not because of his extreme financial imprudence.

Corys turned and looked at him and he saw that he had frightened her again.

'Oh, no, Richard, but thank you very much,' she said, with a manner that made it impossible for him to urge his suggestion. Alarmed, wary, with an air of drawing herself back from dangers half unknown Corys spoke and turned to throw a handful of snow at a sheep, who lay on the snow near by. It stood up, waggled its little jaws at Corys and gave a faint, murmuring bleat, the merest whisper of a baa-a.

'They always talk like that in deep snow,' said Corys.

But Richard was not interested in the sheep.

'I must say I wonder now that you ever sold the land,' said Richard, with a dryness in his tone that Corys recognized with that quick reaction to disapproval which is one sign of youthful uncertainty.

'Ah, but I didn't know what it would be like,' said Corys. 'If I had known I would not have sold it, not for Old John or anybody's sake.'

They walked down again, irritated with each other. It had begun to snow and the white trees showed vague as puffs of mist while the road ahead was hidden by the fast driving flakes. Their ceaseless motion and their whiteness made Richard feel half mesmerized. How much longer would he walk with Corys through a world where nothing seemed real?

'Rudie Sweeting made a jelly the other day and put it in a snow-drift to set,' said Corys, aware that Richard was annoyed about something. 'She was busy. It began to snow and the jelly was buried. She hasn't found it yet.'

CHAPTER XX

Every doctor in the Lake District was exhausted with overwork. With the population three times more than normal and, perhaps, four times more often ill than was normal, owing to one aspect or another of the war, they worked day and night, without a holiday, and took their share also in the duties of the Home Guard or A.R.P. Richard decided that his medical problems were not urgent enough to warrant him laying his heart, like an odd-shaped last straw, on the overburdened shoulders of any one of them. When the weather grew more reasonable he would go to Liverpool, where he had a doctor friend. Liverpool would certainly not have had over population included among its other war burdens.

Richard was glad of the snow which prevented him from going to Liverpool. He knew some change in his life was ahead but he did not want it to come yet. He spent part of each day on the Island, beside a big fire, reading about Bainriggs and how a tenant in 1440 had an unreasonable cow in the wood, eating bark illicitly, and how the de Bainriggs were trying to kill bracken in 1780. He would wonder, pausing in his reading, what Corys' ancestors did when this and that occurred, when the plague came in 1597, and when Rydal Hall was sacked by Cumberland Roundheads in 1645.

Early in the afternoon he would walk back to land, with the snows of Silver How, wan in its own great shadow, ahead and the sunset glow, gold and then a dim rose, on the white eastern fell tops. He would let himself dream, just while the snows lasted and while life in the dale was so strangly conditioned by isolation, and the silent, muffled weight of snow, and the white glare, that seemed to numb the eyes. When the first bus got over the Raise from the north, then, Richard told himself, he would force himself to wake.

Meanwhile, the Lovelys moved up to Grey Craggs, from which the old gentleman and his wife retreated, temporarily, to a friend's house in the village. It had seemed that a move must be impossible in the snow, but Mr. Lovely desired to escape from Lake View before snow water got into it and he directed operations, and paid for them, so well that everything was eventually carried up White Moss, sometimes on a lorry, sometimes in the arms of Robert the builder's men.

Soon after the move Corys paid a call on Mr. Lovely, kicking the snow from her rubber boots on his Shap marble doorstep.

'Isn't the light odd, in snow?' said Corys, her voice gone husky, as usual, because she was agitated. 'The white ground seems to shine so queerly into a room.'

Corys was thinking how queer Mr. Lovely looked, with this white light shining up under his fat little chin.

'Do you like Grey Craggs?' said Corys, trying to speak as one grown-up to another.

Mr. Lovely looked back at her, perfectly aware that the young miss was after something. He was not surprised when, without waiting for an answer to her questions, she asked another.

'Will you be selling Penny Rock, Mr. Lovely, and, if so, what would you want for it?'

Mr. Lovely put the tips of his fingers together and his head on one side.

'I may sell Lake View,' he said, 'and the land, if I can get a good offer for the whole. Or, if I don't get a good offer I may let Lake View and keep the land in my own hands. There's another bit, could be used for a building plot, towards the river. I couldn't take less than twelve hundred for house and land, not as things are, as you may say. There's people'd give me fifteen hundred, straight down, for it, they're that put to it to find somewhere to go, but I'm not one to make profit out of the war.'

'Twelve hundred. Ah!' said Corys, steadily enough, and as if she was not at all astonished, but her face went white, as if the snow glare had suddenly washed all life from it.

Twelve hundred! Corys walked home over the lake, pondering. Her grandfather had left her six thousand pounds. In just over two years she would be twenty-one. Would Mr. Lovely consent to let the property until then, if she signed a paper promising to pay for it on some specified date?

'I must have it!' said Corys, to herself, on the snowy lake, and lifted her face to the icy breeze that was blowing a drift of snow powder low above the frozen surface.

The Sweetings looked beautiful in the snow. In their blue coats, with the silver fur collars fastened close about their throats, hatless, and wearing the inevitable rubber boots, they tramped the valley, day by day, and neglected their housekeeping to do so. Where all was colourless and all things, fells, trees, rocks and roofs, smoothed into the same rounded shapes, the blue Sweetings with their yellow heads moved vivid as jays and elderly war guests who had been house-bound for weeks watched to see them go by.

It was they who found that Miss Trusty was dead. With immense exertions they waded and scrambled their way up Red Bank and past High Close and so, sometimes gliding their little feet along the glazed and frozen snow and sometimes floundering through it, they came to The Hen House, their blue pockets full of sweets for Miss Trusty and their blue coats and pale heads dusted over with snow crystals. The Hen House door was shut, but smoke rose, blue as snow in shadow, in a little wavering thread from the chimney and the snow that had fallen in the night had been dug away from the doorway. The Sweetings knocked, and knocked again. At last, and but timidly, they opened the door and there was Miss Trusty, dead. She sat in her old arm-chair, comfortably, in her own chair, beside her own fire, and fallen beside her lay the light spade with which she had, an hour ago, dug away the snow. The great cold and the little exertion of shovelling snow had killed Miss Trusty and, from the look on her face, it seemed that her body, left here in the cold and loneliness, knew that she had found something long desired.

The Sweetings were frightened. Never before had they seen anybody dead. It had always seemed to them natural that people should be born but most unnatural that they should die. Just so, in the clear freshness of their happy mornings they never paused to think that in the evening they would be tired and glad of rest, glad even to lie in the curious trance of sleep, helpless and still. They ran, stumbling, and weeping, back to Fold-in-the-Wood and Mr. Sweeting had to walk into the village and tell P.C. Smith that Miss Trusty was dead, since, though she might legally be left to live alone, she must not be left dead, alone, above Chapel Style.

Richard heard the news that afternoon from Maimie, whom he met walking back to the Hall after unravelling a pound of wool that an old lady's pet dog had ravelled.

'What does she pay you for doing that?' asked Richard, after he had said how truly sorry he was, for himself and all Miss Trusty's friends, because she had died. 'She was restful, like a rock. You could lean on her,' Maimie had answered, sadly too, for she liked to lean.

'I get a shilling an hour for reading aloud, combing dogs, walking out children (or dogs), paying bills, unravelling wool and listening to old people who like to tell me we are losing the war,' said Maimie, with a demure humour that Richard did not remember her having possessed when she was engaged to him. 'When the combed dogs bite me, I get a little more.'

At this point of their walk the red mail van came rushing along, clanking its chains. They had to climb on the frozen snow that lay in a great bank at the road-side. The mail van charged by, turned too sharply into a gateway and stuck in the snow masses accumulated at the side of the beaten track. The postman, whistling, and thinking about his son in the R.A.F., got out and dug himself free.

'Letter for the Hall,' said the postman as Richard and Maimie came by, having scrambled down after walking on the wall top for a few yards.

Richard took it; it was for Blodwen, from her husband.

'Have you heard that Mr. Lovely is going to sell Lake View to some one who will run it as a tea-house?' said Maimie.

'*What?*' said Richard.

'I heard it at my old lady's,' said Maimie. 'She had it from her landlady, and the boy who brings the oil told her. He takes oil to the Lovelys and walks on Sundays with the Lovely house boy. So it may be true. You know the boy, Richard, a little fellow who looks about twelve. Last Saturday he took out eighty gallons of oil. Cory says the central heating has burst in all the big houses and so they burn oil stoves.'

'A tea-house! Lake View! Did you hear how much Lovely is to get for it?' asked Richard, caring nothing about any boy who carried oil.

'£1500,' said Maimie, 'or so the fish man told me. He came while I unravelled wool and I had to go and beg him for sausages and so we got talking. He says the policeman was told to blow his whistle when there was an air-raid warning, in some little village, I forget its name, in Cumberland I believe. So there came a warning and he blew it, long blasts on it, like they say. And every one came out and stood in the doorways saying, "Poor Mr. Plasket! He's lost his dog again." And now they don't have it blown at all. Why should they?'

Richard had fallen into his old custom of not hearing what Maimie said. He brooded upon Lake View, as a tea-house, with red umbrellas up beside the lake, the wireless on, tea-cups on little tables under the beeches (those that remained), and thin, scratchy pictures of Wordsworth's head on the cups. A car park would no doubt be arranged, at the side of the house. There would be an artistic sign swinging by the roadside; 'Cumberland Teas: rum butter: Grasmere gingerbread,' would say the sign, for most people and, no doubt, all sign painters think Grasmere is in that county.

'Hell!' said Richard, just as Maimie had told him that young Mr. Lovely was home again because he had had a septic finger owing to something to do with a bomb and, anyhow, Easter was not far off.

'I beg your pardon,' said Richard, and Maimie said 'Granted!' primly, just as she used to do.

Corys appeared at Old John's that evening. The way she strode into the kitchen, kicking a mat aside and without greeting either of them made Richard compare her, for the moment, to her tempestuous grandmother. 'After all,' mused Richard, looking at her vivid face, brown with long days in the sunlit snows, 'she has Grandy's blood in her as well as that of Welshmen and all the old de Bainriggs, who seemed to have been at least as savage as their times.'

'Richard! I've just met Jownie Wife and she says Mr. Lovely is selling

Lake View, and all the land, to somebody who will use it as a tea-house,' said Corys. 'Is it true?'

'I don't know,' said Richard.

'Ay, it's true, to be sure,' said Old John, placidly sitting. 'Sit down, Miss Cory, it's a long time since thou's been here.'

'Well, will you please find out?' said Corys, not sitting, and not, apparently, hearing Old John. 'I'll come with you to Grey Craggs and wait outside. I'd go myself, but I daren't—I couldn't ask—'

'Have you heard Miss Trusty's dead?' asked Old John, as Richard rather reluctantly got up. Old John spoke with relish; it always seemed he gained a solid satisfaction from telling news of a death. Yet, he had liked and respected Miss Trusty and would miss her.

'Ay, she's dead,' said Old John, 'and there'll be more now. Deaths always come in threes and I'se heard tell old Wilson Fleming is in a bad way to-night.'

'Miss Trusty dead?' said Corys, with a shrill note in her voice, and she suddenly sat down.

'I believe it is true,' said Richard. 'The Sweetings went up there and found her. I expect this great cold was too much for her, and perhaps her heart wasn't too good, but she hadn't been ill. She must have died all in a moment—'

Richard did not know what more to say. How did one comfort any one about a death? But Old John was not at all put out.

'Ay, you'll be likely to feel it, Miss Cory,' he said, with a grave gusto. 'You'll git nobody like Miss Trusty for your friend now she's gone.'

Corys sat for a moment, in silence, looking at the fire. Then she got up, with the mien of one reheating a fiery resolution.

'Will you come to Mr. Lovely, Richard? And ask him how much he is to get for the sale and ask him, will he, instead, let Lake View, so that I can buy it myself when I am twenty-one?'

It was nearly an hour later when Richard came out of the Grey Craggs gateway on to the snow-covered road and found Corys, standing where she had stood, without moving, since he left her.

'Gerald is home, looking very fit in spite of his finger,' said Richard, with that bright irrelevance that seeks to postpone bad news.

'Mr. Lovely won't wait. He will sell it, now. For how much?' said Corys, her voice low and yet sharp with longing to know the worst.

'For fifteen hundred pounds,' said Richard. 'The man who is buying it is experienced in running what Mr. Lovely calls tea gardens and it seems he expects to make a very good thing out of it. Of course, after the war, he'll have a season of only about three months and I dare say, after the war, when all the strangers have gone home again, it will be shut up all winter.'

'Is he selling it, or is it sold?' asked Corys. 'Because I might, if Grandy were to back me up, but fifteen hundred—'

'It is sold; or rather it will be, directly both parties have agreed on details. Mr. Lovely's solicitor is drawing up an agreement now,' said Richard, glad to put an end to Corys' agonizing financial questionings. 'I told Mr. Lovely you would like to buy it when you came of age but he said he always took a bird in the hand, when he could get one, and now he had got one.'

'A tea-house!' said Corys, in an incredulous whisper. It could not be possible! Anything so awful could not be allowed to happen!

'Good-bye!' said Corys, a moment later, and darted down some steps and so out upon the lake, for they had walked as they talked.

Richard watched her figure, moving, smaller and smaller across the ice, until she reached the Bonfire Hall boat-landing. There was a light wind from the north. It came leisurely through the snowy cup of the Raise from a leaden sky.

'Poor Cory!' thought Richard, and shuddered with cold as he stood.

CHAPTER XXI

'I make no pretensions to be a Christian,' said Grandy, to the three ladies she had rescued, and Blodwen. 'I admit freely that I am not one, though I wish very much that I were. It is contemptible and should be impossible to be a half Christian, but that is what I am, so far as I know. I admit, again, that I don't know much.'

To this only the lady who had wept in Red Lion Square replied, and she did so only because she was still nervous.

'At the work party they were saying that nineteen hundred years of Christianity has brought us to this war,' said this nervous lady, tittering. 'Of course, it was a shocking thing to say.'

Blodwen looked up quickly, expecting that Grandy would now suffer from one of the more violent expressions of her personality. Blodwen sat with the others this morning because she was too happy to be alone. Usually, she found morning calls an intolerable nuisance and, leaving the visitors to Grandy, continued busily at work about the house. But the letter that Maimie had brought her yesterday afternoon had been from her husband and he had written to say that his Government Department, and he, were to move forthwith to Westpool, a seaside resort, where the work of governing would be carried on in a more detached and purely academic atmosphere than obtained in London.

'Darling, darling Miles! He'll be safe,' thought Blodwen, watching Grandy anxiously, because of the nervous lady's remark.

'Nineteen hundred years of *what*?' said Grandy, with astonishing calm. 'Did you say of Christianity? Has any country, anywhere, had one year of Christianity since the world began? Tell me that!'

The nervous lady could not.

'It all depends, doesn't it, on what you mean by Christianity?' she said, tittering again.

'Indeed, it is time some one found out that,' said Grandy, suddenly contemplative, and she fell into one of her alarming silences.

It had not snowed for a week and the ice on the lake had become, mysteriously, almost free from snow, though it still lay deep on the country-side. The frosts had been less severe and it had thawed at midday.

As Richard trudged across to his hogg-house one morning he found it odd to be walking again on dark ice, marked by white cracks, and with snow only in detached cakes, here and there. He reflected as he walked that he would try and go to Liverpool next week. It was time he went. There was a pale haze everywhere; the twigs of buried bushes began to show through ragged holes in the domes of snow that covered them; the snow was slipping off the Island trees so that the tawny oak leaves and dim, ruddy tinge on birch trunks looked vivid and exotic in the white landscape. The ice was groaning; he had heard the formless sounds of its stresses and strains in the night. As the lake waters sank a little beneath it, it sank too, but only with those dolorous moanings that are one of the most grim of country sounds. Already, though it was but ten o'clock, Richard walked through a thin film of water, come whether from the inflowing waters of the river or from the ice itself he did not know.

'Is it really going to thaw at last?' thought Richard, looking up at the dull sky and feeling a breeze, cold but damp as mist, upon his face.

He went into the hogg-house, built himself a big fire and settled down, determined to forget Corys and her trouble, that he now began to feel a little tiresome and even faintly ridiculous. Like her father he inclined to think that Corys was being rather absurd and, perhaps, rather morbid. Or so he told himself he thought.

He had brought his lunch with him and he was pensively regarding a tin of baked beans when Corys burst in upon him, as if his thoughts had conjured up her bodily presence.

'Good morning. Have you a tin opener about you?' said Richard, ardently hoping she would not mention Lake View.

But she did.

'No, and you can't do anything without one. I have tried, but I only cut myself,' said Corys. 'Richard, to whom does Lake View belong now, to-day I mean? To Mr. Lovely or the person who has bought it?'

'To Mr. Lovely. He told me the various formalities would take a day or two to complete,' said Richard.

'Ah, that is what I thought,' said Corys. 'Is Mr. Lovely very rich, do you think?'

'He told me he pays nineteen and sixpence on each pound of quite a lot of his income, which means he is rich, very rich, though it doesn't sound like it,' said Richard.

'Thank you,' said Corys, which she did not usually say.

Soon afterwards, she left, and Richard decided to try boiling his tin to try and make it burst of itself, but gently, he hoped.

Just before dusk he locked up the hogg-house. The tin of beans had not burst, fortunately, and he had found the tin opener so late in the day it had not seemed worth while to use it then. So he felt hungry and irritable and realized he would be glad to get back to land and the sociable comfort of Old John's cottage. There had been gusts of wind as he sat in the hogg-house that sounded strangely after the long calm of frost and snow, and he had heard snow falling from the roof with heavy thuds. Once, when he had stepped out to empty his kettle, he had been astonished to feel a sense of relaxing in the air as if some tension had been slackened, and the hogg-house, when he re-entered it, felt chill and dank in spite of the fire. Now, at dusk, he saw that, once more, there were reflections from the lake. The film of water on the ice had deepened so that Silver How stood upside down in it, its snowy, shadowed bulk oddly criss-crossed by the white lines of cracks in the ice below the water. The Island pines were dark, the thick hoar frost of the night having melted, the rocks were dark again and the patch he had swept bare of snow by his door was green. He thought he had never seen a pleasanter colour after the weeks of arctic whiteness.

A moment later, however, and he began to curse the thaw. It had been rapid enough to maroon him. The ice already supported water nearly a foot deep and as Richard cautiously waded on to it he felt his weight added dangerously to its burden. The ice sheet gave beneath his feet, sagging and groaning, so that the water rose nearly to his knees.

'Oh, dash and blast!' said Richard, and stepped quickly and lightly back on to the Island.

During that day of thaw Gerald Lovely had been very well entertained up at Grey Craggs. This was his first visit to his new home. He felt proud of it. Lake View he had been ashamed of; it had been shoddy, though a temporary convenience. But Grey Craggs, that stone mansion with the furniture from High Castle, St. Helens, opulently disposed about its enormous rooms, was a house he could take pride in. He got up late, because of his septic finger, and the morning was diversified by the falling of the Grey Craggs gutters. These solid, cast-iron troughs had already supported nearly a foot of ice for the past few weeks and now, snow slipping from the roof on top of them, made it impossible for them to support it any longer. So, all through the morning, lengths of guttering, heavily weighted with ice, fell most dangerously, now on this side of the house and now on that, and snow, in great masses, fell with them, or independently, and with a momentum that made it almost as deadly as the falling gutters. It amused Gerald to dodge about, in and out of verandah doors, looking up, taking cover, darting out again and watching over the housemaid's passage to and from the dust-bin. In spite of his care, for she was an exceptionally competent housemaid, she was almost brained by a bit of downspout, that crashed on the back-door step a moment too soon to catch her.

By afternoon it seemed that anything movable upon, or adjacent to, the roof must have descended, and Gerald felt bored and began to telephone to his friends, the wires having just been repaired after the last snow-storm.

'I have a septic finger so will all the girls come to tea?' telephoned Gerald, to the Sweeting girls' nearest neighbour, who cursed aloud before he put down his receiver but took the message to Fold-in-the-Wood because of the girls' lovely heads, through the snow that had now gone heavy, like flour.

Gerald telephoned the same message to the Girl with the Purple Hair, a war guest whose other name was unknown in the village, and to the pretty girl with green eyes, from The Swan, and then he bethought him of that kind, womanly little creature whom Blunt had jilted and who had been nearly drowned in the cloud-burst. Too bad, thought Gerald, idly flopping over the pages of the telephone directory; what was her name? He rang up Bonfire Hall and then he remembered it was Maimie. Would she, and Corys too, come to tea? After a pause Corys answered, in a voice the deepness of which made its abruptness the more noticeable. She would not come, but Maimie would. Thank you, said Corys, and rang off at once.

At the tea-party Maimie told a story about her old lady of that morning, the one to whom she simply had to listen. 'Usually, she talks happily all the morning and I just say Yes, and No, and How marvellous! now and then, but this morning she said some one was snoring up in her loft. So they were; I heard them. She was sure it was a young parson who had been bombed in Manchester and had asked her to take him in, but I said how could he have got up there? So I got a ladder and went up through a trap-door, with a candle. And it was a large white owl, sound asleep and snoring!'

The white light of the snow showed nothing odd or ugly in Maimie's face. When she had finished her little story and they had applauded it the light of humour died at once from her eyes and she sat looking at the snowy slopes of Loughrigg, illuminated by the evening light which shone dimly over Red Bank. 'The light on those snows reminds me of the pale light of the narcissus fields in flower, high above the Lake of Geneva,' said Maimie, looking at Gerald for sympathy and comprehension.

'She's been about a bit,' thought Gerald, who had not, because Mr. Lovely said it was better to see England first and gave Gerald no money for holidays. 'And she's suffered! Any one can see that. Poor kid, what she must have seen in Chelsea!'

He called her a kid in his mind in an unconscious attempt to assert his manhood but he thought of her as a woman, a little, brave woman who kept her end up, even with that fellow Blunt, who had turned her down.

The Sweetings had not come to the party because they still wept whenever they thought of Miss Trusty, dead in her stone hut, but the Girl with the Purple Hair and the pretty girl from The Swan had come as well as Maimie and it seemed to Gerald that it was an exceptionally pleasant tea-party.

'You can't go yet, not for hours,' said Gerald, to his party, after tea. 'I am going to sing to you, but I can't play the piano with this finger. Can any of you? Play it I mean, with your fingers?'

Only Maimie possessed the old-fashioned accomplishment of playing the piano. She was not quick at reading new music and she and Gerald had to go over each song several times before he was at all satisfied. When he was, he sang triumphantly, in his voice that was as lovely as his name, and the others joined in the choruses of the rollicking songs he sang.

'You can't go home till midnight,' said Gerald, rummaging in his piles of music. 'Here, this one, Maimie. We must do this one. Midnight, and I'll see you all home after we've had sausages and sardines, hot and cold, and mixed or not. Now, Maimie, go ahead. ... "Early one morning—"'

The moon was now past the full. Richard, ill-tempered in his hogg-house, thought he would watch for its rising above Rydal Fell, and about eleven he looked out. The moon was not up but there was a pale glow behind the white edge of Rydal Fell. Since midday the woods had lost their whiteness; they now looked vaguely dark upon the snowy hill-sides. The lower end of the lake was filled with their shadowy reflections and they and the black water made a gulf of darkness closing the valley beyond the dim, snow slopes. As Richard stood, listening to the faint whisper of the miniature ripples that washed ashore at his feet, he saw the moon's rim rise above the fell ridge, blurred by a blowing haze. He thought how odd and pleasant it was to hear water stirring, after the long, frost-bound silence of the dale. He hoped the southerly breeze would blow harder, bringing warmth and thaw so that he would soon be able to row himself ashore. The solitude of his Island began to irk him, now that changes lay so near ahead.

Something, he thought a sound so faint that he was uncertain whether or not he had heard it, drew his attention again to the darkness at the end of the lake. After a moment he saw something, in the midst of the darkness. A point of light shone out and then broadened instantly, so that he saw the dark tracery of tree branches black against it. Now he clearly heard the crackling of fire, as he had heard it in the Bainriggs woods on the day he came to Grasmere nearly two years ago. Across the rippled water, that was now beginning to catch the light of the rising moon, he heard fire, crackling and hissing, and saw flames beginning to leap high among the trees.

'Is it, can it be, Lake View on fire?' thought Richard, trying to decide exactly where, upon the lake shore, shone that red-gold, quivering light with the cloud of smoke, glowing red, above it.

'Jownie Wife again?' thought Richard, and instantly another thought came into his mind. 'Nonsense, incredible,' said he, in his mind, and sternly.

CHAPTER XXII

Earlier that evening Gerald had walked, with his three girl guests, down the snow-covered White Moss hill and had got the family small car out of the shed at the foot, where it had been kept since the great snows began.

'Jolly to see the lake thawed at last,' said the girl with green eyes, looking down at it in the dusk. 'It looks so dead when it is all ice. I shall go for a row to-morrow.'

'So shall I,' said Gerald promptly, looking at her.

He drove home the Girl with the Purple Hair and the pretty girl with green eyes and then took the white road Back o' Lake. It was not dark and this road had been snow-ploughed, but the cleared track was only one car wide and Maimie felt alarm at the way he drove. She was aware that Gerald had had at least one cocktail too many but, remembering that it was often said of the Lakes four-in-hand drivers that they drove better when drunk, she hoped for the best. However, he suddenly stopped the car, just before a blind bend, and began to propose marriage to Maimie.

'See here, Maimie, I think we hit it off pretty well, don't you?' said Gerald, putting his left arm along the back of her seat.

He then told her that he was pretty rich already and would be richer later on; that he did not care for young girls; that he had been wanting to choose a wife and had now chosen her.

'As soon as I'm through with the University and before I go into the R.E.s we'll be married,' said Gerald, and was painfully astonished when Maimie said no.

'No, Gerald. You're, you're too young,' said Maimie, carefully choosing her words so as to keep cocktails out of them, but speaking with some haste because she was convinced that a car would come round the blind bend and smash them. 'I could not bear to—to spoil your career. I am so much older than you, and I've no money, and—well, anyhow, no, Gerald,' said Maimie, listening anxiously for the sound of a car's engine. It would be just like Rudie Sweeting to come crashing along, because of a red warning or something. She was besotted about Red Cross work and always drove like mad when summoned to the First Aid Post.

Maimie was even more clearly awake than was Corys to the effect of alcohol on affectionate young men. She would much like to marry Gerald but not as a consequence of a befuddled proposal: it might lead to trouble afterwards.

'If you don't drive me home at once I shall get out and walk,' said Maimie with a shrillness that Gerald rightly put down to fear, though he took it to be fear of him. In his present exalted condition a blind bend had ceased to have any significance for Gerald. The thought that Maimie was afraid of him gave him a solemn kind of joy. What a man must he be if a charming woman of the world like Miss Ozzard sat in bodily fear of his advances!

A little sobered, for, after all, she had refused him ('now did she?' thought Gerald; 'I must be perfectly clear on that'), he drove on, set her down on the Bonfire Hall track, turned with the greatest difficulty, and much wheel spinning in the snow, and drove back to the village.

There, in spite of feeling both subdued and triumphant, for he would get her some day but perhaps not so soon as he had hoped, Gerald remembered that he had promised to run on to Lake View and make sure that all was well there. Old John Benson had been burning brushwood and rubbish, dead leaves and what he called chats in a snow hollow just across the road and Mr. Lovely had been fussing about sparks and flying embers, and the long time an ember might dangerously glow and then burst, even more dangerously, into flame. Until he had the money for Lake View Mr. Lovely did not want it to be burnt down, for though it was insured he was not insured against the loss of the excellent bargain he had made with the gentleman who was to run it as a tea-house. So Gerald drove the little car to the Lake View gate and there, to please his father and because he was truthful and could not tell his father that all was well at Lake View unless he had seen that it was, he got out.

By now the moon, as Richard had also observed, was beginning to swing clear of Rydal Fell. Its white light shone already on the Silver How snows and made them glimmer with an unearthly shining. So high above the dale seemed they that they looked like moonlit mists, separated from the land by the dark gulf of the slopes in shadow below them. Gerald did not look at them. He was looking at Lake View, perfunctorily, and thinking the while of Maimie, and beyond Lake View he saw, without noticing it, the pallor of the rippled lake in a shaft of moonlight that slanted down through a hollow in the hill ridge. He had followed the path of white marble chippings past the back of the house and was beginning to round the corner towards the front door when he heard, as Richard did a few moments later, the rustling whisper of fire, tentatively feeling its way among fuel that would soon flare up into a roaring flame. He ran forward and saw that the farther end of the house already had flames running up its green walls, darting, licking, gliding up as if they were too hurried to consume what they touched but must grasp at the whole house at once.

'I must be going cuckoo,' thought Gerald, wondering if what he thought he saw was really there.

Lake View in flames! Or was it owing to that last cocktail?

His doubts notwithstanding Gerald ran about, energetically trying to extinguish with snow the fire that he soon knew to be real, for it scorched his face and hands and he smelt the little hairs on his rough tweed coat singeing under his nose. He found in a moment or two that his attempt was hopeless. The wood was dry, old and thin. It caught alight in a fresh place every few seconds. Soon flames were enclosing the chimney-stack above the kitchen and dancing, like the feet of invisible devils, up and down the part of the roof that was covered with tarred felt.

Gerald, exhausted and almost stupefied by heat and smoke, stepped back and grasped at a beech trunk to steady himself. Thus, looking along the lake shore to turn his face from the heat, he saw a dark figure spring from behind another tree and begin to run. Immediately the irresistible instinct of the chase seized upon Gerald. The wretched creature must have thought himself discovered by Gerald's turn of the head.

'Silly fool; if he had stood still I'd never have seen him in all these lights and shadows,' thought Gerald as he sprang after the person, who was, no doubt, the escaping malefactor, and left Lake View to burn, as it would have done anyhow.

Gerald was in no state to run fast or far, but the creature he chased was hampered by sacks, one over his head and shoulders and one, apparently, wound about his waist. Also he was probably frightened so that he fled carelessly. Along the base of the retaining wall that holds up the road to the Prince of Wales Hotel lies a narrow strip of lake shore, obstructed by alder and hazel bushes, and made uneasy to the feet by shingle and larger stones. Upon this the fugitive stumbled and nearly fell; in recovering he lost time he could not afford to lose. Gerald's outstretched hand just touched the shoulder sack.

'Ouch! Grrr! Le' go!' said the hunted one, and then did that which gave Gerald a shock he never forgot.

'Got you!' said Gerald, grinding his teeth like a pig with indigestion, but more joyfully.

He was wrong. The creature in the sacks wriggled free from his hand and thereupon, silently, quickly and yet with a kind of dainty cautiousness passed out upon the lake. In a moment it was a yard from the shore, in another two, in another—but Gerald shut his eyes.

Sausages, sardines, the songs he had sung, cocktails, his love-making, the lonely frightfulness of the fire at Lake View, these were enough to make Gerald feel a little lightheaded and uncertain of himself. And now, on top of all the other things, was a person walking on water. He opened his eyes, a very little. He saw that the person continued to walk, sunk just so far that the rippled lake hid his feet and ankles. Gerald felt rather sick and shut his eyes again. Arrived in Grasmere only the day before, told of the thaw that had made open water of the lake, he knew nothing of the ice sheet still concealed beneath the moonlit ripples. He clung to a hazel bush, slowly turned his back on the lake and, forgetting his car and Lake View, on fire, crept slowly towards his White Moss home, which he reached with thankfulness. There he woke his Mamma, who was alarmed at his looks and put him to bed, with aspirins inside him and a cold compress on his forehead.

'He seems quite delirious and keeps talking of a figure walking on the lake,' said Mrs. Lovely, to her husband, who was still in bed. 'Can it be that septic finger?'

On the Island Richard Blunt had stood, watching the fire at Lake View with grave eyes. It seemed to have flared to what must surely be its wildest brilliance when he, like Gerald, saw some one walking on the water. This figure, dark against the dimly lit ripples, came suddenly out from the shadow that hid the main road and the narrow beach below it. He saw it only after it had come some yards from this unlit bank of the lake and out into the moonlight.

'Oh, heavens!' said Richard aloud, observing that the figure made towards the Island and thus feeling that his dreadful suspicion about the Lake View fire was about to be confirmed.

'If it is Cory she'll be drowned,' thought Richard, immediately, and after this he saw only the moving figure on the moonlit lake, listened for the dreaded sounds of cracking ice and swirling water, and heard and saw nothing else.

Now the figure was far out from the land, midway between shore and Island. It moved forward slowly and soon Richard could hear the faint sounds of the ice, scrooping and straining beneath it.

'Oh, God!' said Richard, aloud. 'Don't let it break! Don't let it break!'

'If it is Cory, things are not hopeless,' thought Richard. 'She must weigh only half what I do and she is quick and light on her feet.' Ice that would sink and crack under him might sustain her.

Meanwhile the flames from Lake View sank down to a red glow, the moon shone clear from high in the sky and gusts of the warm south wind came whispering in the Island pines that had been snow-laden and silent.

Corys came ashore. As she neared the Island Richard, holding to a hazel stem, leaned far out towards her. She took his hand, waded in and stamped on the snowy grass as if she had some vague idea that she could dry and warm her feet by stamping.

'I was pretty sure I could do it,' said Corys, apologetically. 'I knew the ice was still thick but, about the middle, it felt a bit awful underfoot. However, it was that or nothing; Gerald had his hand right on my shoulder.'

Corys' voice was husky and her hand felt as cold as her feet must be. Richard said nothing but put his arm about her and took her in to the fire. There she unwound the sacks with which she had tried to make herself unrecognizable, took off her shoes and stockings, and sat down with an exaggerated calmness that did not hide the agitation which was making her shiver more and more, in spite of the radiant glow from the burning oak logs.

'I made a good job of Lake View anyhow,' said Corys, giggling, because Richard had not said a word. Level-headed though she was his silence made even Corys feel that if she did not giggle she would scream. 'And I was perfectly right to burn it. It was wicked, there on Penny Rock, and it would have been worse as a tea-house, miles worse. Mr. Lovely is rich, you told me he was very rich. It won't do him any harm and, anyhow, he must have insured it. Now, he may not trouble to build another house and perhaps one day I shall get a chance to buy back my lovely, lovely land.'

'You were absolutely wrong. I am utterly ashamed of you, Cory,' said Richard.

Richard was angry not only because Corys had burnt Lake View; she had been foolhardy and idiotic in crossing the drowned ice and she had given him a fright that he thought he would never get over. It was bad of her to have destroyed somebody else's house, but worse to have let herself so nearly be drowned.

'I dare say that even half an hour later you couldn't have done it,' said Richard, meaning her crossing of the ice.

'Why not? I wanted to do it when I did because of the moon getting up,' said Corys, speaking of her fire. 'I knew it was rather early but I reckoned on getting away in the dark. And I should have, if I hadn't been so silly. The fire was fascinating. I watched it, instead of slipping off to the footbridge. And then Gerald saw me, by the light of the fire, I suppose, and I had to dart away in the opposite direction. I wonder what he thought when he saw me, walking over the lake!'

Corys giggled again and tried to warm her hands, which were so cold they felt numb.

'I sometimes wonder if you are human,' said Richard, slowly, and there was a tone she had never heard in his voice before.

'Richard!' said Corys.

'And how are you going to feel when Mr. Lovely has you jugged for burning his property?' asked Richard. 'And haven't you any shame for behaving like a melodramatic, spoilt schoolgirl? Just because you wanted something, which you had got rid of of your own free will, you must go and steal from Mr. Lovely. I'd rather be Jownie Wife and burn houses down from revenge than behave like you.'

Richard was in that state of anger which has the recklessness and dignity of all intense emotions. His age, his manhood, the blazing scorn of his anger overwhelmed Corys but did not convince her of error. She was more shaken than appeared by her escape from Gerald and the dangers of the ice. She got, a little shakily, to her feet.

'I can't stand this,' said Corys, in a quiet voice and apparently to herself. She stooped and began to try to pull on her shoes over her cold, bare feet.

'What are you doing?' said Richard, savagely.

She did not reply, but got her shoes on and walked to the door.

'Cory!' said Richard, hurrying after her.

He was only just in time. She fled before him in the moonlight, over the mound of the Island and down to the shore that faced Back o' Lake. She was stepping out on to the ice that, presumably, still lay unbroken beneath the dark, shadowed water when Richard clutched her shoulders.

'Cory! What are you about?' said he, all the anger gone from his voice.

'Curse you!' said Corys, and struggled with such a passion of grief and fury that for a moment he found it hard to hold her. 'Oh, Richard, let me go! You beast! I want to go home!'

CHAPTER XXIII

'Oh, I wish Daddy was here! I do want Daddy!' said Corys, back in the hogg-house.

Richard had never before heard her say that she wanted her father. He had let go of her the moment they were indoors again. Corys had shrunk away from him and huddled herself in the chair opposite his, where she now sat, not looking at him and longing for her father.

'Don't be silly, Cory,' said Richard, uncertain whether to be kind or brisk. 'Your father would have said just as I have, and probably worse.'

'If Daddy were here you wouldn't dare to speak to me like that,' said Corys. 'What business is it of yours?'

'What indeed?' thought Richard. He threw up his hands with a quick gesture of renunciation.

He stood, looking in the fire for a moment, and then spoke in a business-like voice which he tried to make impersonal.

'We have got to get ashore as soon as we can,' said he. 'If you are here when day comes people will think one of two things. They may connect the figure crossing the lake, and hence the fire, with you.'

Corys made no reply and, still, did not look at him. Richard felt a sudden relaxation of his self-control. What was the good of going on, always thinking of Corys, always shielding her from realities of a kind that she would have to face some day?

'Alternatively, they will say that you and I are in love with one another,' said Richard, aware that his words were inexcusable.

With that curious perception that he had of Corys' feelings Richard knew now that he had given her a shock, probably the greatest shock she had experienced in her life. He felt that she drew herself together, mentally and physically, as some animals shrink when touched. For quite

– 189 –

a minute she said nothing but sat still, even her breath quieted after the panting fierceness of the struggle on the Island shore. When she did speak it sounded as if some one cold, remote and impersonal spoke from some part of Corys now withdrawn beyond his reach.

'How can we get ashore?' said Corys.

'By boat, if at all,' said Richard. 'I hope there may be water enough to float it. Of course, we may ground on ice, now and then.'

'We had better go now,' said Corys, standing up.

When he had set his boat afloat Richard hesitated. Should he let Corys go alone?

'I had better come too; two of us may be better able to manage than one in spite of the extra weight. Besides, I shall be glad to be back at Old John's,' said Richard.

Corys rowed. Richard, in the stern, had a fence post with which he thought he might be able to push, on the subsiding ice, and so help their progress. They did not stick, though twice the keel touched the ice. Once ashore he turned down lake towards Bonfire Hall. Corys began a protest but fell silent again, and they walked in silence to the Hall.

'Good night!' said Richard, at once turning his back on her. 'Good night, and thank you,' said Corys and something in her voice oddly reminded him of her grandmother, dignified after one of her rages.

It was about half-past one when Richard got into bed. He lay long awake, thinking of Corys. There had been a moment, in the flood by the footbridge, when, if she had responded to his ardour, he thought the delicate charm she had for him would have taken substance and he would have desired her for his wife, as perhaps, he would never desire again. She had not responded, but had been violently repelled by his emotion. Suddenly, he realized that he was already thinking of Corys as a part of the past, a part of his life in Grasmere, and of a relationship that must be as impermanent as it.

Next day, it appeared that all the valley was convinced that it was Jownie Wife who had set Lake View afire. It could not be proved but, if she had burnt Oak How, which was also not proved, it was not unlikely that she might burn another house. The lack of motive was baffling but people like Jownie Wife did things without apparent motive. Most people were sorry for Mr. Lovely, who was well liked in the village, but they were amused to hear his son had got himself into such a state as to see a figure walking on the water. A very few wondered if the fire raiser could really have got away on the submerged ice, but most thought not. Anyhow, it was an unbounded relief to all the residents that the offensive sight of Lake View was removed from the landscape and it seemed, from what they heard, that no house would replace it, anyhow till after the war. One resident left five shillings for Jownie Wife, at the grocer's.

The Lovely family, while infuriated at the loss of Lake View, were really more upset about Gerald. They were a united family and Myra was sent for from a place called Pontrhydfendigaiad, where she was staying in order to write an article about something or somewhere called Strata Florida. They all felt very anxious about Gerald, who would not believe that the person on the water might have been walking on the ice beneath it. He did not believe there had been any ice beneath it. He said, and truly, that there were no visible signs of ice; he had been told, only that evening, that the lake was thawed. They were only trying to comfort him and make him believe what wasn't true. He knew, too well, he had either seen a spook or else gone queer in the head; personally he thought both these events had happened. He gave up cocktails; suffered increased pain and inflammation in his septic finger; became depressed; sat about, staring at nothing, and was vague in his speech and manner. The doctor, in spite of being overworked, gave time enough to Gerald to decide that he needed rousing from a condition that might lead to serious nervous trouble.

'Who can rouse him?' said Mrs. Lovely, despairingly.

The Sweeting girls went fleetly up White Moss and chattered around him; the Girl with the Purple Hair looked impressively into his eyes; the pretty girl from The Swan told him stories of Grasmere residents that other of the residents would have given much to hear. None of these roused Gerald.

'Try letting him alone,' said the doctor, pausing one day between a coming baby and an old gentleman, going from this world, in a fit.

Let alone, Gerald felt injured. He needed sympathy, and the

affectionate support of some one who admired him. He knew himself to be that phenomenon, so fascinating to patients, that is called an interesting case. No one at Grey Craggs now seemed interested in him. Mournfully remembering his happy state before he saw the spook, Gerald remembered, as well, Maimie and his doubt as to whether or not he had asked her hand in marriage. Might it not be as well to try and find out? His legs were unaffected by his unhappy experience and by his finger, which now kept on healing up too soon. Thus, one evening, he walked Back o' Lake and called on Maimie. His mother saw him go and hoped he would not drown himself.

'Myra, had you better follow him, a good way behind? said his mother.

All this being so, about Gerald, it began to seem that Maimie might expect to have a stroke of luck, some day not very far off.

Two days after Corys had burnt Lake View, Richard, without seeing her again, went to Liverpool. There he saw what he had seen before, in other cities that had been bombed, but after his months of mountain peace he seemed to see it differently. He heard sirens again and the familiar roar of the barrage. He slept in the raid shelter beneath a partly demolished hotel, and slept longer and more soundly than he had been doing, in his silent hogg-house on the Island. On the following morning he saw his doctor friend and found that what he had begun to think must be happening inside him had, indeed, been doing so. Contrary to what the other doctors had said, valves, muscles, ligaments, tissues, nerves, and all the accompanying and remarkable mechanism that influence and are influenced by these objects, had begun to recover, in the case of some of them, whatever they had lost, and, in the case of others, to lose whatever it was they had unfortunately acquired.

'You'll get no doctor to pass you as A1, not now, and not ever,' said the doctor friend. 'But you are as fit as many a man who goes about not knowing that anything is really wrong. For certain types of work you would be perfectly O.K. but you must keep within your limitations. Do this,' said the doctor, 'and don't do that, and you may hope to get no worse and even to improve a bit as time goes on.'

From Liverpool Richard went farther, into the country, to see his mother. Her roof had been put on again but she was much distressed about one of the evacuee children she now harboured. It was a town child and took every opportunity of cutting off the heads of hens.

She seemed pleased that Richard's health had improved but he was more conscious than he had been that, as they both grew older, his mother lost some of her once passionate interest in him.

'So nice to see you, dear. Come again,' said his mother, bidding him farewell when he left, but her eyes roamed past him, to the hens running in the farmer's field across the road. It was not yet time for school; where was Cecil with his blood-stained penknife?

After visiting his mother Richard saw some of his old friends in the R.A.F. He was examined by medical boards. He used all his influence and ingenuity and wangled the old wangles for which he had been noted, even in the Royal Air Force. Eventually he got himself accepted, though not for active service, and so set out for Grasmere, well satisfied.

He had been away nearly a month and it was now the end of May. His train was late and Miss Wilson waited for him three hours in her taxi at Windermere, reading meanwhile a treatise on bee-keeping, for she proposed shortly to keep bees. She told him Grasmere news as they drove beside Windermere, which was calm and still golden with sunset though all the country but the higher fell tops was already shadowed. Two war-guest ladies had quarrelled at a work party and one had wept. The Prince of Wales Hotel was standing empty, once again. Perch-traps had been set in Grasmere and had caught, when pike and eels did not get in, a quantity of perch. The electric light had been off for two days, owing to lightning, and thunder rain, rushing down Tongue Gill, had choked something at the reservoir with bits of bracken and so there was no water in Grasmere one morning.

'The foreman used to go up at night and clear it, but he can't take a lantern now, owing to A.R.P.,' said Miss Wilson, 'and he has to wait till daylight.'

There had been a thunderbolt at Troutbeck, said Miss Wilson. Otherwise there was but little news.

When they got to Grasmere the sky was still bright and blackbirds sang; sheets of wild hyacinths looked like purple shadows in the woods; May trees in flower, each by itself and white as puffs of cloud, stood high on the clear, darkening slopes of Loughrigg and Rydal Fell and Helm Crag; the scent of growing ferns, sweet in the dew, filled the air about Old John's cottage.

'I've heard that all the three Sweeting girls, and Corys de Bainriggs as well, are going to join up,' said Miss Wilson, casually, as she carried Richard's suit-cases into Oak How.

Richard could not sleep that night. How quiet it was! Here, in the quietness, he realized what an enchanted time it had been, his long months on the Island, his walks on the fells, his chair by the fire at Bonfire Hall, and the glamour of Corys, that had at last closed about his senses as the sunlit, clouded fells had closed quietly in upon his hurt and healed it.

And now, soon, he was going back into the war and glad to be going. And Corys, could it be true that Corys was to join up too? He tried to think of Corys away from Grasmere and could not do it; she seemed to him a kind of forest being, bred of waters and the mountain winds, destined to elude, like cloud upon the fell sides, everything that sought to hold her. Would even the army hold Corys? Grinning to himself, Richard thought that it would.

His first meeting with Corys after his absence was made easy by the curious thunder-storms that Grasmere was experiencing at this time. Miss Wilson had talked of thunder and the Sweetings, whom he met next day, told him that there came a storm early every evening, short but sharp.

'It blows up all the telephones; blue flames come out of them,' said the Sweetings, who were delighted to see him again but a little grave and preoccupied because they were going into the Navy. 'The men put the telephones right, and then, next evening, they blow up again. Daddy was in the exchange the other evening and there came a flash and blue flames ran all round the exchange, and shot out of a post-office van, and a bus engine was stopped in Red Lion Square. A transformer has been struck on White Moss and no one has had any light for ages. Did you know, Richard, that Cory is to join the A.T.S.?'

The Sweetings had said this a little hesitantly, because they all knew that the friendship between Richard and Corys de Bainriggs had been of a special kind. Their father had called it sentimental nonsense; their mother moonshine, but they themselves had felt sure it was neither. They had not understood it, but they felt vaguely indignant with Corys. Who was Corys, to bewitch and worry such a man as Richard Blunt?

Richard was so busy establishing himself in his hogg-house, for the time that remained to him before he should be called up, that he did not call at Bonfire Hall till after tea. He walked from Oak How. It was still hot, though Back o' Lake was in evening shadow. Part of the valley was sunlit, but part lay dark under a formless gloom that was spreading out from over Loughrigg. The glistening, sunlit tops of cumulus clouds showed behind Rydal Fell and as he drew near the Hall the air seemed to thicken ahead of him so that Loughrigg was hidden and near by beech trees stood out against this dark haze as if an infinite plain lay beyond them.

Jane Peascod showed him into the long parlour with her usual absence of emotion.

Grandy was there, and the younger Mrs. de Bainriggs. Maimie sat in the lakeside window. Corys was reading in the other window, where the green light of the evening woods lay on her. She was dressed like a girl. Her hair looked tidy. She had her brown hands clasped round her knees, and her back bent over the book that lay limply open in her lap.

When Richard went in they all stood up, except Grandy, who was writing on her knee a letter to *The Times* about the growing abuse of getting petrol by means of cattle food coupons.

'This allowance of corn for Herdwick sheep is another idiotic thing,' said Grandy, looking fiercely up at Richard. 'A Herdwick wouldn't know what to do with corn, if it saw any. As it is, Herdwick farmers draw corn and sell it to people with fowls. How are you, Richard? You look very fit.'

Corys was coming forward, slowly, and looking gravely at Richard as she came. He was about to turn to her, after greeting Blodwen and the lady he had jilted, when there came a flash of lightning. It seemed to shine through each window, equally brightly, with a forked, hard brilliance, and at the same moment there came a sound like a sharp

- 195 -

explosion from the telephone and blue flame darted out of the instrument and seemed to dart in again. As this was the third night in succession on which this had happened the Bonfire Hall ladies took it calmly; the great crack of thunder that instantly followed and which started echoes that reverberated between the fells and clouds would have drowned their cries, had there been any. Richard, standing near the telephone, could not feel calm. He received an electric shock, presumably from the blue flame before it darted in again. There is, for some people, a peculiar difficulty in remaining calm under the impact of an electric shock. Richard did not shriek or make any abrupt movement. He felt, subconsciously, that if he did either the shock would get at him again. He stood perfectly still and shrank in his clothes, making himself tense for whatever might come next, and his tingling arm stayed, half lifted, as it had been that he might shake hands with Corys.

'That beast of a thing has struck you,' said Corys, quickly, seeing a pale stupefaction on his face. 'Sit down, Richard.'

She thought of his damaged heart, and did not know what an electric shock might do to it. She put her arms about him and urged him to a chair and Richard sat down and smiled silently up at her, rubbing his arm as he looked.

'Oh, you're all right!' said Corys, hovering over him and then half withdrawing herself.

Looking up at Corys, with a month of the war-like outside world and then a rather severe electric shock between this look and the last he had given her, Richard realized that Corys was going to ignore all that he had said to her after she had burnt Lake View. She could not have forgotten it; perhaps she never would. But dignity demanded of her that she should ignore it and he thought, also, later on, that she had deliberately withdrawn into that ivory tower of her maidenhood that she believed proof against all assault. Other women, other girls, might be accused of having a lover. Not so Corys de Bainriggs. Richard's words had been a fantastic absurdity; such words could never be applied to her, Corys. He could never have meant that they could. So now she smiled at him, her first uncertain coldness quite banished by the lightning in the telephone, and he felt as if the Corys of old days were back again, his faithful friend.

He told them all the news of his journeyings and his future plans, but no one spoke of Corys' future. At the end of the long evening of happy talk Corys offered to row him to the Island, towing his boat.

'Every one says Jownie Wife burnt Lake View,' said Corys, looking at him, as she rowed, with impish eyes, 'but they can't prove it, so it does her no harm. Gerald Lovely has been ill; he thought I was a spook. I think he is courting your Maimie; she seems to know what to do with him. I never knew. Richard, thinking things over since I burnt Lake View, I have decided that it will do me no harm to go away from Grasmere for a bit. Mummie said Wales, but I said no, the war. The war has been on my mind rather, the last week or two. The Sweetings are going to be Wrens, so I shall be an A.T. I want to do everything quite on my own. And if I'm not bombed, Richard, and I come back again, perhaps I shall feel better, about Penny Rock I mean.'

She faced the western glow and her face and neck were brown against the shining water as she rowed.

'I think you are right,' said Richard.

CHAPTER XXIV

Maimie felt concern for Gerald Lovely. She thought him ill and likely to become seriously so. She had no experience of nervous disorders and when he told her details of his sufferings, details which became increasingly detailed every time he told them, she thought, as he did, that his brain was suffering from some of the affections that may trouble the brains of the learned.

'You see, he has been working very hard at Cambridge,' Maimie would say to Blodwen, in the long parlour. 'And some doctor told him once that the most highly developed parts of our body are the most easily upset. And then seeing what he thought must be a ghost made him think he was going mad. He didn't believe in ghosts, or, of course, it would have been easier for him. I do think it was too bad of Cory! Burning somebody else's house and then worrying Gerald!'

To this mildness of disapproval had weeks of the atmosphere of Bonfire Hall brought the normally moral Maimie.

Grandy chuckled, though she had not been addressed.

'Off-comes must take us as they find us,' said she. 'I must say I should have done just what Cory did, if I had felt as she, apparently, felt about Penny Rock. But you had better not try and cure Gerald by telling him what he really saw or you may get Cory seriously in the soup. I doubt if anybody knows who started the fire, except Old John and probably Jownie Wife, Jane Peascod of course, and possibly half the village. But I wouldn't tell an off-come; you never know how an off-come may behave.'

In spite of this admonition, given more seriously than were Grandy's admonitions as a rule, Maimie did tell Gerald. Those in love are no more generally trustworthy than any other single-minded creature, such as a broody hen or a courting stag, and all Maimie's loyalties were beginning to be centred in Gerald.

When Richard had been back on his Island for a week and Corys had filled up forms about herself, as required for recruits to the A.T.S., Gerald and Maimie walked towards home from Ambleside. They had had tea at the Wateredge Hotel, on the lawn by the lake. The pleasure of the good tea and the sunlit lake made them feel happy with each other; it seemed as if their own good management of their affairs had made the water shine and given the tea an almost peace-time strength. But as they strolled along the Under Loughrigg road and Gerald heard the Rothay, running beside them, his gloom began to close about him again. How sad, at twenty-one, to be going queer in the head!

Mr. Lovely, observing his son's new interest in that young Miss Ozzard, had made inquiries about her, from Richard Blunt. Presumably, if Richard had been engaged to her, she was all right, but Mr. Lovely wanted to feel sure about this.

'A good, straight girl?' said Mr. Lovely, inquiringly. 'Not very brilliant intellectually, but sound enough; kindly I think, and likely to stick to a fellow when she got him? That sort do stick. Their homes mean a lot to them. And if there were babies she'd be a tender mother, or so I imagine? No money, of course, but that doesn't matter, much. I'd rather Gerald married a bit of money and he'd do better to wait a while, but, as things are, mother and I feel let him have the girl, if he wants her, and I dare say she'll do as well for him as most, in the end.'

Thus, Mr. Lovely and his ladies encouraged Gerald in what had become his pursuit of Maimie and it seemed that only Maimie's elusiveness, whether coy or cautious, now postponed her engagement to Gerald.

This sunlit June evening, as Gerald grew gloomy again beside the Rothay, Maimie made up her mind. His desire for her had, by now, had its inevitable response from her impressionable and affectionate nature. Lonely, rebuffed by Richard Blunt, haunted by poverty, both heart and mind in Maimie inclined her towards him. He was young, but she was also, and the extra year or two of her age seemed to her more than counter-balanced by his masculinity and his riches, which gave him a kind of worldly wisdom she was without. In a meadow by the Rothay they sat down. The meadow lay in the evening shadow but the river, rushing under Pelter Bridge, seemed to bring light as well as sound with it from the golden west. Its quiet murmur, as monotonous and yet as varied as the sound of waves falling on some lee shore, gave Maimie an enchanted sense of rest and security. She felt all her being turn towards Gerald for without him, there beside her, there would be a gap, unnatural as half a pair of blackbirds, in the golden peace of the country-side.

'Gerald, you need never be worried again about your mind, or what you saw that night, on the lake,' said Maimie, hesitating, as well she might, but determined to hesitate no longer. 'You thought you saw some one walking on the water. So you did, but the some one was walking on the ice under the water.'

'So every one says,' said Gerald in a voice that he contrived to make as haggard as his look.

'But they were, I mean, she was,' said Maimie. 'Gerald, it was Cory. You were chasing Cory and to escape you she took to the ice. She knows the lake too well to have made a mistake. The ice bore her. She went across to the Island, and Richard rowed her to Back o' Lake as soon as he could get his boat to float clear. This is true, Gerald. Cory told me herself.'

Gerald, this evening, was rather enjoying his sad state of health and even more the concerned regard of Maimie, sitting so close by his side. They argued for a long time, Maimie maintaining her truthfulness, he that she told such a story only to ease his sufferings. Finally to convince him it seemed necessary to Maimie to reveal that Corys had set Lake View on fire, so she revealed it.

'Phew!' said Gerald, whistling. 'The young rip! Wanted to buy it back, did she, and when she couldn't she set it alight! My Gosh! What living in a place like Grasmere does for some people! Seriously, Maimie, that kid ought to be kicked out into the world for a bit. She'll get above herself, if she isn't already. Cory, to burn Lake View! I don't altogether blame her, I must say.'

The swearing of Gerald to absolute secrecy about the misdeed of Corys took some time, for Maimie was a pleasant sight, when pleading. When this was over Gerald thought of something else.

'Gosh! Now I know I am sane we'll get married,' said Gerald. 'I didn't like to suggest it when I thought I was going all bats in the belfry, not to say cuckoo. But now— see here, old thing, let's get it over at once, while the parents still think you are saving me from wherever it is they put them in Westmorland. Not that they'd have any objection to you but they might pretend to have, just because they're so rich. Maimie, angel kid, what about next week?'

'I will not be hustled into marriage against your parents' wish,' said Maimie, still elusive, though she experienced a happiness so astounding that she felt it almost unbearable. As Corys had once asked how an unbearable grief could be borne so Maimie now wondered how she could support the dazzling burden of her joy.

Thus it came about that, next day, their engagement was announced and the marriage was to take place just after that handsome young Mr. Lovely had taken his degree at Cambridge and consequently just before he joined the Royal Engineers.

'I was never really worried about Maimie,' said Richard, placidly smoking his pipe in the long parlour. 'I knew she would soon find a fellow who liked curls.'

'Are you going to be one of those men who never fall in love?' asked Blodwen.

Richard paused.

'I think that eventually I may be like some one who has never had measles,' said Richard, considering his metaphor as he spoke. 'They say people who have never had measles really have. They have had a dose, at some time, so slight that they felt merely a bit off colour and did not go all measley, but this slight dose self-inoculated them against any more attacks.'

'Well, I doubt if Maimie, dear girl, would have been the right wife for you,' said Blodwen, after making sure, in her mind, that Richard really meant to say he had been half in love, once.

Grandy said nothing. Instead she cocked a too expressive eyebrow and looked from Richard to Corys, who was filling in more forms for the

A.T.S., and back again. Her look spoke so clearly to Richard that he felt, in alarm, that she must have said in words what must not be said.

'Well, it is time I cleared off,' said Richard, hastily rising. As he rowed back to his hogg-house he wondered had he, inadvertently, spoken the truth about his feeling for Corys?

Three days later he received orders to join his squadron and learned, unofficially, that in a month or two he would probably be sent on a special mission to the Near East. He had had nearly a fortnight on the Island and he would not be sorry to leave it. For him, restored to moderate vigour, there could be no peace in the green stillness of the June nights and no solace in the eternal shining of the lake waters. There was a job he could do and gladly would he go and do it and come back some day, if the Lord so willed it, to a Grasmere he had done all he could to earn.

He left Windermere next morning by the 6.35 train. Clouds blew along the fell slopes and the lake was dark with waves. There was a sweet scent of damp woods and meadow flowers and the air was full of the sound of running water and the gentle splash of wavelets. Corys came with him to the station to see him off. She was pale and grave. He knew, as he knew so much about Corys, that she hated his going. He wondered if she would cry, for her voice had gone small and husky as it had done, long ago, when she could not tell Old John of her sale of Penny Rock. Poor Corys! What troubles had she had!

'Good-bye! Cory, my dear!' said Richard, his hand on the railway-carriage door.

Corys' lips moved but she said nothing. He had told her, but no one else, that he would be going abroad in a few weeks. She looked up at him, her eyes wide and dark and frank as the eyes of a sad child. She made a little movement towards him and Richard bent and kissed her forehead and felt her dark hair soft against his own.

'Cory! my dear!' said Richard again, but in a different tone. He pushed her hands gently from his shoulders and got quickly into his compartment. He put his suit-case on the rack. Then he leant out.

'Good-bye again, old thing!' said Richard, and his voice sounded almost gay. 'Give my love to everybody, and the best of luck!'

The train drew out and Richard, sitting still, wondered how truly had he spoken about measles, and love. He thought he had been right; never again, thought Richard, could he feel for any woman what he had felt for Corys.

He saw her once more, nearly a month later. He had been walking up and down Preston Station, waiting for his train to the South. It came in, from Carlisle and the north. As Richard hurried along its immense length he saw two girls in khaki get out of it, just ahead of him. One was a rosy cheeked, slender creature, lively, with gay, roguish brown eyes that looked brighter for her peaked khaki cap. The other was Corys. Corys looked like a child that had cried itself sick overnight but had already begun to feel that the night was a long time ago. Bewildered, but intent, looked Corys and the determination that had fired Lake View was clearly to be read upon her pale but sunburnt face.

'Silly! Where on earth do you come from?' said the rosy girl, seizing Corys by one arm, and her manner made Richard surmise, and rightly, that the girls had first met at Lancaster, only half an hour ago. 'Don't go mooning off that way, unless you want to go on the engine. This is the way. Come.'

Neither of them looked at Richard but, upon this, they scampered away, up the long platform and the distant stairs.

Richard got into his dining-car and sat, thinking of Grasmere and his life there as set in a ring of shadowy fells and shining water. These fells, that secret water, had enclosed his Island and his dreams of Corys.

Sighing, and then smiling at his sigh, Richard drew the menu towards him.

'What on earth does one eat in war-time trains?' thought he.

※ ※ ※

Afterword

※

When you think of a UK 'home front' novel from the Second World War, and the effect of war on women's lives, you probably think first of something set in London – perhaps during the Blitz. Images that come to mind could be of bombed-out buildings or barrage balloons. But, of course, the whole nation was at war. Even far away from London, in Grasmere, a village best known for being the home to poet William Wordsworth, the war has an impact.

Most obviously for the plot of *Forest Silver*, it has had an impact on the central male character, Wing-Commander Richard Blunt. He is a newcomer to the village and has been invalided out of the Royal Air Force but not before being awarded the V.C. – the Victoria Cross, the highest decoration of the British honours system, awarded for 'most conspicuous bravery, or daring or pre-eminent act of valour or self-sacrifice, or extreme devotion to duty in the presence of the enemy'. Being 'no more use' to the RAF, Blunt has come to the Lake District in search of some sort of peace. And he comes quoting a poem to himself (though Yeats, rather than Wordsworth): 'I tire of winds and waters and pale lights!', from the 1894 play *The Land of Heart's Desire*. Indeed, poetry pops into Blunt's mind on several occasions as he gets to know the community. Mrs Sweeting has 'named her girls Cecily, Gertrude and Magdalen, in the hope, so far disappointed, that they might be followed by a Margaret and Rosalys', in reference to a list of Mary's 'five handmaidens, whose names / Are five sweet symphonies' in Dante

Gabriel Rossetti's 'The Blessed Damozel' (1850). Meanwhile, when meeting Corys at her home – after an initial rather abrupt encounter – this is Blunt's impression:

> Mr Blunt felt himself bewildered and wondered if he was bewitched. This tall creature, in stained blue overalls, with a muddy smear across its right cheek and hands that looked as if they had just delved into those various mucks so delightfully eaten by the ducks in the poem, had a strong resemblance to the clean girl in shorts who had dropped tears on Jet yesterday.

The poem referenced is 'Ducks' (1919) by F. W. Harvey – 'Or finding curious things / To eat in various mucks / Beneath the pool, / Tails uppermost' – a poet from the previous World War. Blunt is nothing if not eclectic in his reflections.

At first, Blunt is only able to view this community through the lens of an outsider – equal parts natural splendour and poetic heritage, with not enough understanding of the way it operates, or how the war is affecting day-to-day life. And it's true that one of the joys of reading the novel today, as it was at the time, is Ward's keen eye for the timeless beauty of the Lake District. Throughout the book, she describes the striking landscapes, the drama of the mountains and lakes, and the pervasiveness of the weather.

> It happened to be one of those days, rare at the Lakes, when the falling rain, the low and formless sky and the sodden country-side were all of the same colour. The valley pastures were grey-green, the sky of a greenish grey, and the rain that joined grass and cloud, being transparent, appeared of the same sallow hue. The road glimmered with a metallic brightness in the gloom, reflecting a light that was nowhere else perceptible, and the full river swept beside it with a heavy sound that drowned the watery patter of the rain.

Such things are eternal and unchanging, as recognisable to the Grasmere resident or visitor in the 2020s as in the 1940s. But Grasmere is not standing still, and the distant war is making its presence felt. Not just in the people who return from bomb-damaged Liverpool or stints of urban fire-watching, or even in the knowledge that Gerald intends to join the Royal Engineers. It is there in many aspects of everyday life – and, being the home front, these are the changes that women predominantly experienced while men went to the front line.

For one, the villagers must adhere to the same blackout regulations as their city counterparts. People ask one another, 'How far can a German airman see a cigarette', but it is bonfires that seem more of a threat than the insufficient drawing of curtains to conceal household lighting. Jownie Wife, the terror of the village, set light to mounds of leaves 'long after black-out and brought P.C. Smith on his bicycle to scold Miss de Bainbriggs for showing a light'. When Old John's house burns down, the A.R.P. (Air Raid Precautions) wardens are 'more worried about the light than the flames since an enemy plan was known to be prowling nearby'. They even have air-raid practice, though this is a moment where Ward satirises the effort:

> Another test was made of the local air-raid siren, which was tootled by hand, but no one, fortunately, was able to hear it except two households on the same side of the valley who thought it was a bus changing gear on the Raise.

Perhaps the most significant wartime effect, and the most frequently mentioned, is the arrival of 'war guests'. Even during the war, the village attracted summer tourists eager to see where Wordsworth wrote and to sample the 'famous gingerbread' (still available all these years later). But while the community would usually return to some sort of quiet insularity after the summer, the presence of the war guests means that outsiders become a year-round presence.

Some are evacuees (including the factual detail of the entire student body of London's Royal College of Art being evacuated to nearby Ambleside); others have evidently chosen to make their way to relative safety, altering the dynamics of the community for better or worse. They 'gave concerts and recitations' and 'taught the natives and each other whatever seemed most suitable'. They provide local opportunities – 'Maimie spent the autumn in reading to old war-guest ladies, taking war-guest children for walks, acting as secretary to a war-guest financier, and helping in the Gift Shop' – but also take up doctors' appointments (in a world before the National Health Service) and 'being wealthy, were forever wanting to do things in a Bank'. They are clearly considered a different breed to people like Corys, who are lifelong residents of the area and deeply familiar with its ways. These outsiders are less hardy, staying inside and hoping the rain stops, rather than stomping out in all weathers. And they are also afforded fewer privileges by a self-protecting community.

"It is very hard for all these newcomers," said Blodwen, who had understood the looks of both fish man and greengrocer man. "They get only what is left over when all of us have had what we want."

"Self-preservation, that is," said Grandy, striding along with her fine head held high to meet the breeze. "The tradespeople do the best for those of us who will be still here after the war – why bother about the others whom they may never see again?"

Whatever their reason for being in the village, these outsiders are grouped by a term peculiar to the region: 'off-come'. As Grandy says, "Off-comes must take us as they find us. [...] You never know how an off-come will behave." You'll still hear the word in use today, though 'off-comer' is now a more common variant.

These outsiders are not just walking examples of urban foibles, or obstructions at the bank. They can threaten the way of life of people in the community.

> "Is it for sale?" said Corys, horrified, as are all Grasmere people when any old house is for sale, because who knows what an off-come may do to it?

One of the signs that Blunt has become immersed in the life of Grasmere is his instinctive horror, towards the end of the novel, about what might happen if Lake View is bought and turned into an attraction for tourists – sounding not unlike the tea room at the heart of another title in the British Library Women Writers series, *Tea Is So Intoxicating* (1950) by Mary Essex.

> He brooded on Lake View, as a tea-house, with red umbrellas up beside the lake, the wireless on, tea-cups on little tables under the beeches (those that remained), and thin, scratchy pictures of Wordsworth's head on the cups. A car park would no doubt be arranged, at the side of the house.

Mr Lovely might comment that nobody 'wants building land in war time', but the buying and selling of land is one of the main themes of the novel. It runs to the heart of who Corys is: both that she has to sell land, and her desperation to get some back.

> "Cory will never get over the sale of Penny Rock," said Blodwen […] "By that I mean that her grief at its loss will affect her growth, mentally and spiritually. It will become a part of her as a bit of metal railing sometimes becomes part of a tree trunk, that grows around it and hides it, but it is there all the time."

In a period during which so many people were experiencing actual grief, it is striking to include this form of mourning in the novel. Even the title looks back to agreements about land. On the surface, it may sound like a poetic way to consider a certain sort of natural beauty, but as Richard and Corys discuss, 'forest silver' was a genuine term for a payment. Though apparently well known to the residents of Grasmere, and visitors like Richard, 'forest silver' probably isn't something contemporary readers will recognise. Indeed, even in 1941 it was a very niche reference to use for a novel's title. This 'forest silver' tax isn't a nationwide phenomenon; the term was only used by people in this region and referred only to land that had been part of the medieval Forest of Kendal. Blunt defines it as 'the tax that was paid for letting beasts run in the forest': in practice, in the thirteenth to sixteenth centuries it was a payment taken through other measures that then permitted local residents to rope off 'common' land for their own animals.

In Ward's novel, 'forest silver' thus hints at a wider, metaphorical meaning: who has the right to land? What does ownership of it entail, and how does that affect the long-established community? Wartime tears up the usual rules and expectations in Grasmere. Perhaps the prospect of a cheerful, kitsch tea room is not anathema to most readers. It would be unsurprising to find the tea room Blunt envisages today in many Lake District towns and villages. But it is an image that leads Corys to arson.

Corys is the most unusual and memorable character in the novel – particularly in a history of the portrayal of women in twentieth-century novels. Throughout *Forest Silver*, both from Corys' viewpoint and other people's, she is considered somewhere between a woman and a man. She 'had always felt herself more boy than girl', and says "I hate being a girl". She is drawn to 'boys' pursuits' and in order to do them must 'dress as a boy'. The more traditionally feminine Sweeting sisters ask her why she pretends to be a boy, and 'told each other what a scream Corys was, a boy one day and a girl the next'. Even Grandy says, "She's not in

❧ ❧ ❧

the least conscious of being female and won't be, perhaps for years at the rate she is going."

Some might read Corys as a non-binary or even a trans character, decades before these designations became commonplace. It's impossible to rule out such readings, though they were probably not in Ward's mind when she created the character: rather, like many other young women of the period, she was pushing against the role that had been predetermined for her by all the generations leading to the 1940s. Particularly in wartime, as women took on traditionally masculine jobs and tasks, there were many who were shunning 'girls' clothes' and adopting more utilitarian outfits. Corys has always felt more at home in 'unfeminine' occupations, and wartime gives her an opportunity to adopt a role that isn't bounded by gender.

While the novel is firmly set in wartime, the reader hopes that Corys will never allow herself to be trammelled to the feminine stereotype in the later 1940s and beyond.

Simon Thomas

Series consultant **Simon Thomas** created the middlebrow blog Stuck in a Book in 2007. He is also the co-host of the popular podcast Tea or Books? Simon has a PhD from Oxford University in Interwar Literature.